# CONFIDENCE

# CONFIDENCE

**MINDS SHINE BRIGHT**

ANTHOLOGY 2022

**MSB**

MINDS SHINE BRIGHT

Editor: Amanda Scotney
writing@MindsShineBright.com

Published by Minds Shine Bright in 2022
PO Box 1042
Windsor, 3181, VIC, Australia
Website: www.MindsShineBright.com
Twitter: @MSBwriting
Facebook: Minds Shine Bright page
Subscribe: www.MindsShineBright.com/minds-shine-bright-blog/
Copy editing by Kim Astill
Book design and layout by Ampersand Duck
Cover artwork by Michael S. Lang
Printed by IngramSpark
ISBN 978-0-6455231-0-2 (print)

The views expressed by Minds Shine Bright contributors are not necessarily those of the editors or publisher.

Minds Shine Bright acknowledges the people of the Kulin Nations, the Traditional Custodians of the land on which we live and work and where we have created this anthology. We pay respect to their long history and culture, and their Elders, past, present and emerging.

Special thanks to my friends and family who have supported and encouraged me behind the scenes; the arts and writers' organisations and libraries that have helped to promote the Minds Shine Bright writing competition and created safe havens for the writing community; and each of the writers who have submitted their work to the Minds Shine Bright writing competition.

This publication includes strong themes, images and language. Parental guidance is recommended for young readers.

# CONTENTS

# INTRODUCTION

Welcome to the first Minds Shine Bright anthology, *Confidence*. It's with some trepidation and much joy that this book is launched.

This collection includes the winning and commended entries from the inaugural Minds Shine Bright writing competition. While each piece stands alone, woven together with other interpretations of confidence, they form a story about our environment, our times and what it means to be human. From universal elements and the cycle of life to the inner workings of a mind, *Confidence* takes the reader on a journey.

Minds Shine Bright is an arts business that runs two writing competitions each year and publishes books. The Minds Shine Bright *Confidence* writing competition is held annually from October to February. Our aim is to capture and share how fiction writers explore and interpret the theme of confidence in stories, poems, and scripts over time. The second competition, *Storm*, is the first of our revolving-theme competitions that will run from June to September each year. The aim of *Storm* is to showcase a smaller set of writers.

Over the next few months, we will be spreading the word, highlighting some of the award-winning writers and connecting with local communities.

## LOOKING BACK

As an adult in my mid-fifties living in Australia, I'm grateful for the largely quiet and uneventful times in which I have lived for most of my life. When I was a child, there were constant reminders of the World Wars—old black-and-white pictures on walls and mementos of great uncles I never met—and the Vietnam War ended during my childhood, impacting a generation of young men.

There have always been bushfires and floods here. Mother Nature throws drought at us too. These natural events seem to be increasing in intensity, and their potential to cause havoc is more often realised as the climate changes.

At the start of 2020, a huge amount of Australia was on fire. At the same time, there was growing concern at the rapid emergence of a new virus in Wuhan, China.

Jumping forward to September 2021, when Minds Shine Bright opened for entries, we were in our second year of dealing with the global COVID pandemic. Many of us had experienced multiple lockdowns, and rising case numbers and deaths were, and still are, having a profound impact on the health system, our mental health and on the arts.

These factors, as well as imagination, the literary canon and innate creativity, shaped the first Minds Shine Bright anthology, *Confidence*.

## INTERPRETATIONS OF CONFIDENCE

Minds Shine Bright writers are a diverse and highly imaginative group. The countries that are represented include Australia, New Zealand, Canada, Germany, United Kingdom, Ireland and Romania. Published writers range in age from teenagers to octogenarians, and two category prizes, one for scripts and one for flash fiction, were awarded to writers who were under eighteen.

The classic interpretation of confidence, across all entries, was a person with an artistic talent, often a young person but not always, who lacked self-confidence. They were often anxious about performing their talent in front of others, sometimes facing harsh criticism for wanting to express themselves creatively. With encouragement and guidance, life experience or sheer determination they were able to overcome their fears, find their sense of self and embrace their talent.

Some of the entries focused on the environment and its insurmountable challenges. Characters came to terms with their place in chaotic circumstances as fire, floods, storms and drought all took their toll – testing relationships, taking the lives of loved ones and destroying homes. However, the environment provided an element of nurturing and healing too as characters found a strong sense of self and connection from the natural places they identified with most.

What a crazy mixed-up world we live in since COVID-19 reared its ugly head. Many writers considered confidence through the lens of health, and there were frequent references to breathing and sore throats.

Writers who were under eighteen tended to be very open and clear when discussing their worries and fears.

Coming-of-age interpretations of confidence focused on identity, diversity, self-image, boredom, anxiety, the impacts of alcohol and drugs on youth culture, risk-taking, misplaced confidence and leaps of faith.

Humour, fantasy and fairytales were all used to step out of the day-to-day world.

Sadly, family violence was one of the most written-about topics. The impact of domestic violence on the lives of families and children, the erosion of self-esteem, the loss of identity and freedom, and the struggle to walk away and find a safe place was explored many times. But writers also drew upon the idea that the domestic is a haven, a safe space; somewhere to bake, to garden, to negotiate family politics and to make difficult life decisions.

Explorations of death and dying, decisions and choices, nursing homes, loss of memory and loss of self were key threads. There were also poignant observations about finding inner strength, coming to terms with the loss of our faculties as we age and coping with the losses of loved ones.

Despite the challenges, hope rose from the darkest places and spaces. The hope that things would be better, that we could get through today and that we might live to tell another story tomorrow and truly shine bright.

## ABOUT THE EDITOR

**Amanda Scotney** is a writer, poet, independent filmmaker and the Founder of Minds Shine Bright. She was born in Hobart, Tasmania and now lives in Melbourne, Victoria. Amanda is passionate about promoting the arts and writers and is the judge of the Minds Shine Bright Writing Competitions. She is proud to release *Confidence*, the first publication by Minds Shine Bright.

# THE WINNING ENTRIES

There were many talented writers who submitted their work to the Minds Shine Bright writing competition. While many entries left a lasting impression, the winning entries for 2022 are:

**OVERALL WINNER**

'Red Bikini' by FRANÇOISE THORNTON-SMITH. This amazing short story transports us back to the day when much of Australia burned. It masterfully explores confidence on multiple levels, including the individual responses to the fire and the protagonist's journey of recovery.

**FLASH FICTION WINNER**

'Flying Free' by POPPY BRAZIER is a visual, powerful piece that explores overconfidence in young people coming of age.

**SCRIPT WINNER**

'Beaucoup Bills' by JED STANLEY is a highly visual, action-oriented screen play about a group of young friends who rob a casino and the consequences of misplaced confidence. It captures the essence of Perth.

**POETRY WINNERS**

'Dahlias' by KEVIN DYER captures the topsy-turvy craziness of our last couple of years and 'Emergence of Voice' by MICHAEL LEACH explores the growth of confidence from boyhood to manhood. These two poems both make me cry.

**SHORT STORY WINNER**

'All the Pain and All the Joy' by ALEXANDRA SVOBODA is the celebratory tale we all need. At a cracking pace, it celebrates women's football as a safe place to achieve success and to build inner strength to tackle workplace bullying and low self esteem.

# OVERALL WINNER

## FRANÇOISE THORNTON-SMITH
### WARTOOK, VIC, AUSTRALIA

Françoise Thornton-Smith is a writer and volunteer fire-fighter. She is particularly interested in the relationship between nature and humans. Her work has appeared in *Fire* (Margaret River Press) and *Write Now!* 2011.

# RED BIKINI

Arlette touched her chest through the long, loose t-shirt. She ran her fingers down her sides, over her hips, across her abdomen. The t-shirt felt comfortable and amorphous. Almost a hospital gown, except that it had no ties. She should feel really positive now, she knew that. They were back at Tamm Inlet, where they had enjoyed that wonderful holiday ten years ago, all sunny, cheerful memories. She remembered being happy on the beach and in the water, going on bushwalks, working on her translations in between, board games with the children. Had she really done all that? Was she capable of doing anything now?

Only Pete was watching her. She knew. She didn't turn around, but felt his gaze x-ray her shirt. Her hands, his gaze, swept gently over her body again. Her stomach. Her chest. Her thin legs, skinny arms. Her short hair. Repellent? Pitiful? Get over it, she told herself. She closed her eyes briefly and then walked stiffly down to the river to join the others. The sensation of the cold water shocked her. When had she last swum?

'I felt a fish. It touched my legs!'

'Catch it, silly. We can eat it for dinner!'

Fiona and Marg splashed Arlette and dived under in the slowly flowing river. Arlette gingerly went deeper. Now the cool, dark water felt cleansing and pure. She ducked her head under the surface and came up again. She swam over to the other two, surprised that her arms and legs made the right movements, albeit jerkily. This was nice. Laughter echoed between the tall eucalypts leaning over the water. Marg swam downstream to where the two men were fishing. Arlette and Fiona did a slow breaststroke upstream and then floated back down, on their backs. Arlette glanced at Fiona's comfortingly chubby, solid body next to her. Fiona had substance, had presence. Arlette felt thin and transparent. She could not imagine herself working again or doing any kind of meaningful activity. Maybe it was too soon to think of that. But she was even uncertain about the simple things, like how to talk to the people she was holidaying with. She and Pete were expected to make a meal one of the days down here. She hadn't cooked a meal in two years, let alone for six people. She floated and worried. Fiona lifted her arm and pointed out an egret standing on an overhanging branch.

'Egret,' Arlette repeated dumbly. She stared at it as they floated by. What was an egret to her? 'Oh, wow, of course, gee, an egret!'

It was warm when she got out of the water. Was anyone looking? She felt too visible in her clinging t-shirt. She pulled on a long-sleeved blouse. Against sunburn, she could say. To avoid the looks of pity from the others, she could say. Stop it, Arlette told herself. It's alright. Nobody is looking at you. Nobody expects anything of you. Neither do you. Could that be the problem?

Marg had laid lunch out on the front of the boat: crackers, cheese, tomatoes and some fruit. Arlette ate three crackers and a mandarin. Now she was full. She patted her flat, taut stomach. Pete watched her. Did he like the new Arlette, no chubby curves any more, twenty kilos lighter? Did she? Arlette usually avoided the question. She seemed to be avoiding so many things, these days. And that was strange, wasn't it, now that she was better? She did quite like being thinner, if she was honest with herself. That was positive, she supposed. She just didn't know what being normal was any more.

Arlette sat down beside Pete on the sand. Something white fluttered out of the sky and landed on her hand. Ash. She looked up.

'Bushfire.'

'Thought so.'

They stayed there, flicking the ash off their hands and legs every so often, watching the others. Pete was used to sitting with her for hours. The cicadas kept up their incessant din. A kingfisher darted across their field of vision like a jewel. In the peaceful atmosphere they heard birds warbling in the trees. The river kept flowing and the ash kept falling, soft, weightless, harmless. Arlette leaned back and looked up at the sky. Bright whitish blue, nothing special. Like the ceiling in a hospital treatment room. She could smell the smoke though. Her decades of CFA experience kicked in.

'Forty kilometres away, wasn't it? asked Pete. 'And the ash here already.'

'Yeah, something like that. The wind is the wrong direction, of course. But not very strong.'

Pete leaned back on his elbows too and stretched his legs. 'I think my toes are sunburned.'

'I still want to swim in the sea. It's important.'

'I know. You'll get a chance.'

Marg came out of the water, laughing loudly. She grabbed her towel and rubbed down her arms. Her movements slowed. She held out her arm and turned to Arlette and Pete with a look of horror.

'Ash! The fire's coming! My god, we have to leave. Oh my god. Steven, Steve, hurry up! Get the boat going!'

Fiona lifted her head from the water. She was floating downstream yet again. 'What?'

'The bushfire! It's here!'

John and Steven hurried back from their fishing spot further downstream. They had heard the fear in Marg's voice. John started giving orders. You lot pack up the food. You do the fishing rods and gear. You collect any leftovers. He got to Arlette and Pete. There was nothing left for them. You pack your own things.

It took only five minutes to be back on the boats and heading downstream again. The cicadas kept up their deafening racket. A pelican glided in over their heads. The eucalypt branches swayed in the breeze. Marg sobbed. Fiona tried to calm her down; the fire was far away; this was just the wind bringing some ash. Marg's anxiety was infectious. They could not leave that tranquil riverbank fast enough. All they wanted was to be back at the beach house.

Arlette and Pete had arrived at the beach house two days earlier. It looked the same as ten years ago: still secluded on the edge of the bush, tucked away among the trees. Nobody would know you were there. The house was quiet and cool. Arlette went through the whole house, checking every room. She wanted to recognise everything the way it had been, but the house was not the same. The bathroom and kitchen had been renovated. Why did it have to change? Arlette was not the same either. She didn't like thinking about how she had changed.

Arlette unpacked their clothes and laid them out neatly on the large table in the bedroom they had chosen. She put their swimming gear on the corner. The towels. His bathers. Her bikini. Red. She had made it on the sewing machine when she could still only sit upright for about half an hour a day. It had to be something she made herself. She ran the fabric through her fingers. Red, lycra swim-wear, ordered on-line. Her sister Liz had helped her with the sewing, via email and telephone. Basically, she had made the bikini on her own, for that body of hers. Red, a colour she would previously never have chosen. A daring, challenging colour to hit you in the eye. A bikini—something she had never worn before. Here I am. See me. But she wasn't ready to wear it yet. It was difficult enough for her to look at her body, let alone display it for others.

They went out on the boat again the day after the river picnic, this time to the lagoon. The wind had shifted, taking the smoke and ash away; the danger was no longer visible, and the others seemed to forget its existence immediately. John took Arlette and Pete fishing on his boat. Ten years ago, it had been their own children who had held the lines; now they did. Arlette enjoyed it. She felt a fish tug the line.

'Pull it in, fast! Now! Keep pulling, keep the line tight!' John was as excited as she was. He steered the boat and yelled instructions at the same time, gesturing, trying to help, passing a bucket for the fish.

Her first fish. It flopped in the bucket, still alive and desperate not to die. Arlette considered that for just a moment. She knew the feeling. But it looked like she was meant to catch that fish today. Arlette smiled and laughed out loud. Then Pete caught his first fish as well. John said that was enough: one each. John cooked the fish for them, for their lunch. They felt like kings.

Arlette rested on their bed. She was often tired but today it was pleasant. Tiredness from activity. Later she went out to the veranda and sat on the bench with Pete, looking out to sea. The waves were higher on the lagoon. She stood up and looked intently at the moving tree branches.

'The wind's shifted again.'

'Yes. I expect the smoke will come back soon. It will get closer.'

She sat down. Pete put his arm gently around her shoulders. His proximity disturbed her. It felt too intimate, and made her feel small and vulnerable, while she was trying to become more independent and stronger again. They both knew they made a good team. They had been great together, the past couple of years. Recovery seemed to be more difficult than illness. She sighed.

Fiona came out of the kitchen. 'I've put the radio on. ABC Gippsland. There are fires everywhere! The Princes Highway has been cut; we can't get away even if we want to. What should we do? What do you think, Arlie?'

Arlette was surprised by the appeal to her CFA experience and knowledge. She hadn't done any firefighting the past eighteen months. She still knew a thing or two, she supposed.

'I don't see us defending this house. We need some kind of escape plan if the fire gets this far. The boats? Could we go to the beach?'

'Yes, great idea! We can take food and water with us. Tents. Head out to the sand bar. We'll be safe from the fire there. I'll make a list.' Fiona went back inside.

Arlette and Pete continued to sit. Pete took Arlette's hand in his. She was comfortable now, leaning against his arm, but she had had enough of sitting; it felt like waiting. Waiting had meant bad news several times. 'Let's play a game,' she said.

'Good idea. Great idea!'

They were halfway through Scrabble when Marg burst in.

'The bushfire! It's only 15 kilometres away! The emergency radio says we all have to go.' Marg moaned and tore at her hair. Arlette stared. She had never seen anyone tear at their hair before. And she was perplexed. Marg was so scared—why? There was no immediate danger.

'It's safest to stay put, Marg. We can go to the beach if it reaches us. The track is closed, the highway too. Where would you go? You might end up stuck on the track. Fallen trees, burning trees and bush. It's too dangerous. Just stay here. It's almost evening; fires slow down then. We're probably safe for the night.'

'No, no, I have to go.' Marg almost screamed. Fiona put her arms around her, but Marg broke free and ran to her room. 'Steve! We're going!' Arlette heard Marg banging around and imagined her throwing clothes and belongings into her suitcase. She admired Marg's decisiveness; however foolhardy it was. Marg had decided that there were options for her, she had a choice: stay or go. Shit had happened to Arlette in the past few years, and it had always been beyond her control. There hadn't seemed to be any choice: you either accepted the treatment, or you died. Was this the same situation, with the bushfire bearing down on them? Do something or die? Arlette sat up a little straighter. She had survived, thus far. And now, perhaps, she could make her own choice. She might not feel as decisive as Marg, but she was used to long-term uncertainty and danger. She had fire sense. She could make sensible decisions. Maybe she did have something to live for? Maybe she had something to offer?

Arlette and Pete packed the Scrabble game up, with some regret. The atmosphere was too tense for games. Arlette lay on the bed for a while. Fiona packed things, vacuumed and mopped floors and cooked a meal for everyone, all at the same time. She found comfort in motherly activities. She forgot about the meal. The smoke alarm in the kitchen went off. Marg screamed and came back, believing the bushfire was here now, all around them—it must have set the smoke alarm off. Fiona spoke to her sternly and showed her the blackened saucepans. 'Oh,' she said. Her shoulders slumped. Arlette and Pete could only watch, and wonder at the tension and fear. Arlette realised again that she was not prone to panic. Still, she was glad Fiona hadn't asked her and Pete to cook.

The afternoon light disappeared as the clouds of smoke thickened above them. Ash and burned leaves and twigs were falling everywhere now, and the air was hard to breathe. 'Still kilometres away,' Arlette murmured to Pete. He nodded. They moved their car to the middle of the lawn in front of the house. It was the safest place they could think of. They packed a few things in a backpack, and went back to playing Scrabble, but in their room. The radio in the living room was set to its highest volume so everyone in the house could hear the emergency broadcasts.

Residents of neighbouring holiday homes dropped in to compare notes on preparation. Several parties were preparing to go out to the sand bar. Others were staying in their houses. All agreed it would be sooner rather than later.

When the first burning embers fell, Arlette breathed more deeply and felt a calmness wash over her at the same time as the adrenalin began to flow. She looked into the sky and willed the embers to become bigger, thicker. Danger to life. Also, willingness to die. She could handle all that. Wasn't she good at that?

They sat around the long table, looking out the windows at the thick, grey air swirling around. The sun went down, an evil, glowing red orb in the brown sky. Nobody spoke much. The radio said enough. The radio reported that the wind was shifting again. They would be safe for the night, possibly the next day too. Marg yelled 'Yippee!' They agreed to play a board game together, all of them, except for John who never played games. It was smoky even inside the house, but they ignored it.

'The wind seems to change a few times a day,' Arlette said to Pete later.

'I know. So, I don't think this place will still be standing tomorrow evening.'

Only two cars were going down to the jetty the next afternoon for the evacuation, carrying the heavy stuff: tents, eskies, boxes of food, water containers. Pete and Arlette were to walk down. Before she hopped into the car Fiona turned around and gave Arlette a big hug. Arlette tried not to flinch. Fiona was crying. She wiped the tears from her cheeks, leaving grey streaks like some kind of grisly clown make-up.

'You've been great, so strong, such a good support for me. I don't think I can handle it. Oh dear.' She sniffed and looked for a handkerchief in her pocket.

Arlette was embarrassed—she was cheerful. It was her automatic reaction to bad situations. She couldn't stop smiling. She had been cheerful all day, while the situation worsened. She patted Fiona on the back and pushed her gently into the car.

'See you down there.'

Pete checked their own vehicle one more time, wiping drifts of blackened leaves and ash from the bonnet. More leaves fell even as he swept them away. They looked out towards the sea and the lagoon, but visibility was down to around fifty metres. All they could see, feel, and breathe was the thick, dark smoke swirling around them.

'She thinks it's the last time she will see the place.'

'That's probably true,' replied Arlette, 'I can't comfort her.'

'I know. Although, I don't understand.'

He rolled over and gently ran his fingers along her arm. She smiled, without opening her eyes. Or had she grimaced? She hoped his eyes were shut too. His fingers slid slowly over her left breast. A strange sensation: she could feel it, but also could not feel it. Her whole chest felt, to her, like rubber. Not even like pins and needles. Just dead, I guess, she thought to herself. But not dead.

Pete's fingers found the scar across her abdomen. He traced the scar. He poked his finger in her new belly button. Then his fingers went up to her new breasts and traced all the scars on and around them. The scars in her armpits. He stroked her hair. She liked that. She liked the new soft, fuzzy down on her scalp. Like a newborn puppy, she thought dreamily. Not a monster.

Pete was getting excited. He caressed her stomach, cupped each lumpy, little, new breast in his hand, ran his finger around the elastic of her underpants. He was aroused, but her body had no idea what was happening. How could this be her body? She rolled over to face him and opened her eyes. His expression: a mixture of lust and repulsion, desire and pity. She moved her hand to his underpants and began to pull them down. He helped her. He pulled her pants off.

All the while, thousands of grains of sand blasted their tent by the lagoon at high speed, a terrible sound. It was excruciatingly hot in there, but better than outside in the ceaseless whirlwind of sand, ash and smoke that howled over the water, over the mountains. Arlette pulled her red bikini from under her head and held it tight in her hand, her talisman. She kissed Pete's mouth. Was he doing this for her sake? Was he still attracted to her? She had to believe that. They both shut their eyes. He moved on top of her.

'Look how the whole sky over that way is red now, like a painting. And the sound! My eyes are killing me. All that sand in my eyes, the smoke. But I need to see. It can't be long now.'

The little tents on the beach all leaned precariously one way and then another, buffeted by the fierce winds. One had already lifted up and blown away. Fiona sat in front of her own tent, hugging a towel around her shoulders to protect against the stinging sand, talking to nobody in particular. She faced the lagoon, looking through the swirling smoke at the little hamlet of holiday houses on the other side. Arlette squatted beside her. She marvelled at Fiona's stoicism, but also revelled in her own feeling of strength and power now that the fire storm was upon them. She was wearing her red bikini. She felt naked, but strong. The air was dark orange-brown and full of threatening thunder. It was four-thirty in the afternoon and hard to see anything, but they did see the first trees up the hill behind the houses burst into bright flame, like an instant giant blowtorch. Arlette touched Fiona's shoulder gently and went down to the lagoon. The water moved, an ash-covered animal pelt. She touched it with her toe and recoiled. Not a puppy. A monster.

She turned and trudged up the dune, past the group of people who stood there watching the houses in the hamlet start to burn, one by one. A man nodded at her. She smiled back and felt good. Over and down the other side, to the ocean beach. Here the waves pounded in, hit the beach with a thud and spread out again. A familiar sight and sound. Nobody was on this beach. They were all watching that disaster on the other side. Arlette looked at her red bikini-clad body. Not bad, from that angle, in that light. Not a monster. Not a puppy. A kind of woman. She had skills and experience. She loved and was loved.

This was the moment. Arlette walked into the waves. She wondered whether she should just sit down there or go in further? She went in deeper and dived under the next wave. The seawater caressed her. She rolled around and smiled. Treading water, she looked back at the flaming mountains. It was a silent movie in eery sepia colours. She only heard the water lapping her and thumping on the steep beach. She turned and looked out to the open sea. She could swim into oblivion. She had been considering that. She suspected that Pete knew, even if he did not understand. And yet, and yet. Arlette moved her arms and legs, swam, and went back to the beach. She walked over the dune. She felt comfortable in her red bikini, not naked. There was Pete, gazing at the conflagration. It was difficult to see now through all the smoke. She wrapped her arms around him and pulled him in to her. He ran his fingers up one strap of her bikini and smiled at her.

'We're going to be fine. I'm sure of it.' She kissed his arm, then went over to Fiona to discuss further safety and evacuation measures. This was her. In her red bikini. This was what she could do.

# TREADING ON WATER

## CHARLOTTE FINN    BULLA, VIC, AUSTRALIA

You're treading on water
Arms arching up along with the waves
I watch from underneath the surface
Aching for the day I too can make castles out of crumbled caves

I wouldn't dare ask you to lift me to the air
It would disturb your dance
Instead I'll struggle and observe
Not uttering a single opinion until I hear your stance

I memorise every movement
Long for when I can glide and soar
Firmly staying a dream
Brought back to reality by the water's deafening roar

I cut my feet on the rocks
I still wish to walk as you do
Run, even, never faltering
Perfecting every art form I pursue

I have seen you stumble
Now that I look at you from a distance
No longer blinded by that ever-burning light
My lungs have screamed long enough, I must rise to the surface
    this instant

I now tread on water alone
Water rippling at my feet
Falling through the dance I've seen mastered
Finally seen, finally complete

# MICROBIAL

**CLAIRE DALKIN**   HOVE, ENGLAND, UK

Water laps against the hillside, barely visible through the haze. Even halfway up, residents have to build their dwellings on stilts. Since the floods, millions of homes have been lost. New wetlands form, new reefs, and the wildlife that comes with them has caused the last humans to retreat into tight, little urban pockets. They build vertically: stacks of flats, farms and offices, like heavenly in-trays for the Almighty.

Down on the promenade, which is now doing a good job as a seabed, ancient hire bikes float just above their tethering stations. All along the skywalks, despite the poor air quality, people are milling about, a moving mosaic of colourful robes and gas masks. At the edge of the crowd, head bowed, hood up, a woman makes her way. Dressed in earth brown, with gumboots, she looks like an autumn leaf amongst summer blooms.

Celeste takes the Sky-train to her 'office'. Apparently, the world once looked like a blue marble. She shakes her head. She remembers when her mother told her about how work was all sharp suits and stiletto heels, which caused GBH to the wearer, and she half-smiles, observing her muddy boots. Her mother also described sunbathing, beaches and breathing unaided. The Sky-train slides into the port, depositing Celeste upon a springy, sedum-cloaked platform, to face the unblinking eye of Security. Every day, this causes such discomfort that she makes as little eye contact as possible, by allowing her gaze to shift diagonally to the floor. Every day, Security forces her to wait, until she raises her head, no matter how briefly. Once admitted, she pads along the corridor to emerge into a vast, transparent dome.

Above the haze, sunlight hits glittering panes of tinted graphene. The Domes are stuffed with life: supported by vines, forests, meadows, pools and waterfalls. At the entrance, Celeste removes her headdress and overcoat with its cumbersome oxygen mask. Next, her clothes are placed into a cleansing basket, and a fine mist sprays over her, killing harmful pathogens, begetting good bacteria. Celeste closes her eyes against the soft spray, breathing deeply, thankfully, allowing billions of tiny lives to thrive on and in her bodily city while the water soothes tiny welts and scratches on her skin.

*You had ice cream and kitten heels, Mum, but could you wear nothing at work and have no-one bat an eyelid?*

Now she is immersing herself in temperate rainforest. Other humans work in the Domes, but they keep mostly to themselves, and Celeste can work for weeks without seeing anyone. Birds and small mammals whistle, chuckle and screech, snug in the greenery. Slivers of insects glisten around her, curious, hungry; some come for a sip of her blood, others, like the butterflies, come to drink the beads of sweat that form on her upper lip; forming a psychedelic, tickly moustache. She fills the hanging bird feeders. A nightingale sings its thanks from the edge of a nearby bench, and soon, bees are fussing around her while she prepares their energy snacks.

As she works, she sings, or hums along with them. The bees drink, buzz their approval and move on. She has just turned her attention to the seedlings when out of the corner of her eye she notices what appears to be a crow, thirty metres away. She turns sharply; no, it is a cyberpriest, hunkered dark and thrumming against the green, with various symbols etched in gold across its body. A high-pitched wail floats down through the air. She looks up at the platform by the Domes' entrance, where mourners, weeping, in multi-coloured fabrics, bear a shrouded body. Many of the cemeteries around the coast are now flooded, so other arrangements have to be made...

Slowly, the platform is lowered towards the earth where the 'priest' hovers at the head of a long, shallow bamboo box. This is piled high with sticks. The relatives sing as the deceased is lifted onto the pile, a few words are spoken while foliage and dark grains are scattered over the body, layer upon layer until it is covered. The singing dies away and the mourners stand in silence, holding one another. Five minutes more, and they are rising back up to the Domes' entrance. Celeste turns back to her work, but her brow is furrowed. She does not watch as gardeners arrive to pour fast-acting fertiliser over the mound and starts when something lightly touches her arm. It is the cyberpriest.

'Celeste?' it buzzes gently.

She nods, eyes widening.

'Do not be afraid,' it intones. 'You are an invaluable resource, and now you can always be with us.' The bot turns towards the mound. 'When is it you retire?'

Celeste is trembling violently, but she manages to whisper, 'Friday.'

'I will collect you,' says the cyberpriest, 'and you may bring a companion to comfort you in your last hour.' It rises and accelerates away. 'Enjoy your last days, dear Celeste!'

She feels her legs give way. Two other gardeners have been watching, and they make their way over to her, gently helping her up. One of them hands her a hot drink.

'I don't need to retire,' she splutters. 'I'm not sick; I'm strong; I work hard!'

The workers nod sympathetically, but neither of them can be more than eighteen.

'There just aren't enough jobs or places to live anymore,' says one apologetically. 'You're amazing,' she adds. 'None of this would have happened without you.'

'Yeah,' says the other, 'you've worked so hard to help build this place, and you never complained about anything. We learned everything from you.'

Celeste manages a small, tight smile.

'We'll always remember you,' he adds, patting her arm awkwardly. They back away slowly.

As the humans retreat, fear and grief advance. Celeste misses her mother every day, and the feeling is still raw. The world she lives in now is one where old friends have disappeared or have moved hundreds of miles away because of the new safety rules. It was her mother who helped her navigate life, kept her safe when she could not manage to look after herself. But it was only once the Domes had accepted her that she found her place. Celeste lives for nature, revels in it, believing these animals and insects to be her true family, her tribe.

But now...

*Who will save me?*

*The bees?*

*The birds?*

She looks down; her cup is empty.

Outside, the mist turns to rain, clearing some of the yellowing smog from the lower slopes and the sea swells thick and dark. The humans clock off work for the day and head for their shelters. Celeste stands motionless beneath the green canopy, picturing her body petrifying into stone; the solid image helps to slow her heart.

*Perhaps I'll stop now.*

She moves deeper into the foliage and, leaning into thick creepers, closes her eyes. Mosquitos head in for their evening meal and, although the bites are uncomfortable, Celeste smiles.

*I'm still useful.*

Apart from her own bed, Celeste has never stayed anywhere overnight. Her heart thumps joyfully in the darkness as sky turns to cloud, turns to stars, turns to cloud...

The moon peeps through and sends split beams through the Domes. One lights up Celeste's left foot, and she gasps as though someone has touched her.

The following morning, Celeste is back at work, checking her vegetables, feeding her bees, chattering to the birds. The weather is changing outside: the winds are rising while deepening banks of cloud sail ever faster over the Domes. Soon, rain hurls itself, as though enraged, against the panes. She looks over to the forest area and misty waterfalls but sees no-one. Not even a shadow is moving. For the first time in many years, she feels lonely, but then a hospitality bot leads two new recruits past her plot, and she can see that they are no more than eighteen. Shining eyes and glowing limbs momentarily turn her way. She grimaces.

*Saplings. Enjoy the next forty years.*

It is her penultimate day at work. As she clocks off, for the first time ever Celeste slowly raises her chin to stare hard into the onyx eye of Security, waiting for something—a word of thanks or explanation, maybe. It remains silent and then, to her astonishment, lowers its gaze diagonally to the floor. Celeste feels her mouth stretch itself into a smile.

*Well, I'll be off then.*

Watching her city through the Sky-train windows, as it hurtles her through various levels of living quarters, she racks her brain for options.

*I just won't go back. I'll lock myself in. I'll get up extra early tomorrow and move on. No. It's my apartment; I can stay there. I just won't go in to work anymore. I've got some savings...*

The Sky-train is slowing down for her stop; second from the lowest level, where her block looms, grey and dead-eyed. If buildings could be psychopathic, this would be one of them.

Celeste and her mother once lived here together, in an optimistically labelled 'garden flat'. This means a drab bedsit with enough room for a bunk bed, one cooking ring and a fridge big enough to put a jar of pickles in. The bathroom is shared with ten other inhabitants and is rarely clean; the electricity is equally dirty, flickering constantly; and the one window looks out onto a mouldy yard, housing one dead tree. The tenements here are tightly packed, so sunlight is rationed. On bad days, killer smog steals into the space just outside her window, which remains tightly shut.

Beneath the bunk bed, an oxygen cylinder lies in the shadows, just in case.

From the top mattress, Celeste looks at her life and wonders how she might spend retirement.

I'll try out new recipes. I'll listen to music. I'll read a book. I'll grow an indoor garden. I'll—

Every ten minutes a train rattles above, causing the room to shudder. Her phone never has any signal here, and she struggles to read much of her mail while the outside world passes her by. The block has been designed so that people rarely see each other, just muddy footprints that appear here and there, or a new stain on the lino in the hallway.

*I can run away. Go travelling...*

She laughs out loud. She had been inseparable from her mother, who was her only living relative and close friend. The people who run away are fugitives or thirty years her junior; itinerants following work. The streets and hills are humming with drones, pursuing anyone who leaves their natural daily course. She has never really thought about the future; her retirement plan was left to her mother, and Celeste never had the confidence or foresight to ever ask what it was. Since her mother's death, she spends longer and longer at work each day, submerging her loss in the abundant life around her.

Celeste sits up. It is past midnight, but the trains are still running. Pulling on her overcoat, mask and boots, she runs from the building and doesn't look back.

The Sky-train takes her above the gloom to an indigo firmament, draped in swathes of stars, with the moon shining its spotlight on her as she pulls up to the Domes' platform. She flings off her coat and kicks off her boots. Running along the corridor, Celeste drops her mask onto the sedum floor to stand tall before Security: the computer blinks its eye once, opens the doors, and as the moonbeam follows her down into her domain, she feels like a queen.

All her birds and bees are asleep.

Celeste drinks from a flask of water and pours the remainder over a patch of loam. Next, she buries her hands within the mud and begins to smear it over her body, washing her hands as though with soap, rubbing it in her hair, everywhere she can reach, using her toes to wiggle her feet firmly into the earth.

*Now I'm home.*

Tall and wide as the mountain in her imagination, she waits for morning.

*Sunrise.*

Celeste walks. She breathes in the perfumes of nearby flowers; brushes against long, feathery meadow grasses; strokes the furry backs of bumble bees and a velvet pipistrelle bat that has fallen asleep before it reached its roost. Its little heart quickens at her touch, and she moves away. Reaching the waterfall, Celeste stands beneath it and feels shriven as the water pummels the mud away. Her hair is matted, but she doesn't care.

She has a sudden desire to wear something as colourful as the blooms around her, knowing her mother would have approved. Slowly, she wanders back towards her plot, where the birdsong seems to be the loudest. It is too early for the first shift, but she picks up her watering can to drench the sunflowers. The slightest of breezes alerts her to the approaching cyberpriest.

'Good morning, dear Celeste! Are you ready?'

She nods and wordlessly follows the small, shining orb through the grasses and flowerbeds to the lift, where they rise to the higher platform.

'There will be company, unless you really wish to be alone,' says the priest.

They are in front of a metal door.

Celeste tries to calm her thudding heart as the door slides open.

'If you would like a sedative...' begins the bot, but she shakes her head and steps through.

The room is bathed in soft, warm light, as though the sun is setting. Three multi-coloured forms float before her.

'Celeste!' they speak as one. 'We are here to help you transition. There is no pain, only love.'

Before she has time to say anything, they are encircling her with flower-bright gauze; the priest thanks her for her selfless work and repeats that she will always be part of life in the Domes. He gestures to a tiny wafer and vial on a tray.

'Eat and drink of these, in order to become one with the body of the Domes.'

The last physical sensation of Celeste is the taste of dark cherries.

The figures flow around her, moving faster and faster until she and they become a rainbow blur.

As the room disappears, Celeste knows her feet have left the floor.

She seems to be growing, spreading, dispersing. From far off, a crowd is cheering, clapping, and in the distance, she hears the priest saying, '...to mark the passing of a selfless woman, who served the planet in life and death. All creatures and bacteria rejoice, for through her, other worlds are born....'

As all around her fades, she senses, rather than sees her mother.

If you ever visit the Domes or work there, you will meet Celeste. She is in the air, in the plants, in the tiny worms as they forge their way through the warm earth. She will look at you through the eyes of birds, she will call from their throats and dance through the waterfall as you pass by; she shivers with delight through the flowers; and just listen to the bees; they are humming along with Celeste as she sings.

# ACORN

**KATE FOULDS** BENDIGO, VIC, AUSTRALIA

Inhaling the sweet scent of recent rain, I sit on the wooden bench beneath our acorn tree.

The earthy aroma reminds me of Imogene's small grubby fingers unfurling, 'Look! Mummy! I found a tree maker!'

Her train won't be arriving for another fifteen minutes. I cast my mind further back.

I see myself hacking through cape brooms at the station. My sister, an unwavering comrade, by my side.

Somehow we managed to carve steps into the mudbank, forging a staircase for our hideout, long before the tourist train mob steamrolled our platform.

Mum said she would have had a blue fit if she knew what we were up to.

'You could have buried yourselves alive!'

At the time her only concern was filthy pants left on the bathroom floor.

We pedal as fast as we can along the gravel track towards our hideout, carrot red hair streaming behind me, untamed, 1980's style, not a helmet in sight.

A violent late spring wind whips a willy-willy of red dust in the ploughed spud paddock, thirsting for rain.

Drifting deeper, further now, I stand before the park's imposing wrought iron gates, a mother myself.

Robbie rounds back towards me. I lift his sunhat and kiss him briskly on the forehead, giving Imogene a distant wave.

'Put your listening ears on for Uncle Trev and Auntie Sue, and be nice to your sister. See you after lunch.'

Then they were gone...

... Legs sinking, helicopter hovering. Robbie's prostrate body steadied by neck blocks, onboard, breath fading.

You don't have to be in a war zone to be blown apart.

Days turn to weeks, turn to months, turn to years, turning, turning to 2020 where borders are closing, jobs are freezing, Imogene's expecting...

'Mum! Let's go!'

Imogene pulls me to my feet from beneath our acorn tree, sunlit eyes searching beyond the confines of her mask.

'It's time.'

# GRANDMOTHER

**JENNIFER HARRISON**   WINDSOR, VIC, AUST

In one story she was holding up the earth,
all its landscapes, with sturdy laurel fingertips
(so she imagined when the labour call
came through on WhatsApp). In another,
she was hopeless, distant, and far away
as they hurried through the morning traffic
only for the nurses to send them home again
to pack a bigger, better Netflix night bag.
In that story, she was cast aside like a fishing
line no one needed yet—but soon enough
an ocean of pain was rising like a tightening
fist, a daughter leaning into the womb's
esurient spasms. The old story of empiricism:
life-as-almost-death, the cosmos watching
desire becoming new history. And now,
the oldest story of all: true agony     *intense*
*that was intense     intense*     my daughter whispers
and who hears her speak of it but me?
It's a story I'll never find again but I don't
yearn for that kind of labour: a page neither
blank nor blurred by time or forgetting. I feel
as shipwrecked now as I did then. More
than love is expected of us. And how might
I have prepared her better for the double sphinx
that guards the entryway to nurture? Earth
lonely, not in the least lonely, but the loneliest
a woman will ever be? *Labour*     such a manly
word for stone and jackhammer and splitting.

I should have warned her that this will be
a test of all pain but what kind of woman
says that to a daughter? A betrayal the same. . .
*that pain was more pain than pain*     she tells me
her voice an exhausted lambent flame
*I think I died     I wished I could have died mum*
and she looks amazed at the blanket-bound
bundle wrapped sleeping in her strong arms
*that was intense that     was intense     intense*
*why do we suffer for hours before an epidural?*
*I don't think a man would countenance that*
and here on the edge of covid FaceTime
despite virtual cards and popped champagne
I'm quiet because I knew it would be *hard*. . .
and what might she recall now that she knows
there is no forgetting? Now that she has given
her life a new membrane forever—not lonely
but the loneliest loneliness she will never name,
the lonely confidence of blood-knowledge:
that she is a mother and will never be the same.

# MORNING CHORUS

**C SULLIVAN**   QUEENSLAND, AUSTRALIA

In the depths of the night is when I felt it the most. No. Depths would imply layers; a beginning and an end. Time expanded and distorted. I no longer measured it in hours and minutes but with the frequency of feeds, the pitch of cries, and the number of sways and pats.

Sometimes, after he'd finally settled, I'd still sit holding him, too tired to get to my feet and return him to the bassinet. Everything still, except for the warm, salty tears that descended my cheeks and dropped off my face. Too much to bother wiping. I'd always been an ugly crier.

My eyes wandered the bedroom walls until my gaze fixed on a cobweb in the corner of the room. Other mothers would have tidy bedrooms. Vacuumed carpets and clean sheets with matching pillowcases.

His body still fit in the space between my fingers and the crook of my arm, but only just. He was growing. I was glad he was getting what he needed but wondered how long it would be until I could say the same.

I turned my attention to the window. The gaps between the blinds still revealed black. Soon, the outside world would start to stir. First light would seep in, and the birds would begin to sing their morning chorus as though all was right with the world.

Then, I could leave the room.

# JESSICA AT FIFTEEN

**MOCCO WOLLERT**   KEPERRA, QLD, AUSTRALIA

'I'll be the President of the World!'
Of course, she will be
because one can be anything at all
at age fifteen.

Dancing at *Blue-Light Discos*,
feeling adult, in her own power,
she is a kaleidoscope
of endlessly moving colours.

She shines with beauty,
enhanced by innocence.
Seeing her riding her horse
is like watching
a perfect *pax de deux*.

# CATCH AND RELEASE

**KAREN LETHLEAN**   HEATHCOTE, NSW, AUST

The first time I saw the kid, he would have been twelve. Caleb Johnson, little ferret, into everything, sharp and quick, was keen to talk to me one afternoon in the school holiday crowds.

'What kind of rod is that, mister?'

'Old one, sonny, automatic caster.'

'And your float—never seen one like that before.'

'It's a bubble. Watch. When there's a bite, it goes under. I pull, not too sharp. Here we go.'

Out came an under-sized bream, not the day's first. Caleb reached out, with those skinny, scabby, slightly sun-burnt arms, to grab the fish.

'Wait a minute, lad. Let the flipping die down a bit. Now hold the thing around its belly so it can't spike you. Not everything out of the ocean is trying to hurt us.'

Caleb watched as I disengaged the hook, then frowned when I went to toss the tiny fish back.

'What's wrong? It has to go back—it's undersized.'

'Yeah, I know it's small, but can you put it back gently? Fish must get a shock when they're tossed back.'

'Sure,' I said, thinking this was way too Buddhist for me.

We watched bright silver dull to grey once submerged, then the bream gasped, orientated itself and disappeared.

Caleb looked up with giant pebble eyes, so I asked, 'Want a try?'

'Can I?'

Caleb's bike had a bashed-up seat, a dirty, semi-rusted chain but swanky wheels. Maybe he nicked them? I immediately chastised myself for being judgemental; not all kids are petty thieves, rotten to the core. Just like all old men fishing near caravan parks aren't paedophiles.

Waiting for bites is a time for small talk, so I asked, 'How long you down here for?'

'Couple of weeks. My dad says an ocean holiday is cleansing.'

'He's right.'

'You live here?'

'Yep, shack up the hill, used to be more fun when my wife was alive.'

'My mum's dead too, car accident, so dad says...'

Right then the bubble vanished, and we repeated our catch and release.

'S'good to get bites, even undersized ones, eh?' I said.

'Yeah, this is fun.'

'You never been fishing before?'

Surely this, sandcastles, and surfing are essential family activities on the coast.

'Dad has heaps of times.'

A small crowd gathered. Always the way; those not dampening a rod, hang round those who are, a bit like hunter-gatherer tale sessions. Caleb beamed and lapped up their attention.

I noticed a large, beer-gutted man looming, with a brown-paper-bagged, half-drunk bottle in hand, directing an ownership leer at the boy. Soon as Caleb saw his expression, the kid jumped on his bike and vanished, skinny arms sticking out of an oversized shirt. Hair with a dishevelled, too-much-saltwater, beach-holiday look.

Caleb showed up on the pier every day for a fortnight. Animated, real chatterbox, not surly like older lads. Sort of grandson I'd always wished for. Gave me something to look forward to in next holiday's season.

Almost didn't recognise him one year, on account of his growth spurt. Hair shaved almost painfully close to his scalp, he'd grown spider arms and legs but still showed a collection of scrapes and bruises.

Didn't expect Caleb to hang around the shop with other teenagers neither. Surprised me when he spoke.

'You still got that rod and bubble, Dennis?'

Wandering back through a crowded Lakeside Caravan Park, I spied an exchange. Caleb was dragged off his bike; lots of shouting and a king-sized whack across the kid's ear. Didn't strike me that the lad ever did anything to warrant such punishment? Caleb fell to the ground, but his father not letting up, put the boots in.

Then he yelled in my direction, 'What you looking at, you old perve? I seen ya. Think it's OK to touch up little boys? That's right, bugger off, ya old weakling.'

Had my hand over the phone, not too difficult to find a number. Right there, front of the directory, under Abuse and Assault. Then alarm bells rang.

... So, you know the lad from... And how often do you see him... Where exactly does this boy live...

How bad I'd come across—like some old guy who'd taken a disgusting fancy to Caleb. That's when I knew I couldn't make such a call.

'What happened to your face?' I asked the poor kid, trying not to stare at his cracked lips.

'Slipped and fell off me bike.'

'No, you didn't.'

Caleb clammed up, stared out into the tiny swell tossed up by the nor'-easterly. Breeze came up early, bringing promise of a thunderstorm. Then he turned tear-brimmed eyes to me.

'I think it's great how when we catch small fish, we place them back, don't you?'

'You're sixteen now, aren't you?'

'Yeah, why?'

'I think you can leave home if it's not safe.'

He turns back to stare at the water, as if somehow it's sending out messages.

'Then where would I go, Dennis?'

'Come down here. I have plenty of room.'

'Get real, I couldn't even afford the bus fare.'

'Couldn't you get a paper run, deliver catalogues to letterboxes on your bike, do some odd jobs and save up the cash?'

'Nice ideas, Dennis, but there aren't those kinds of chances for a kid like me. Everyone thinks I'm going to nick something, or I want money to buy smokes.'

Now I'm the one hopelessly staring at my hands.

'Look, I know Dad,' continues the boy, putting his warm hand over mine. 'If I'm not there, he might lash out at something likely to get him into real trouble. I'm sort of like a small fish taking bait, getting pulled in and then released, compared to the shit we'd be in if some giant marlin or shark took the hook.'

Told me so much about the boy. Might never cross paths again, but I sure hope I get to see him grow to manhood. Probably be the nurse emptying my bedpans.

# THE LAST HEADY DAYS

## JULIET GUTHRIE   BOX HILL STH, VIC, AUST

laughing is sundust
shakes and heart lurches
mask zits.
i am a spry live-wire
a pale cut of meat
the desperate highs and pulling
lows
i am the smartest person in this
 room;
ha! i am inadequate
this is it
i glow

# FOSSIL

**CLARE LE**  THORNLEIGH, NSW, AUSTRALIA


Fingers trailing tender, riding ripples
Rowlocks clunk and squeal at heaving oars.
Her gaze sinks beneath the filmy surface
In amongst the mangrove roots and darting fish.

Her father has rowed steadily up the river
Freckled arms braced against the flowing tide.
Gingernuts melt slowly in her cheeks
Wedged firmly in the upside-down hollow of her jaw.

Peace. Pure peace
Aching warmth seeps through her chest.
The water is cool—a dragonfly darts across the meniscus
It's gone as soon as it's arrived—happiness is like that.

He is happy here, she is safe
Home is harder, it keeps her floundering—a fish in a red bucket.
Cold tail flaps. She spins, she's caught in motion
Scales sparkle and slide until he flips her out again, into this river with
     him.

Together they make their way further into the mangrove forest, oars
     gently prodding
'We can't break the finger roots—that's how they breathe', he says.
The mud smells rich, it's home to baby fish and crabs and water gnats
She breathes it in and rests her chin on the side of the boat.

In my child's mind I promise to never forget this—so I fossilise it
But it's not cold like the fern fossil I found at camp—this fossil is alive.
My father lives there too, and he is always happy
It's why I keep my fossil and sometimes crack it open a little—just to
     know.

I'm quiet now, I'm drowning in this faded bucket—there are only drops
     left
My tail is still, and my scales are starting to splinter.
I have been left on this pontoon for a while now. Where is he?
A shadow blocks the baking sun.

Tender fingers trail along my scales—and gently lift me.
Down I glide, down into the murky mud flats.
As I rise and near the glittering surface, I see her face
Even through the blue mosaic I can tell she's free.

I am confident of that.

# FIRST PRIZE, FLASH FICTION

## POPPY BRAZIER

BRISBANE, QUEENSLAND, AUSTRALIA

Poppy Brazier is a writer in her final year of high school who takes inspiration from her hometown Brisbane and its surrounding areas. In her story 'Flying Free', she explores the notion of teenage arrogance and overconfidence through the backdrop of nearby Stradbroke Island. Poppy loves the nostalgia writing can bring and loved bringing the Stradbroke Island landscape to life, as she has many fond memories on the island with friends and family. She hopes that readers can recognise teenage invincibility and relate to the disregard of mortality in pursuit of excitement.

# FLYING FREE

Click.

The sound of the car doors locking echoes into the crisp October night. The headlights fade out and the barren carpark fills with darkness. As we walk to the edge of the trail, our thongs squelch and squeak over the rocky bitumen, the only reminder of yesterday's late afternoon thunderstorm.

'Beat you there,' yells Noah as he sprints down the North Gorge path, its terrain flattened by the thousands of tourists and locals. I push myself harder, following in his cloud of dust, wishing that that my scrawny body would sprout wings and fly. The trees on the side of the path become a blur. Faster.

Nearly got him.

As Noah starts gloating about his win, Olivia catches up, muttering 'idiots' under her breath. The crashing waves echo like sledgehammers in the distance, pounding against the secluded cliff face. Beckoning me.

I take a running start and soar over the mottled wooden fence on the trail edge, the only barrier between me and the thrill that awaits. The others follow, the fence effortless to step over, even though Noah's towel catches the splintering wood. If they really want to stop something, surely a larger fence would help?

Trekking through the coastal brush to the rocky outcrop above the water, the terrain changes under my feet—wet scrub to igneous rock. The sharp edges nearly pierce through my well-worn thongs.

I peer over the windy cliff to the other side of the gorge. The surf lifesaving club and its mint-coloured paint now a forest green in the dark of the night. But it's not the only thing changed by the ascent of the moon. The lights are out, and the island is asleep.

We are truly free.

I throw my stuff under the screw palm, etched with our initials from a couple of summers ago, and follow Noah and Olivia to the edge of the rock wall.

It is a place prohibited by protective parents.

We have climbed these cliffs a million times over, ever since we stopped swimming between the red and yellow flags. So, it became our nest, a place to hide out and return to at night. Weaved with the memories of summers past, and now the longing to escape from our incoming futures—going to the city and leaving this place behind.

As we pass the steepest part of the decline, the handholds become more defined, worn with time. I can see the rocky outcrop in the middle of the gorge, a meeting place for white-bellied sea eagles in the spring.

The body in front of me slips.

I scream for her, 'Olivia'.

Noah whips around so fast I think his head might detach from his body.

Thankfully, her hands stay on the volcanic rock wall, and her legs find footholds.

'Don't do an Ava and fall,' taunts Noah, just as she regains her balance.

'Christ mate, do you always have to be so bloody crude,' I retort.

'It's a joke, we aren't that fucking stupid.'

Silence falls like a thick blanket. Only Olivia's deep breaths can be heard. I can see her hands running over her legs, scanning her body for cuts and bruises.

Even I notice the crimson ink pouring from the gash in her thigh, yet she moves on, as she looks at the smooth sheets of rock above her. Not a single handhold in sight, but she couldn't climb on that leg even if there was one. Past the point of no return.

I stand frozen, gazing into the black depths below me. An idiot's mistake.

Like a rabid wolf, the sea froths at the mouth, white caps form over the southern side of the gorge. Lapping, the waves lick the rhyolite below me. Blackened by the moonlight. Crashing. Weathering. Wave by wave.

'It was on the other side of the gorge, you know, nothing will happen to us,' Olivia turns back to face me, snapping me out of the tension that is beginning to build.

I grip my handholds tighter, fingers turning white, trying to keep my mind off the oceanic mongrel below, ready to snap me into its depths.

Just ahead I see Noah reach the jump point, where the cliff juts out like a worn headstone.

'Olivia and I are going to jump; she needs to get to shore to stop the bleeding', he yells out to the night; voice caught by the strong winds.

Surprisingly, instead of doing his usual arrogant backflip Noah takes Olivia's hand and they take a graceful leap into the depths below. Within seconds their bodies are swallowed. Consumed by the all-powerful creature.

I move forward to the jump spot. My knuckles begin to flush with colour again, no longer clinging for dear life. I peer back down, waiting for them to surface.

5 seconds.

10 seconds.

20 seconds.

Their initial splash has disappeared.

30 seconds.

40 seconds.

I get onto my stomach, knees scraping and drawing blood, trying to get a better look.

This can't be happening.

Another minute passes. Frozen. The rocky spires of the cliffs below bare themselves like teeth. Taunting. A monstrous wave crashes into the cliff face, causing tiny rocks to ricochet into the night, snapping me back to my isolation.

I know what must be done.

Already wasting precious time, I stand on the edge. The inky depths are beckoning me, but I know the truth of below. The only one who can save them is me.

So, I leap.

Soaring through the air.

Wind whipping my hair.

Salt spraying my face.

A bird in motion.

Prey for the sea.

# BEAUTIFUL THINGS

**ELLA MITCHELL**   WELCOME BAY, TAURANGA, NZ

Nail polish,
Half scraped off wonky toes
That bear the stories of childhood adventures
And misadventures.

Cellulite populated thighs
That imitate craters of the moon,
 Just as uneven and milky pale,
But nowhere near as mesmerising.

A belly that harbours soft rolls and curves
Like rolling hills and valleys.
'More to love,'
But too much to truly like.

Prematurely arthritic fingers
That point out each unsavoury landmark
On the map of the body I'm supposed to love.
And I do.

Sometimes.

I think of all of the beautiful things
That have come before me,
And all of those that will come after,
And it pains me to think that I am not one of them.

Not because of crooked toes,
Or dimpled thighs.
Not because of the baby fat that never quite wore off,
Or the bony fingers that prod at it.

No, not because of anything I do have,
But because of the one thing I often don't.
Confidence.
Barely a shred.

Perhaps if I possessed a little,
Then it wouldn't be so hard
To love each imperfect aspect,
Or at least to be at peace with them.

If only confidence would come as a more frequent visitor
To the body I call home,
Then perhaps the notion of becoming a beautiful thing
Would not be so unattainable.

# SARAH

**LENI MAAG**   MUNICH, BAVARIA, GERMANY

Her hair was blue. Her skin pale. The heels of her black, shabby, chained boots clocked on the floor; you could hear them from inside the classrooms when she was walking down the hallway, just like you could hear the teacher approaching. She had a dark red, washed-out backpack, and most of the time, she wore shorts and tops. She was small for her age, or maybe average height, the blue spikes of hair, rising from her head, making her appear taller. She wasn't necessarily popular, or even popular at all, in the common definition, though everybody at the school knew her name. She barely talked to anybody, barely raised her hand in class. Most of the time, when allowed, she had her headphones on. She walked through the school and slid through the days and classes as if she wasn't quite in tune with the reality of the other students, as if she was visible to them but actually moving in another sphere, another frequency, another reality. At lunch, she sat on the bleachers at the rugby field, headphones in, all by herself, eating her sandwich. Everybody knew who she was, though nobody knew anything about her. She was a presence whose presence was noted and whose absence made people turn their heads and whisper quietly behind their palms to each other. She was the quiet definition of confidence.

# CHILBLAINS

## DAVID EDWARDS    O'CONNOR, ACT, AUSTRALIA

The quivering beetle was better than Valium. Vibrating in the passenger seat, I was back in the womb. Or at least my infancy. Back when dad would drive Henry and me around the block. Sometimes over an hour, just to get us to sleep.

'That ice won't scrape itself, William.'

I waved a hand in front of his face. Swollen and scarlet, my fingers glistened as though varnished with Vaseline.

'Oh no, you're not using chilblains as an excuse again.' He turned his head away. 'Henry had them too, but he still chipped in.'

Exhaust smoke lingered in the rear-view mirror. I watched it mingle with the morning fog before opening the glove box.

'You know I can't be late today,' I said, retrieving the blue, plastic ice scraper. 'And Henry hated it when you made him do this.'

The winter air had christened every window with crystals. They shimmered in the changing light as my mother's wedding ring once had. We never found out what she did with it.

Hacking at the ice in fits and bursts, I embraced the burn that throbbed in my fingers. Until I saw those figures on the driveway. The family stickers that had adorned our rear windshield. Now discarded with unwanted frost. Mother and child lying atop a bed of ice.

'C'mon, William, do you want to make that exam or what?' Dad said, leaning out the driver's window.

I didn't look up. Just worked the remaining window in long and languid strokes, letting the ice mound upon my hand.

Pulling out of the driveway, I looked at the empty patch where the figures had rested. It's possible they stuck to the tire when dad ran them over. Two apparitions, spinning together beneath our feet.

'Where should I drop you off then?'

'Exam's in the library.'

He kept glancing at my fingers as he drove. My right hand shone beside the gearshift, singeing his peripheral vision.

'And what subj—'

'I need to concentrate, Dad.'

'Fine, we're here.'

My writing hand cramped on the first page, sprouting a spasm in that fleshy mound between index finger and thumb. Blistered by chilblains, I couldn't shake it out.

I tried diverting the pain. Digging a toe against my orthotics, clenching my jaw. Thinking about my mother; my brother. Stuck against the wheel, turning over in progressive revolutions. Tasting asphalt as they faded into ever-fainter versions of their former selves.

'William Mackellar,' Mrs Horvat called. 'If you can't stop fidgeting, I'll ask you to leave.'

'If that's what you want,' I said, standing from my chair.

'Pack your things and get out.'

I inhaled a lungful of literature, placed my thrombosed hand in the nearest bookcase, and walked the straightest line. Books tumbled to the floor like a crop of oranges shaken from their evergreen. Fifty sets of eyes on the back of my neck.

# RITE OF PASSAGE

**JAYDAN SALZKE**   MIDDLE RIDGE, QLD, AUST

Slipping through the shaving gel, the razor, aged yet sharp enough, slices my skin. I'm painfully aware that this is the exact same spot on my neck that I nicked only a minute ago. Blood begins to drip and mixes with the white of the gel to create a slightly orange concoction. I wipe it with the towel I have on standby, already damp with blood in various spots, and reveal the cut underneath. It's irrefutable evidence that my first-ever shave is not going well.

Resting the razor on the lip of the sink, I pause, close my eyes and take a deep breath. I draw on every ounce of patience that I have within me before looking again to my reflection. Shaving gel still covers the majority of the face staring back at me. It torments me with the fact that I'm not even a quarter of the way done.

I sink to sit on the cool tiles in defeat, ready to throw in the towel. It's not like I have much in the way of a beard anyway. I'm not some forty-year old who neglected the need to shave for the past twenty-plus years. I'm a sixteen-year-old locked in a battle with this so-called rite of passage, and I'm losing. Miserably.

My dad's words echo in my mind, and I try to latch onto them. He'd say, 'Jos, it's not about the times you fall down. It's about the times you stand back up.'

I know I must keep trying. Partly because I would look ridiculous leaving the bathroom with this shaving gel beard, but mostly because I want to—no, I need to—look my best tonight. 'Look good, feel good' or whatever. I'm mainly interested in not looking like some pubescent yeti, but I'll take any extra help I can get in feeling good too. The styled hair and freshly ironed button-up apparently aren't quite enough.

Standing again to face the mirror, I attend to the seeping blood of my most recent cut once more. Then it's just a case of staring down my enemy and uttering three, hopefully not baseless, words: 'stand back up.' The look of determination in my reflective counterpart's eyes fills me with a surge of confidence.

I reach for the razor and bring it to my face once again. Pulling the skin tight with my left hand, I follow it with a gentle stroke of the blade that I hold in my right. Slow but steady, I maintain light pressure and lift the blade from my skin when there's no more gel to glide through.

Success!

Looking at my handiwork, I've managed to mow one crooked patch of facial hair away.

Not wanting to push my luck, but also needing to celebrate the triumph, I take the opportunity to rinse the blade. I'm grinning like a fool as I wash the gel and few strands of facial hair from the blade.

I'm about to press the razor to my face when I hear a jangling of keys at the front door. Embarrassed and slightly panicked, I rush to move all the shaving equipment—I have quite the elaborate setup going on—out of sight. Soon, though, I realise that a face covered in shaving gel, or, alternatively, a partly-shaved one, will give me away anyway.

I resort to straightening everything again on the bathroom bench as the door closes and footsteps approach. Then, following the familiar sound of grocery bags slumping onto the kitchen counter, I'm greeted by the reflection of my mother's inquisitive face in the door.

She's still wearing her scrubs from work.

'Whatcha up to, honey?' she asks.

'Isn't it obvious?' I turn to face her. 'I mean, isn't it painfully and embarrassingly obvious?'

'Oh my,' she says, noticing the blood on my neck from one of my many incisions. 'You're making a bit of a mess of it, aren't you?'

'I would've thought that was also painfully and embarrassingly obvious.'

Her face fills with motherly worry as she steps closer to examine the cut. With care, she wets my bloodied towel and applies it to my skin. I let her. It's warm and soothing. I wonder if this is what her patients feel when she attends to them.

'Where did you even get this stuff?' she asks, eyeing the shaving gel and picking up the razor from the bench with her free hand.

'I found it in the bottom drawer. It looked alright, plus I really needed the shave so...'

As I speak, the look on her face softens from worried to dejected, and she casts her eyes to the bottom drawer. They linger there, and I feel like I've lost her for a second.

'Must've been your father's,' she says after a while, placing the razor and damp towel back on the bench. It's a solemn statement, and I can tell it's painful for her to recall memories of him.

'Oh. That makes sense.' It's a dumb reply that emphasises how especially dumb it was that I didn't think of that in the first place, but it's all I can manage.

I, too, have been sucked into reliving memories of my father. Amongst the intense chess matches and late night reading sessions, my mind drifts, as it often does, to the last time I saw him.

We're moments away from slaying the Deviljho when a shrill call breaks through the noise of slashes and explosions. I exit the game from my end and am met with groans through my headset.

'One second,' I say to the voices: Harrison and Skye's.

Adjusting the headphones to keep only one cup over my ears, I'm welcomed back to reality by Mum's repeated call, 'Jos! Dinner!'

After calling back, I replace my headset and adjust the microphone. Though I won't be joining the others in finishing off the Deviljho, I know that Harrison was right: travelling the New World in *Monster Hunter: World* was the perfect distraction.

'I gotta go, guys,' I say, expecting them to be disappointed that I'm cutting the campaign short. It's not disappointment I receive though.

'All the best, Jos,' says Skye.

'Yeah,' Harrison follows it up, though he pauses. He understands the magnitude of this more than anyone else. 'You've got this, man.'

Signing off, I wear their support as a backpack and make my way down the stairs to the dining room where Mum, Dad and three plates of perfectly square lasagne and side salad await me.

Whilst it's not unusual for our family to eat at the table, it's become increasingly difficult with Dad's work as of late. He's an anthropology professor at the local university and has just been selected to undertake field work in Greece. Like, the country Greece.

It's a really big deal for him, the first time he's had the chance to complete field work in years, but it's meant late nights of planning and preparation, either locked away in his study or on endless phone calls and video chats.

The stress clearly wears on him. He's developed dark patches under his eyes, and I never see him sit down. Most nights, Mum, just off a shift, plates her meal and mine at the table, but leaves his in the oven.

It means that tonight's dinner has an aura of significance around it. Mum's changed out of her scrubs, and Dad has exchanged his work attire for a polo shirt—a small change, but a meaningful one to show he's present with us. I've dressed up too. I wear my go-to navy jeans and white button-up with a pair of brown leather suspenders.

It's like each of us have our own reasons for why this dinner is an important one. I can't help but wonder if they've caught onto mine.

The two of them look up as I enter the room and invite me, with their eyes, to take a seat at the third plate. We go through the pleasantries of 'looks good' and 'I added broccoli this time' before eating.

With each forkful that I lift to my mouth, I feel the nerves begin to rise in me again. One butterfly grows to two, and two to three, and before long there's a colony fluttering around in my stomach. My hands, too, perspire, and I have to wipe them on my jeans just to make sure I can firmly grip the cutlery.

Finding a break in the conversation, I make sure to start before I lose my courage completely.

'I've actually been meaning to tell you both something,' I say.

They look up from their meals and the enormity of the moment—the sheer no-turn-back reality of it—hits me.

'I've known for a while that –' but I'm interrupted. Not by anything they say—in fact neither of them say anything—but by what I see. 'Dad, are you okay?'

Though before he was happily grazing on his meal, he now clutches a hand to his chest and is struggling for air. His eyes have widened, and his posture completely slumps. Something is very, very wrong.

The moment slips behind us as time speeds up. The next few minutes rush by in a cacophony of chaos and sound.

A clang. Mum's dropped her cutlery to be by his side.

A thud. He's gone to get out of the chair, and he and it have fallen to the floor.

A panicked voice. Mum's on the phone with emergency services.

I'm both frozen in place and rushing around urgently.

Somewhere in the mayhem, my eyes meet Mum's. Both are filled with fear.

His passing later that night sent shockwaves through my system and our family. I remember every detail of it, like it's seared into my memory.

I remember, too, the chaos of the next couple of weeks. Between visits from extended family, funeral arrangements and grief counselling, there was hardly any time to breathe.

Mum returned to work, she couldn't afford not to, and we ended up having to move from our two-story house into an apartment to help make ends meet. She wouldn't let me contribute, as she wanted me to stay focussed on school. But while she spent most of her time at the hospital, I spent most of mine anxious and scared.

My friends came through where she couldn't, especially Harrison. We would go on walks or play *Monster Hunter: World* late into the night and just talk. He seemed to know when I needed our conversation to be light and meaningless—and he would engage me in a Skittles versus M&M debate accordingly—or deep and philosophical. Most importantly, though, he also seemed to know when I just needed silence. For him to just be with me. Us together.

When she could, Mum and I would sit together at the table and eat and cry. Or we would go sit in the movie theatre and watch just anything to feel normal. Talking about Dad never got easier, though. It's not that either of us has nothing to say, or that we don't want to say it, but it doesn't feel right.

And that night? Whilst I'm sure both of us have relived that night in our memories over and over in the past few months, neither of us have brought up the unfinished conversation. Harrison says that it'll come up again when the timing is right. I'm still anxious about it, not sure whether she's forgotten or if she's waiting for me or what.

But, as I stand here, shaving gel dripping down my face, I watch her stare intently at that bathroom drawer and know we're both thinking about it now.

That night. That conversation. Dad.

She snaps out of it before I do.

'Well, honey. What's the occasion?' She's once again looking at my shoddy shaving attempt, and I can tell she's trying to lift herself out of the memories, so I follow suit. 'Do you have a date?' she jokes.

'Actually...'

'Shut up! My son has a date? How did I not know about this?'

I feel my cheeks flush despite my attempts to not let her totally embarrassing behaviour get the best of me.

'Who with? Is it someone from school?' She's practically jumping up and down at the thought. I'm relieved to know she approves. That, like me, she's ready for some sense of normalcy in our lives. Though, to be clear, me having a date is not normal.

'Yeah, someone from school,' I say.

'C'mon. You've got to give me more than that! Who's the lucky girl?'

And there it is. The perfect setup.

I feel the choice materialise before me: follow the usual pattern and lie. Or take the road untravelled. Tell the truth. Tell her what I've wanted her and Dad to know for the longest time. Tell her before I lose the chance to.

My insides scream that it has to be the second option. And though I did not expect this conversation to occur in a bathroom where my blood and hair are spread out behind me on the bench, I want to take the risk.

But just as the shaving gel that clings to my face reminds me of the dismal failure that is this afternoon's shaving attempt, so too does this conversation remind me of last time.

Until three words cut into the cloud of doubt: stand back up.

'Actually...' I say.

Mum's inquisitive look returns, and I have to quell the colony that has emerged in my stomach once again. Tears form in my eyes—something I cannot control—at the thought of finally saying it.

Wiping my hands on my pants, I say, 'His name is Harrison.'

'Oh, Jos.' The words appear to slip out of her mouth before she can stop them. I'm unable to draw any connotation from them, which only furthers my anxiety.

Then, the pieces come together. 'That's what you were trying to tell us that night, isn't it?'

'I've been wanting to tell you for longer,' I say. 'Both of you.'

'And Harrison. He's the boy that you play *Monster Fighters* with, right?'

'*Monster Hunter*,' I correct. 'But yeah, he's in a few of my classes at school.'

'Jossy...' She pauses and my stomach tightens, threatening to murder any remaining butterflies. The tears fall, and I feel them collect at the bottom of my face and mix with the gel. I almost can't look at her as I wait for the rest of the sentence. But I can't look away either.

'Jossy, that's wonderful. I am so happy for you.'

Immediately, a weight lifts, and although the tears continue to flow, their purpose has changed. They're contagious too; Mum's crying with me.

I'm exhausted from the confession and unable to find any more words, so I step forward and wrap her in a hug. And she hugs me back. And I get shaving gel all over her scrubs top. She holds me there until the tears run out.

Stifling sniffles, we step back again, and Mum compares her gel-covered shoulder with my face. Then, she springs straight into action.

'Well, you can't go on a date looking like that. We'll need to clean you up real good.'

'We?' I ask, 'You know how to shave?'

'I've never shaved a face, but legs are basically long and skinny faces, right?'

'No, Mum,' I laugh. 'That's a definite no.'

She runs some hot water and gets to work preparing the razor—and re-preparing my face—for the shave. It takes some time, and more input from her than I'd like, but soon I'm fresh and clean from nose to neck.

Mum stands back to admire her handiwork, though I won't be admitting that it's hers to anyone, especially not to a boy on our first date.

'Not bad,' she says. 'You look handsome.'

I feel my cheeks redden and resent it a little but allow myself to revel in the triumph with her for a moment. I've passed the rite of passage. I'm a man.

'Harrison will think so too, I reckon,' she adds.

I feel my cheeks redden again—rightfully so this time—and smile wide.

'I'm proud of you, Jossy,' she says, 'of who you are.'

Tears threaten to fall once more, but she's not finished.

'Dad would be too.'

# PARTY SONG

## SADIE YETTON  AUCKLAND, NEW ZEALAND

The moon is tired of adolescent juvenescence
Party tricks tire when all you can do is overdose
The thrill expires after half an hour or so
I should know better... but I'm still gonna get drunk tonight

Call all your friends, come round to mine
Get all your drinks, it starts at nine
Bring your girlfriend, your other one, too
Not your boyfriend, he's a douche
Hades is taking names at the door
My head is in a thunderous storm
You asked me: 'When can we go to bed?'
'We'll sleep when we're dead, there'll be time to sleep soon'

We kill ourselves for recreation
And stop breathing for a reaction
To feel alive you have to die
God, I'm on such a fucking high
Let's get incoherent
I love you when we're in the moonlight
Let's be friends forever
If infinity stops at the end of the night

I'll do anything to cause a scene
You should know that about me
Hold out your cup and make a speech
Drink to our immortality
I'll turn water into wine
I'll convince you you're divine
Don't worry yourself to death
There's plenty of time for that, yet

We kill ourselves for recreation
And stop breathing for a reaction
To feel alive you have to die
God, I'm on such a fucking high
Let's get incoherent
I love you when we're in the moonlight
Let's be friends forever
If infinity stops at the end of the night

People are faceless
I can't keep track of all the secrets
I've been told in the hazy hold
Of a bathroom in somebody else's home

Children are wasted
We turn into something sacred
When the moon glows high in a darkened sky
The ghosts of old drinks come back to life

We kill ourselves for recreation
And stop breathing for a reaction
To feel alive you have to die
God, I'm on such a fucking high
Let's get incoherent
I love you when we're in the moonlight
Let's be friends forever
If infinity stops at the end of the night

# FIRST PRIZE, SCRIPT

## JED STANLEY

REDCLIFFE, WESTERN AUSTRALIA, AUSTRALIA

Hi, my name's Jed Stanley and I'm a 15 year old
from Perth. Around the time I wrote the script for
the competition I had seen Oceans 11 and Casino
so I guess those two movies were in my mind and
I wanted to write something along those lines that
would also fit in with the theme of Confidence; set
in a familiar place (Perth) and also just something
that I wanted to write. Hope you enjoy it.

# BEAUCOUP BILLS

1     **EXT. FAST FOOD RESTAURANT - NIGHT**        1

We open onto a typical, 24-hour fast-food joint.
Late at night. The Perth skyline can just be
made out in the background. A beat-up old
Commodore pulls into the near-empty parking lot.

A MAN wearing a hoodie, face obscured by
shadow, steps out of the car. He approaches the
door to the restaurant.

2     **INT. FAST FOOD RESTAURANT - CONTINUOUS**        2

The man walks nervously through the dining
room, clutching a pistol. The few customers
in the restaurant look up from their meals –
but no one speaks. There is nothing but the
sound of FOOTSTEPS and the easy-listening MUSIC
playing from the store's speakers. It does
nothing to ease the tension.

The man raises his gun. Through the cashier's
eyes, we see straight down the barrel of the
gun. Then --

                         MATCH CUT TO:

3     **INT. FAST FOOD RESTAURANT - MORNING**        3

Straight down the 'barrel' of a plastic spray
bottle. A quiet SQUIRT replaces the bang of a
pistol.

REVERSE TO REVEAL a round, marble-look table;
on it a puddle of sanitiser fluid from the spray
bottle. A hand, holding a rag, comes into frame
and wipes the table clean.

The hand belongs to JACK GOLDFINCH, 19. He is
dressed in a yellow, short-sleeved button up
work shirt, denim jeans, leather boots and a
yellow cap with the logo of the restaurant on
it. Under that, we can see he has long, messy
brown hair.

He walks into the kitchen, throwing the rag
on a counter and putting the spray bottle down
next to it.

                    MANAGER
          Jack, take front.

Without a word, Jack spins back around and
finds himself at the front counter. A police
officer stands opposite him, waiting to order.

                    JACK
          Hey, what can I get for you today?

                    OFFICER
          Yeah, can I get a, um, coffee frappe?

                    MANAGER (O.S.)
          The machine's not working.

                    JACK
          Yeah, sorry, the machine's not
          working. Would you like a, uh, iced
          coffee instead?

                    OFFICER
          Oh, yeah, that's alright.

                    JACK
          Sorry 'bout that. Was there anything
          else?

                    OFFICER
          Nah, thanks.

                    JACK
          All good. Total comes to seven-fifty.

4      INT. FAST FOOD RESTAURANT: CREW ROOM - LATER      4

          ELLIOT KELLER, a couple years older than Jack
          - 23 - sits, bored, on his phone. He has neatly-
          cut short brown hair, pale skin, and he's
          dressed in the same work uniform as Jack.

          Jack walks into the room. Elliot looks up.

                    ELLIOT
          Hey, Jack. You on break?

                    JACK
          Nah. Finished. What time do you
          start?

                    ELLIOT
          5 minutes. Then I'm off at seven.
          By the way - you hear about the guy
          that held us up?

                    JACK
          Nah, what about him?

                         ELLIOT
          Cops caught him. Nicole said they
          found a Commodore that matched the
          description on a 'routine patrol',
          they waited for him to get in and
          they arrested him.

                         JACK
          Damn. Is he guilty? Like, does he
          have to go to jail now... yet?

                         ELLIOT
          No idea. But he didn't even wear a
          mask or anything, so they'd have his
          face on camera surely.

                         JACK
          Pretty pathetic. I'd be a better
          robber than him.

                         ELLIOT
          For real. Not like it would be that
          hard, right? Just don't leave any
          evidence, yeah? What are the cops
          gonna do then?

                         JACK
          And he still managed to cock it up.
          This isn't exactly Fort Worth.

                         ELLIOT
          Isn't it Fort Knox?

                         JACK
          Dunno. Don't care.

     Elliot stands up.

                         ELLIOT
          Anyways, I've got to start. Are you
          working Friday night?

                         JACK
          Yeah.

                         ELLIOT
          See you then, then.

                         JACK
          Later.

                                        CUT TO:

5    EXT. ELLIOT'S HOUSE - EVENING                    5

          A single-story, exposed brick, house - looks to
          be early seventies. Palm trees sway behind it,

but the front yard is far from lush - the only
vegetation is grass, and that's all died in the
December heat.

A beige station wagon pulls up to the drive.
Jack gets out, walks up to the front door, and
knocks.

COLE - Elliot's housemate, roughly the same age
as he and Jack - pulls the door ajar.

>                    JACK
>            Hey Cole. Elliot here?

>                    COLE
>            Yeah, he's out back.

Cole pulls the door fully open for Jack, and we
move to:

6     **EXT. ELLIOT'S HOUSE: BACKYARD - MOMENTS LATER     6**

The yard is large but empty. Elliot's standing
in the middle, watering the patchy lawn. Jack
calls out to him.

>                    JACK
>            Elliot!

>                    ELLIOT
>            Jack? What are you doing?

>                    JACK
>            What are you doing's more like it.

>                    ELLIOT
>            What do you mean, what am I doing?
>            What does it look like I'm doing?

Jack looks around.

A beat.

>                    JACK
>            There's no grass here. You're just
>            wetting the dirt.

>                    ELLIOT
>            Shut up, Jack. Why'd you come here,
>            anyways?

>                    JACK
>            I just... I had an idea, is all.

Elliot nods.

>                    JACK
>            I...

Jack paces around the garden for a bit before moving closer to Elliot. He speaks now in a quieter voice.

> JACK
> Remember yesterday, at work, what we were talking about?

> ELLIOT
> 'Bout the robber getting caught?

> JACK
> Yeah. Well, nah, kind of. Not the 'getting caught' part. The 'no evidence, nothing the cops can do' part was more what I was, um... thinking about.

> ELLIOT
> So... you wanna go rob someplace?

> JACK
> I'm just saying, we don't - wouldn't have to hurt anyone, and if we were
> --

> ELLIOT
(Interjecting)

> Hypothetically.

Jack looks at Elliot for a second.

> JACK
> Yeah, hypothetically... If we were hypothetically smart about it, then, the cops have nothing to work with.

> ELLIOT
> I didn't expect you to be actually serious about the whole robbing thing. I'm not a criminal. Most illegal thing I've done is like, jaywalking.

> JACK
> Exactly! So, the police have no reason to suspect us, no files on us or anything! It's the bloody perfect crime.

Elliot sighs.

> ELLIOT
> What's the plan, then?

                    JACK
          You're in?

                    ELLIOT
          I didn't say I'm in, just...

Jack moves closer to Elliot. He now speaks
almost in a whisper.

                    JACK
          We go to some, servo or something,
          next to a highway, probably one on
          the other side of town.

                    ELLIOT
          Then?

                    JACK
          Then, we'll have gloves, masks, we'll
          use my car, but we'll make it look
          different somehow, yeah? Remove the
          plates and all that. And then we'll
          just use the biggest kitchen knife we
          can find, and the cashier will give
          us the money. And then we'll be gone
          before the cops can catch up.

                    ELLIOT
          Okay, but... Wouldn't the cops find
          the car as we drive back?

                    JACK
          Well - we can always use side streets
          or something, I s'pose.

Elliot thinks for a second.

                    ELLIOT
          Aight. I'm in.

                    JACK
          Damn, man, let's go!

                    ELLIOT
          Whatever, Jack. Anything you need me
          to do?

                    JACK
          Yeah, um, you get us both some
          Halloween masks or something?

          Whatever's fine. I'll handle the
          gloves.

                                        CUT TO:

Two mugs lay on a marble bench. Jack pours a pot of tea into them both.

> JACK
> You take milk?

> LADY (O.S.)
> Just a touch, thanks hon.

> JACK
> Sugar?

> LADY
> No, that's alright.

Jack enters a cosy lounge room. Floral sofas. Watercolour paintings on the walls. A neat bouquet of roses in a vase on the coffee table. Nothing on the TV. In the corner of the room, there's a Christmas tree with presents underneath it.

On the couch, the lady who the voice belongs to: ROSEANNE 'NANA' GOLDFINCH - Jack's grandmother, mid-70's. Jack walks over and places the tea on the table in front of her.

> JACK
> Careful. It's hot.

> NANA
> I will be, sweet.

Jack sits down with his own tea. Nana takes a sip.

> NANA
> Well! It's nice to see you! Oh, Jack, I was just going to say that I have all these leftover chocolates and, you know, I can't eat them all, so you can take them with you if you want.

> JACK
> Nah, that's alright Nana. I was going to ask if I could borrow a couple pairs of gardening gloves?

> NANA
> 'Course you can, darl. Why'd you need them?

                    JACK
          Oh, there's a heap of weeds at my
          place, so me and, um, Elliot's gonna
          come over, and we thought we'd pull
          them all up and they're pretty tough.
          So, I thought I'd just come here and
          ask, rather than buy some new ones
          that I might not use again.

                    NANA
          Oh, yeah. Well, there's a couple
          pairs in the little shed out back.

                    JACK
          Thanks Nana. I'll go get them in a
          bit. And um, I'll bring them back
          soon, OK?

                    NANA
          No rush, Jack.

                                        CUT TO:

8    EXT. SHOPPING CENTER: PARKING LOT - DAY            8

          A small, somewhat run-down shopping strip by a
          busy highway. Noon. There's not a cloud in the
          sky. No vegetation to be seen. Sun bakes down
          on the asphalt.

          An old SUV pulls into a parking lot by a party
          goods store. Elliot hops out and walks towards
          the door.

9    INT. PARTY STORE - CONTINUOUS                      9

          It's a small store, barely anyone in it.
          Sunlight floods in through the windows. There's
          plenty of stuff on the shelves, mainly Christmas
          decorations. Elliot walks around and picks up
          two off-brand 'Grinch' latex masks.

          He walks up to the cashier's desk, chucks the
          masks down. The cashier - KELLY a few years
          older than Elliot: purple singlet, arms are
          tattooed, light blue jeans, chewing gum - looks
          bemused.

                    THE CASHIER (KELLY)
          Getting into that Christmas spirit?

                    ELLIOT
          Sure.

>           THE CASHIER (KELLY)
> Thirty-one ninety-eight. Cash or
> card?

>           ELLIOT
> Cash, thanks.

Elliot rifles through his wallet and hands out a
ten dollar note, a twenty dollar note and a two-
dollar coin. He grabs the masks, and we see the
cashier watch him walk out the store and hop
into his car.


10    INT. ELLIOT'S CAR - CONTINUOUS                10

Elliot's sits in his car, door ajar, tapping at
his phone. He brings it up to his ear.

>           ELLIOT
> (To phone)
>
> Hey, Jack, mate I got the masks ...
>
> Yeah, just some like full head
> covering, yeah latex grinch ones
>
> ...
>
> Sure,
>
> When? ...
>
> Ok, I'm just in like, Vic Park area,
> so I'll be maybe fifteen.
>
> ...
>
> Yeah, seeya.

Elliot twists the key in the ignition and the
engine fires up.


11    INT. FAST FOOD RESTAURANT: DINING ROOM - DAY    11

Jack and Eliot sit opposite each other at
a table. We're in the corner of a fast food
joint's dining room, no-one in earshot.

>           JACK
> So...

>           ELLIOT
> So, I got the masks. Do you have
> gloves or something we can put on
> our hands?

                    JACK
Yeah. I borrowed some gardening
gloves off my nana.

                    ELLIOT
What?

                    JACK
Said me and my friend were gonna
pull up some weeds.

                    ELLIOT
Whatever man. So, what's the move?

                    JACK
Maybe tomorrow night. Doesn't really
matter where we go, as long as it's
by a highway so we can get there and
back quickly.

                    ELLIOT
Thought we were gonna use side
roads.

                    JACK
Yeah, on the way back, I dunno. I
guess like, the cops will think we'll
be using the highway or whatever.

                    ELLIOT
I guess we're using your car?

                    JACK
What? Why?

                    ELLIOT
Cause it's faster, and you've got a
garage.

                    JACK
Faster doesn't matter. And why do we
need a garage?

                    ELLIOT
We'll have to take off the number
plates. Can't do that in the open.

                    JACK
Right. But um... We can use your car.

                    ELLIOT
Bro, what?

                    JACK
It's way more average looking!
There's gonna be a lot less matte

grey sportscars than Foresters in
Perth, aren't there. No evidence,
right?

                    ELLIOT
          Fine. But I don't wanna drive.

                    JACK
          Cool, man. I'm happy to.

As Jack finishes speaking, an elderly couple
enter the frame carrying a tray of food. They
sit at the table across from Jack and Elliot.

                    ELLIOT
          I'll bring my car over to yours
          tomorrow at ten, yeah?

                    JACK
          Yeah.

Elliot gets up and pushes his chair
in, and Jack follows.

                                        CUT TO:

12    INT. GOLDFINCH GARAGE - NIGHT              12

The garage is dingy and dark. Elliot's twenty-
year-old SUV is parked next to a non-descript
sedan, the Goldfinch family car. MUSIC plays on
a tinny stereo.

Jack is on the floor, tugging on one of the
car's hubcaps, in order to remove it. Elliot's
round the back, unscrewing the licence plate.
One screw to go. He twists round a screwdriver
and --

It CLATTERS onto the floor.

                    JACK
          Shut up. My parents will come down
          and ask what we're doing.

                    ELLIOT
          Ok, jeez. Not my fault.

                    JACK
          If it's not your fault, then whose is
          it?

                    ELLIOT
          Shut up, Jack.

Jack eventually manages to tug off the hubcap,
and places it in a pile with the other three.

> ELLIOT
> Where are we gonna put all this
> stuff? What if your parents come
> down and see the plates?

> JACK
> Don't worry, they won't. Why would
> they come into the garage this late?

A beat.

> JACK (CONT'D)
> Though maybe we should be safe, hey.

They look around the room. Jack eyes an old
fridge left in the corner.

> JACK
> We'll chuck everything into that
> fridge. Doesn't work. Don't know why
> we don't just throw it out.

Jack stands up with the four hubcaps. He opens
the fridge door; no light comes on and its empty
inside. Places the hubcaps in there. Elliot's
still sat on the floor. He clutches both the
plates in his hands.

> ELLIOT
> Catch.

Elliot throws the plates at Jack one after the
other. Jack catches them both and chucks them
in the fridge with the hubcaps.

> JACK
> So that's everything. Weird to be
> actually going through with this.

> ELLIOT
> For sure, man. I don't know why I'm
> doing this thing.

> JACK
> Let's just do it. No reason to wait
> any longer.

> ELLIOT
> Yeah.

Jack switches off the stereo in the Garage. They
both climb into the car.

13    INT./EXT. ELLIOTS'S CAR / PERTH STREETS - NIGHT    13

> It's late at night, and the streets are empty.
> The streets, and Jack and Elliot themselves, are

bathed in the yellow glow from the streetlights.
A slight, low fog hangs around the street.
It's an atmosphere reminiscent of the opening
robbery at the fast-food restaurant.

It's a quiet ride. Jack and Elliot don't say a
word. The soundtrack to their heist: the numbed
drone of the car's engine, punctuated by the
occasional tick-tick-ticking of the indicators.
Eventually, Jack attempts to strike up a
conversation.

>                    JACK
>          Hopefully... hopefully there's no cops
>          on the way.

>                    ELLIOT
>          Yeah. Cos of the plates.

>                    JACK

A beat.

>          Right.

>                    ELLIOT
>          Where are we gonna hit?

>                    JACK
>          Just feel like somewhere a bit of a
>          ways away would be the best way to
>          go, yeah? Most little thefts like
>          this, people wouldn't drive far away
>          from wherever they live. So, the cops
>          will mostly look around, wherever it
>          is we decide to rob. My thinking, at
>          least.

>                    ELLIOT
>          Here far enough?

>                    JACK
>          Sure. Somewhere round here.

Jack continues driving. Wide eyed. Ahead of
them, a large service station. A few cars
filling up with petrol, a few more parked by the
side.

>                    JACK
>          Here?

>                    ELLIOT
>          Nah, Jack. Not here. Too many people,
>          too risky.

                    JACK
          Can't be far till the next servo, I
          guess.

The drive continues. Driver and passenger
equally alert. Soon enough, there's another
candidate, and unlike the last service station,
this one is practically empty. They pull up on
the other side of the street.

                    JACK
          Here we go.

                    ELLIOT
          Chuck on the masks now. Don't want
          cameras catching our faces in the
          car, yeah?

                    JACK
          Yeah. Gloves are in the glovebox.
          Guess that's where they're supposed
          to live.

                    ELLIOT
          The knife is too.

                    JACK
          You're holding that.

                    ELLIOT
          What? Why me?

                    JACK
          I'm driving!

                    ELLIOT
          Fine, I'll drive on the way back.
          That's the more important way,
          anyway.

                    JACK
          Like hell you will. I won every time
          in Mario Kart. So, I get to drive.
          That was the deal.

                    ELLIOT
          Whatever, man. You have to ask for
          the money, though.

                    JACK
          Fine.

They both slip the oversized gardening gloves
on. Elliot grabs a large kitchen knife from the
glovebox, and Jack takes a small backpack from
the back seats; slings it over his shoulder.

14     EXT. SERVICE STATION - CONTINUOUS                 14

        Elliot and Jack get out of the car, fully geared
        up in Grinch masks and gardening gloves. They
        walk over to their target: a service station,
        with not a customer in sight - for the moment.

        The lights from around the station cast down a
        harsh, white light. The sky is pitch black.

                        ELLIOT
        (Under his breath)

                Here we go.

15     INT. SERVICE STATION - CONTINUOUS                 15

        Inside, the ATTENDANT watches as the pair near
        the entrance to the building. He senses what
        is about to happen but doesn't know what to do
        about it. He is completely still.

        The automatic doors slide open. A door chime
        sounds as Jack and Elliot enter the building
        and approach the attendant.

        Elliot raises the knife. It glints in the
        artificial light from overhead.

        Jack doesn't really know what to say. Clearly,
        these two haven't rehearsed the robbery itself.
        Elliot nudges Jack, and so he blurts out in
        a strange, unconvincing attempt at a French
        accent:

                        JACK
                Hand over the money.

        Elliot gives him a look. Jack swings the
        backpack to right in front of the attendant and
        unzips it. The attendant fumbles around, but
        soon manages to open the till and empty its
        contents into the bag. Jack and Elliot dart out.

16     INT./EXT. ELLIOT'S CAR / PERTH STREETS - CONTINUOUS  16

        The pair bolt for the car. Jack slings the
        backpack into the passenger footwell, and Elliot
        stows the knife away in the glovebox.

        Jack hits the accelerator. Jack twists the
        steering wheel and drives like he never has
        before. They get thrown around in their seats
        as Jack corners hard, out of the lot, onto the
        highway, and finally onto the side streets.

They're driving down a side street now. No cars
other than theirs. Inside, the mood shifts from
full on panic to jubilation. Elliot breaks the
silence.

>                    ELLIOT (LIGHT-HEARTED)
>          Man, what was that voice?

He mimics the voice Jack spoke in during the
robbery.

>                    ELLIOT (CONT'D)
>          'Hand over the money.' Bro, what?

>                    JACK
>          Shut up, Elliot. We did it!

>                    ELLIOT
>          I know, Jack! Easy as, man. You were
>          right.

A beat.

>                    ELLIOT
>          Nah, but like, seriously, what were
>          you thinking with that accent?

>                    JACK
>          He'll tell the police I'm French now.

>                    ELLIOT
>          That was supposed to be French?

>                    JACK
>          Doesn't matter, we did it, Elliot. Oi,
>          grab the bag.

>                    ELLIOT
>          Where'd you put it?

>                    JACK
>          I chucked it in the back.

Elliot unbuckles his seatbelt and climbs
round to look in the back seats of the car. He
rummages around and grabs the black backpack.
Sits back down in his seat and unzips it, to
reveal--

>                    ELLIOT
>          Twenty, forty, fifty, fifty-five,
>          sixty-five, sixty-six, sixty-eight,
>          sixty-eight fifty. Um, sixty-eight
>          seventy-five.

>                    JACK
>          What, each?

ELLIOT

No, genius. Sixty-eight seventy-five
total. What's that; like 35-ish each?

Jack looks slightly disappointed.

ELLIOT

Nah man, come on! We did it! The
money doesn't matter! We're criminal
masterminds, bro.

JACK

Yeah, guess you're right. I'm kinda
pumped, man! All the adrenaline.

As Jack is talking, the smile is wiped off
Elliot's face.

ELLIOT

Shhh-Shut up.

The only noise is the hum of the engine. Then,
we hear: a distant police siren. It increases
in volume. It's getting closer. Down the street,
we can see onto the highway. Barely any traffic.
The noise continues to crescendo, until --

On the highway, a police cruiser whooshes past,
sirens blazing. The noise fades away.

Jack and Elliot breathe sighs of relief. Taking
the side roads was a good move. Jack puts his
foot down and the car zips up the suburban
street.

CUT TO:

17    INT. GOLDFINCH GARAGE - LATER                  17

Jack is around the front of the car, screwing
the license plate back on. Elliot is in the
background, leaning on a shelf, doling the cash
out into two separate piles.

ELLIOT

Jack!

JACK

Yeah, what?

ELLIOT

Who gets the extra seventy-five
cents?

JACK

Shut up.

Jack finishes up with the license plate. He chucks the screwdriver onto the bench next to Elliot.

CUT TO:

18    INT. PARTY STORE - MORNING                    18

The party goods store where Elliot bought the 'Grinch' masks for the robbery. The same cashier sits at the desk. This is KELLY PIETERSON.

Kelly's the only one in the store. Scrolling through her phone. In the corner of the store, on the wall, there's a small, old TV. A breakfast news program is playing, not loudly, but certainly audible. The presenter is standing in the isle of a grocery store.

> PRESENTER
> The expansion, which has reportedly been in the pipeline for two years, was scrapped amidst disappointing returns last quarter. The news comes as rival operator Kingfisher Australia, who run the Platinum Casino in Perth alongside other smaller ventures, have surpassed Orelium to become the most profitable gambling group in Australia. Back to you in the studio, Matt.

The news program switches back to the studio. Kelly remains disinterested.

> NEWS ANCHOR
> Thanks, Ginny. Police are looking for two suspects involved in an armed robbery at a Malaga service station in the early hours of the morning.

Security camera footage of Jack and Elliot's robbery is now shown.

> NEWS ANCHOR (CONT'D)
> The bizarre robbery involved two men donning Grinch masks, as well as gloves.

Kelly looks up from her phone. Diverts all her attention towards the TV.

> NEWS ANCHOR (CONT'D)
> The pair threatened the cashier with

a kitchen knife before taking off
with a small amount of cash.

Security camera footage shows them speeding off
in an old red SUV.

Kelly stands up from the chair she was sitting
on. Walks towards a door at the back of the
store.

> NEWS ANCHOR (O.S.)
> If anyone has any information, they
> should contact Crimestoppers at--

19      INT. PARTY STORE: BACK ROOM - CONTINUOUS      19

The room is dark, dingy and cramped. Kelly
walks in, flips on the light. There is a
calendar from 2017 on the wall. She sits at a
desk and logs onto a monitor. Opens up File
Explorer. There are countless security camera
videos. She begins to type:

> KELLY
> (Typing into computer)

*cam _ 3-ext-09-12-22-0900/1500*

It opens up a grainy security camera video
showing the parking lot outside. Kelly begins
to skip to different points in the video. After
enough guessing, she manages to find what she
was looking for. It's Elliot's car, the one just
mentioned on the news, the red SUV.

> KELLY
> What...

She is taken aback. A moment passes, then:

She pulls out her phone and snaps a photo of
the video, zooming in on the car and its number
plate. She rests the phone on the table, closes
the video, and types into the computer once
again:

> KELLY
> (Typing into computer)

*cam _ 2-int-09-12-22-0900/1500*

The camera now shows the inside of the store
from behind Kelly's desk. She skips to the same
point she skipped to in the other video. Sure
enough, there he is: Elliot, with the two Grinch
masks in his hand. She takes a photo of this
too.

20      INT. ELLIOT'S CAR - DAY                          20

Elliot is cruising down a highway in his car, dressed in his work uniform. There's an air freshener dangling from the rear-view mirror and palm trees pass by in the background. A 90's pop song blasts from the stereo, and Elliot SIGNS along to the chorus.

21      EXT. SERVICE STATION - CONTINUOUS                21

Elliot pulls into the service station. He grabs a pump and begins topping up his tank.

                                        CUT TO:

22    INT/EXT. KELLY'S CAR / SIDE STREET - SAME TIME     22

It just so happens that Elliot isn't the only one to drive on this highway on the way to work. Kelly is driving along in the middle lane when she catches a glimpse of an old red SUV at a service station. There's a side street next to it, and she turns hard into, cutting across the highway and causing a few cars to honk their horns.

Kelly pulls to a stop opposite the service station. Whips out her phone, opens the Gallery app, and compares the car to the one she caught on the security cameras. License plates match up. That's her car.

She closes that app and scrolls through her contacts: clicks on a 'Shawn'. Brings the phone up to her ear.

                     KELLY
              Come on, pick up.

                                        BACK TO:

23    INT. SERVICE STATION - SAME TIME                  23

Elliot is second in the queue to pay for his petrol. He holds a small bottle of iced coffee in one hand. He looks around, impatient. Eyes a rack of sunglasses and picks out a pair of casual black ones. By now it's his turn to pay.

                     ELLIOT
              Hey, it's just the sunnies, the iced
              coffee and the, um, Pump Two.

                         CASHIER
               All good. Just sixty-two o-five.

                         ELLIOT
               Yeah.

He reaches out his card to pay.

                         CASHIER
               Have a good one.

                         ELLIOT
               Yeah, you too!

                              ZOOM OUT TO REVEAL:

24     INT. KELLY'S CAR - CONTINUOUS                24

          Kelly is eying Elliot from inside the car while
          her phone is still up to her ear. Still ringing.

                         KELLY
               Shawn? Hey, I can't make it to work
               today [.    ]

               Yeah, sorry it's such short notice,
               it's just, my car just broke down,
               and - yeah. [.            ]

               Um... Yeah, I can maybe see 'bout
               that, but Mum's at work so I dunno,
               um, I can ask Jay [.         ]

               Yeah ok, I'll seeya' on Monday then.

          She hangs up. Chucks the phone on the passenger
          seat. From her window we see Elliot leaving the
          service station and getting into his car.

                                       CUT TO:

25     INT. ELLIOT'S CAR - SAME TIME                25

          Elliot puts on his new sunglasses. Checks
          himself out in the rear-view mirror. Then he
          has a sip of his drink. Twists the key, and the
          MUSIC continues to play.

          Elliot drives off and the same time, begins to
          sing along:

          The verse concludes and Elliot takes a swig of
          his iced coffee. On a beat:

                              SMASH CUT TO:

26     EXT. FAST FOOD RESTAURANT: PARKING LOT - LATER    26

          Elliot's car pulls into the parking lot of the

fast-food joint that he works at. So too does Kelly's blue hatchback - she's been tailing him, but he hasn't realised that.

Elliot gets out of his car. Grabs his work hat, iced coffee, and slams the door shut. He makes his way towards the store when--

> KELLY
> You.

Elliot glances around and keeps walking.

> KELLY
> Yeah, you.

Elliot spins around this time. They are both standing just outside the entrance to the restaurant.

> ELLIOT
> Yeah?

> KELLY
> D'you remember me?

> ELLIOT
> Um, nah, sorry.

> KELLY
> Well, I remember you. And I know what you did. You came to buy two Grinch masks, remember?

Elliot stands still for a moment. He soon manages to collect himself and says:

> ELLIOT
> Nah, sorry. Wrong person.

> KELLY
> I need to talk to you, alright?

> ELLIOT
> I, ah... I can't talk. I've got work in a couple minutes.

> KELLY
> Work can wait. Else I go to the cops.

> ELLIOT
> I've done--

At this moment, a family of four open the door and walk out the restaurant. Elliot and Kelly move out of the way.

                    ELLIOT
          Sorry.

They remain silent until the family is out of
earshot.

                    KELLY
          Look, bro, I don't know who you are,
          but I know what you did, and I have
          the pictures to prove it. Now come
          inside and I can talk to you 'bout
          what I want to talk to you about.

                    ELLIOT
          I-- They'll make me go back to work
          if they see me. And it will be busy.
          I, I mean... You probably wanna speak
          to me in private, right. If you
          haven't gone to the cops yet.

                    KELLY
          Your loss, not mine. If you don't
          want to talk to me... I'm sure the
          police will.

Elliot stands there, dazed, before we move to:

27   INT. FAST FOOD RESTAURANT: DINING ROOM - LATER   27

          Just like when Jack and Elliot discussed the
          service station hold-up, we are in the corner
          of a dining room with no-one in audible range.
          This time, though, things are a lot more tense.

                    ELLIOT
          I'm telling you. I don't know what
          this is all about, ok?

                    KELLY
          Yeah. Sure seemed like it, out there.

                    ELLIOT
          I was just--

                    KELLY
          Shut up. You know I know it's you. I
          was watching the news and there it
          was, gas station robbery with two
          Grinch masks. Who buys two Grinch
          masks? I thought it was weird.

                    ELLIOT
          That's just a strange coincidence. I
          have to get to work, ok? That's it.

                    KELLY
Nah nah nah. So, I knew it wasn't
enough evidence to go off of. But the
store has security cameras. It was a
red SUV in the robbery and a red SUV
you used to buy the Grinch masks in.
That's no coincidence. And then I saw
your car on the way to work, plates
matched up and all, and so I tailed
you. And here we are.

                    ELLIOT
Why though?! Why find me, why not go
to the cops?

                    KELLY
Because I had a better idea. Next
time you go robbing someplace, you
take me. And most importantly, give
me a cut. Fact I don't care if you
take me or not, just so long as I get
a cut.

                    ELLIOT
What? Seriously? I'm not a criminal!
I can't... I'm not robbing anywhere
else.

                    KELLY
Yeah, right. Look. The deal is, you
give me a nice juicy cut of wherever
you decide to rob next. We'll say a
third. And if I see there's been a
robbery on the TV and I'm not getting
a slice of it, I'm going straight the
cops.

                    ELLIOT
What? What if it's not us that did
it?

                    KELLY
Keep your voice down, mate. Or it
won't be me that turns you into the
police. Anyways: I don't care. So,
you might wanna hurry.

                    ELLIOT
Jesus...

                    KELLY
One more thing. This can't be a
little servo hold-up. I'm talking a

proper job. 'Nuff for an Evo or maybe
a home loan deposit type thing.
Haven't quite made my mind up. But
um...

Kelly gets up from her seat. She pulls out an
'Audos Air Chartered Flights' business card and
flips it over to reveal that she's scribbled her
number on the back. Then she pushes it across
the table towards Elliot.

                    KELLY
          When you've decided what you're
          doing, or, I guess, what we're doing,
          then call me.

She walks away leaving Elliot a bit dazed.
Elliot is sitting alone at the table now.
Glances down at his watch: 2:03.

                    ELLIOT

(Under his breath)

          Psycho.

28      EXT. GOLDFINCH HOUSE - EVENING                28

It is late in the evening. Sky is blueish-grey.
Elliot stands outside the house of Jack and his
family. It's a fairly regular two-story suburban
house. A warm glow comes from the windows.

Elliot walks up to and knocks on the door. It's
answered by MRS GOLDFINCH, Jack's mother.

                    MRS GOLDFINCH
          Oh hi, Elliot. Here to see Jack?

                    ELLIOT
          Hi, Mrs Goldfinch. Um, yeah. Could
          you ask him to come out for a
          second?

                    MRS GOLDFINCH
          Yep, just a minute. Are you sure you
          don't wanna come in?

                    ELLIOT
          Nah, um, I'll only be quick.

She shuts the door and Elliot is left standing
outside alone for a bit before Jack walks out.

                    JACK
          What?

                    ELLIOT
We're screwed.

                    JACK
Nah...

                    ELLIOT
The whole 'leave no evidence' thing
didn't work. Cos we left evidence.

                    JACK
How do you know? What's happening,
what evidence? Are we gonna be
arrested?

                    ELLIOT
Basically... It's not the police, nah.
It's this girl, this psycho. She was
the cashier from where I bought the
masks.

                    JACK
Wait, shut up.

Jack moves away from the house and into the
middle of the front yard. Beckons for Elliot to
follow.

                    JACK
Ok, wait... psycho?

                    ELLIOT
I need to tell you everything, bro.
So the cashier saw on the news, two
robbers with Grinch masks, whatever.
And she looked through the security
camera footage and my car is the one
in the robbery. And then she stalked
me or something, dunno how, and, she
said we need to rob somewhere again.

                    JACK
What?

                    ELLIOT
Yeah, she said like — she wants to do
a robbery with us or else she goes
to the police.

                    JACK
OK, well... Could be worse. She could
have gone straight to the cops.

                    ELLIOT
Yeah, I guess, but... She said it had
to be big.

                              JACK
                 What... Like, a bank or something?

                              ELLIOT
                 I dunno, probably, yeah. And um...

A hint of a grin can be seen on Jack's face, but
it is pushed away as quickly as it came. Elliot
pauses for a second, as if waiting for his
friend to interrupt - but he doesn't.

                              ELLIOT (CONT'D)
                 She said that if she sees another
                 robbery on the news, and she's not
                 in on it, she'll assume it's us and
                 go to the police. So, we have to do
                 something soon.

                              JACK
                 Serious?

Elliot nods.

                              JACK (CONT'D)
                 Jeez. Um... You have her number or
                 like, a way to contact her?

                                                    CUT TO:

29      EXT. VACANT WAREHOUSE: PARKING LOT - DAY              29

        It's about noon at a run-down warehouse in a
        semi-industrial area. The Perth hills lie in
        the background. The warehouse is empty, but the
        parking lot isn't - a grey Japanese sportscar;
        90's; is parked directly in front of the
        entrance. Jack's. It is soon joined by Elliot's
        red SUV, which pulls up right next to it.

30      INT. VACANT WAREHOUSE - MOMENTS LATER                30

        Elliot shoves open the double doors and enters
        the first room, the reception. It's eerily empty.
        No sign of Jack, though, so Elliot moves on to
        the main warehouse area.

        It, too, is completely empty, aside from a
        modular office in a corner.

                              ELLIOT
        (Calling out)

                 Jack?

        The office door swings open and Jack pokes his
        head out.

JACK

Over here, bro.

The modular office is the only room in the
warehouse that isn't completely devoid of
furnishings. There's an old wooden desk at one
end that clashes with the sterile white steel
walls. Jack is sat at an office chair, with his
legs up on the table.

JACK

Great, innit?

ELLIOT

How'd you find this place?

JACK

It's been abandoned forever. I've
rode over here and explored a couple
times.

ELLIOT

So, we're planning the robbery here.

JACK

Yeah. I've got parents, you've got
flatmates, we can't keep discussing
it at work. And maybe we'll get like
a crew together or something. It's a
good place.

ELLIOT

You're really going balls deep in
this robbery thing. It's like you're
excited, like the psycho girl.

JACK

Yeah, so what? Same idea as before.
No evidence. Just like, more money
this time around.

ELLIOT

Whatever.

Their conversation is interrupted by Kelly
yelling out from the main warehouse area.

KELLY (O.S.)

Yo! Are you in there?

ELLIOT

(Calling out)

Yeah.

Kelly comes in through the door to find Jack on the chair, feet on the table, eyes glued on her. Elliot is standing apprehensively in the far corner of the donga.

> KELLY
>
> (To Jack)
>
> You look more chilled than the other guy.

> JACK
>
> Thanks, I guess.

There's a brief moment of silence.

> KELLY
>
> Guess we should know each other's names, right?

She points towards Elliot.

> KELLY (CONT'D)
>
> You first.

> ELLIOT
>
> Nah.

> KELLY
>
> Why nah?

> ELLIOT
>
> Cos, I don't want to tell you my name. We could use codenames or something.

> JACK
>
> Too confusing, bro. I'll just keep calling you Elliot accidentally.

> ELLIOT
>
> Nice, Jack.

> KELLY
>
> Alright, Elliot and Jack.

> JACK
>
> So, now it's your turn.

> KELLY
>
> I'm Kelly.

> ELLIOT
>
> Alright. Seeing as we're all acquainted now, I guess, what're we gonna rob?

                    KELLY
          Straight into business. I like it.

                    JACK
          Yeah well, you're the one
          blackmailing us into pulling a heist.

                    KELLY
          I'll help too!

                    ELLIOT
          As if that makes it any better.
          Just makes you seem like more of a
          psycho.

                    JACK
          Whatever. So Kelly, got any ideas?

                    KELLY
          I don't know, like a bank or
          something.

Jack takes his legs off the table, and plants
them firmly on the ground.

                    JACK
          What bank? There's a lotta banks in
          Perth.

                    ELLIOT
          I'm not robbing a bank, anyway. The
          guards'll all have guns.

                    KELLY
          Fine.

They sit in silence for a while, contemplating.
Eventually Jack is struck with an idea.

                    JACK
          What about the casino?

                    ELLIOT
          The Platinum?

                    JACK
          Yeah.

                    KELLY
          That's not stupid.

                    ELLIOT
          Seems a bit stupid. That's like... a
          big thing. Just cause we've robbed a
          servo we're not criminal masterminds.

                    JACK
Nah, hear me out bro. It's not like
they'll be expecting a robbery.

Cause like, it's never been done.
And plus - the idea is the same as
before. We take our time planning
and it'll pay off — we leave no
evidence.

                    ELLIOT
We'd have to get a crew. We can't do
it with three people.

                    KELLY
I still get a third.

                    JACK
Who said you were getting a third?

                    ELLIOT
She did, and I couldn't argue.

                    KELLY
Damn right.

                    JACK
Fine, whatever.

                    ELLIOT
So, we really doing this? We really
robbing the Plat?

                    KELLY
Looks like it.

Jack stands up from his chair. He's eager to
do this thing, though he won't say it. Both
he and Kelly look full of confidence - Elliot,
meanwhile, is still noticeably apprehensive.

                    JACK
We'll need plans, then. We could go
there, scope it out. I reckon I could
even make some money there while I'm
at it.

                    KELLY
You even old enough to gamble?

                    JACK
I'm nineteen, thank you very much.

                    ELLIOT
Just going there won't be enough.
We'll need the floorplans. I really

              doubt they'll be online, so you'd
              probably have to go to the Planning
              Department or something to get 'em.

                      JACK
              Right, well I can go to the Platinum
              and you can get the plans.

                    ELLIOT
              Bro, what? I'm not getting them - you
              can.

Jack looks over at Kelly.

                    KELLY
              Nah-ah, not me. Not today.

                      JACK
              Why do I have to do it, then?

                    ELLIOT
              Cause, we both say so.

                      JACK
              Fine. Where'll they be again?

                    ELLIOT
               The Planning Department, it's in
              the city. You'll be allowed in,
              just, won't be allowed your phone or
              anything.

Jack looks down at his watch: 1:38. He walks
over to the donga door.

                      JACK
              Can't believe you're making me do
              this.

                            CUT TO:

32     **EXT. DEPT. OF PLANNING - LATER THAT DAY**     32

        A street in central Perth just outside the
        Department of Planning: a forgettable mid-
        rise office block, probably from the sixties or
        seventies. Jack's grey sportscar from earlier
        pulls up to the curb across the street and he
        gets out, walking across the street and inside.

33     **INT. DEPT. OF PLANNING: LOBBY - CONTINUOUS**     33

        Inside, it's more of what you would expect -
        granite floors, eggshell walls, some old-timey
        paintings hung up on them and a bored looking
        RECEPTIONIST standing behind a dated monitor.

Jack approaches said receptionist, a bit excited, mostly nervous.

                    RECEPTIONIST
          Hi there, how can I help you?

                    JACK
          I'm here to see the floorplan for the
          Platinum Casino.

                    RECEPTIONIST
          Okay, and you're aware that any
          reproduction of the plans is a
          criminal offence?

                    JACK
          Yeah, course.

                    RECEPTIONIST
          Alright then. The other thing is
          you're not allowed any recording
          devices past this point. I can take
          your phone for you if you have it,
          and I'll keep it here until you're
          done.

A pause.

                    JACK
          Uhm, yeah, that's cool.

He fishes his phone out of his pocket and hands it over to the receptionist. She takes it and stores it somewhere out of sight.

                    RECEPTIONIST
          Ok, that's all good. So, the Platinum
          Hotel and Casino - plans are on the
          5th floor. Straight down the hallway
          after you get out the lift, then hook
          past the toilets. You'll find them in
          the Hotels and Entertainment section.
          Hard to miss.

Jack nods his head to the receptionist and we move to:

34   INT. DEPT. OF PLANNING: ELEVATOR - MOMENTS LATER   34

Jack stands idle in the elevator, which is slowly moving upwards. He glances at the floor indicator:

3...

4...

On 5 we move to:

35     INT. DEPT. OF PLANNING: 5TH FLOOR - CONTINUOUS     35

The elevator doors slide open, and we find that
it's more of the same - dated décor and void of
all but a few people.

There's a hallway that stretches down the
length of the building, and so Jack walks down
it as per the instructions given to him by the
receptionist. He takes note of the security
cameras.

He turns a corner past the toilets and heads
down another shorter hallway to the place he's
looking for, Hotels and Entertainment. It,
unlike most of the other rooms in the building,
has someone in it: an older MAN wearing a suit.
He's examining some files. Jack opens the door
and steps into the room. eyes the man for a
second.

                    MAN
          Oh, sorry, I'll get out of your way.

                    JACK
          Oh nah, that's alright, I was just
          looking for something over here
          anyways.

He walks over to a filing cabinet, which has 'P-
R' scrawled on it in permanent marker. He rifles
through the folders and selects one that reads:

PLATINUM CASINO - FLOOR PLAN

Jack pulls it out of the cabinet and begins
examining the files - biding time until the
suited man leaves. It's not long before exactly
that happens, and with the room to himself, Jack
quickly scans the walls for cameras - there are
none - and then grabs the pages in the folder
and shoves them under his shirt. He puts the
empty folder back where he got it.

36     INT. DEPT. OF PLANNNG: LOBBY - MOMENTS LATER     36

Jack is walking to the exit somewhat hurriedly
when the receptionist calls out to him.

                    RECEPTIONIST
          Any luck?

                    JACK
          Wha? Oh, nah, I couldn't find 'em.

                    RECEPTIONIST
          Really? I can go and have a look if
          you want.

                    JACK
          Nah, it was just... Well, the folder
          was there, Platinum Casino Floor
          Plans, but there was nothing in it.

     The receptionist looks at Jack for a moment.

                    JACK (CONT'D)
          Probably just got misplaced or
          something. It's no worry, I don't
          need 'em urgently or anything like
          that.

                    RECEPTIONIST
          Right, well um... Sorry about that.

                                        CUT TO:

37   INT. VACANT WAREHOUSE: OFFICE - DAY          37

     Elliot and Kelly are back in the portable office
     in the warehouse, awaiting Jack, who soon walks
     in with a grin on his face and three pages of
     floorplans in his hands.

                    JACK
          Alrighty then, no need for applause,
          but I've done it. Got 'em.

                    ELLIOT
          Nice stuff!

                    JACK
          I was basically James Bond back
          there, bro.

                    KELLY
          Let's have a look then.

     Jack lays the pages out on the desk. All three
     of them crowd around it.

                    JACK
          Each one's for a different floor.
          There were like 15 others but they
          were all rooms and restaurants and
          stuff, this is what matters.

                    KELLY
          Alright, so we got the casino floor
          here... What're the other two?

                    JACK
          Right, so, I had a look in the car
          and:

He points at the one on his right.

                    JACK (CONT'D)
          This one's the one that really
          matters. The cash room.

                    ELLIOT
          Level minus 2.

                    JACK
          Right. Then the other one isn't as
          important, but the stairs between
          the casino floor and the cash room
          go through here so I guess it's best
          we got 'em.

                    KELLY
          Generator room?

                    JACK
          Yeah, so that presents some like,
          opportunities, I guess.

Elliot moves his finger back to the page on the
right, the floorplan of level minus 2. Which
also happens to be level with the underground
parking garage.

                    ELLIOT
          I see an opportunity right here.
          See this hallway right here? It's
          connected to the cash room and
          there's only a little wall between it
          and the parking garage.

                    KELLY
          Right, so we could get a sledgehammer
          or something. Or even like explosives
          from the mines up north maybe.

                    JACK
          Actually... I reckon I've got an idea.

                    ELLIOT
          Yeah?

                    JACK
          We could get a car, like a big ute
          or SUV or something. And we'd have a
          whole big range to choose from 'cause
          we'd be in the parking lot.

                    KELLY
And they put all the keys to them
someone, the valet place. That's
actually pretty bloody smart, Jack.

                    ELLIOT
So, we just would, like, crash into
the wall?

                    JACK
Yep. And then we could drive straight
away afterwards.

                    ELLIOT
You know how we were talking about a
crew before?

Jack and Kelly both nod.

                    ELLIOT (CONT'D)
We could... well, not exactly crew,
but we could pay off the valet to
take a piss or something at the
exact time we come so we could take
the keys easy.

                    JACK
Yeah, that works. We just need to
find someone, get them on board, all
that.

                    KELLY
Alright, so we're just gonna drive
into the basement and get cash from
the room? Wouldn't there be heaps of
guards there?

A beat.

                    JACK
What about a distraction? They had
this robbery in, like, Sweden or
somewhere, and what they did was
they blew up some cars outside and
then all the guards inside ran out
to take a look. I dunno, that could
work.

                    ELLIOT
Yeah, nah. Maybe some would go and
take a look but probably not the
guys underground guarding all the
cash. And they'd all still be nearby

anyways, so it wouldn't be ideal even
if it did work.

                    KELLY
          I reckon I've got an idea.

The boys wait for her to continue.

                    KELLY (CONT'D)
          What if we did another robbery
          at the same time. We could get a
          crew, and make it more like, sloppy
          looking. They'd just go and rob the,
          um, croupiers. Then all the guards
          would come out and focus on them
          and we could get into the basement
          silentlyish.

                    JACK
          Alright, yeah, that works. Then we'll
          need to get some people to do that.

                    ELLIOT
          And we'll get a bit of money from
          robbing the croupiers as well. Win-
          win, I like it.

Jack looks at Elliot with a grin on his face.

                    JACK
          You're excited for this, admit it.

                    ELLIOT
          Fine, a bit. But I also think it's
          stupid as.

                    KELLY
          Confidence, man. So, we need a couple
          people to do the distraction thing,
          need a valet to look the other way
          while we take a ride, and we'll need
          some guns. No idea how we'll get
          those.

                    JACK
          Alright, well, look, I reckon we
          start with the valet, that seems like
          the place to start.

                    ELLIOT
          Tomorrow. Me and you.

Kelly nods.

                          JACK
                  Sounds like a plan.

                                          CUT TO:

38  INT. ELLIOT'S CAR: UNDERGROUND PARKING GARAGE – DAY 38

        It's sometime the next day. Elliot's car is
        parked up in the underground parking garage
        at the Platinum Casino. Inside, it's obvious
        they've been there for a while. Elliot is in
        the driver's seat, scrolling through his phone,
        while Jack is in the passenger's seat with his
        feet up on the dash.

        Through the car window, we can see the valet
        booth. There's a VALET inside, a tall man of
        roughly 30 wearing a grey suit with 'Platinum'
        embroidered on the collar, and a bowtie.

        Another valet walks into the booth and the
        two men have a short conversation, and though
        we can't make out what is being said it still
        catches the attention of Elliot, who looks in
        their direction.

                          ELLIOT
                  Oi, Jack, look. I reckon our boy's
                  shift is finished.

        Jack takes his feet off of the dash and joins
        Elliot in eying the two men. The tall valet
        they've been watching disappears through a door.

                          JACK
                  Took him long enough.

                          ELLIOT
                  Wait, d'you reckon he'll come back?
                  Surely, he's left his car down here,
                  right?

                          JACK
                  Don't know, just chill. He'll come
                  back through the door; he's probably
                  just getting his stuff.

        Nothing happens for a few seconds. But then: the
        valet walks back through the door and towards a
        car parked in the space nearest the booth.

                          JACK
                  There we go.

        The valet gets into the car and pulls out
        of the parking lot. As soon as it disappears

behind a concrete wall, Elliot puts his car into gear and drives out after it.

Elliot tails the valet's car as it drives up the ramp to street level of the parking garage. It's noon, and the sky is cloudless. Both cars drive out of the garage and onto the street.

39    EXT. ELLIOT'S CAR / PERTH STREETS - CONTINUOUS    39

The road past the Casino runs parallel to the Swan River, and it's lined with neatly trimmed grass and trees. The valet is driving down the road, with the boys a couple car-lengths behind him.

                    ELLIOT
          Where are you taking us...?

The valet's car rounds a corner and joins a main road, and we cut to:

40    EXT./INT. VALET'S HOUSE - AFTERNOON    40

It's now the early afternoon. We are outside a block of cream-brick townhouses. The valet's car pulls in and parks in the driveway of the nearest one. Not long after, Elliot and Jack come into frame and park across the street. The valet, now out of his car, looks at the red SUV, but then ignores it and heads inside his house.

                    JACK
          All right. Wasn't so hard.

The boys approach the house and, after a second of hesitation, Elliot knocks on the door.
There's a moment of awkward silence but then the valet cautiously opens the door.

                    VALET
          What do you want from me?

                    JACK
          Let us inside. We have a, uhm,
          proposition.

                    VALET
          What? Go away.

                    JACK
          Nah, nah, just, we wanna talk.

                    VALET
          I'm calling the cops.

ELLIOT

No, you're not. Let us in.

A beat.

JACK

We're not gonna hurt you, bro.

41    INT. VALET'S HOUSE - MOMENTS LATER                41

Inside, the house is tidy but dull. There are
two couches - on one, Jack and Elliot, and
on the other, the valet is sitting; tense,
trembling.

VALET

This is so stupid. What do you want?

ELLIOT

You're a valet at the Platinum?

VALET

Yeah, you know that. You followed me
home from work.

ELLIOT

You work often? DO you have a roster
or anything?

VALET

Why are you asking me this? Please,
just go.

JACK

Nah, not happening. You are gonna
give us your roster and then we will
be in touch.

VALET

Can you please just tell me what this
is all about.

JACK

Ok, look: What's gonna happen is you
are going to quickly run off from
your station, have a piss, and when
you come back the casino will've been
robbed.

VALET

What? No, no, I'm not a criminal.

JACK

You're not doing anything criminal.
Just taking a quick break at a
specific time and getting paid for
it.

                    VALET
        But it's illegal...

                    ELLIOT
        Nothing illegal about going to the
        toilet.

                    VALET
        Nah, I... Why did I even let you into
        my house? Should've known you were
        trouble. Please, can you just go?

                    JACK
        Look, I'm gonna explain this to you,
        alright? You're gonna be at work,
        right, and at a certain time you're
        gonna go and take a quick break,
        and when you return a set of keys
        will be missing but other than that,
        everything's gonna be the exact same
        as usual. You'll get a couple grand
        for doing absolutely nothing at all,
        nothing illegal.

A moment of silence passes.

                    ELLIOT
        Take that as a yes. We'll be in touch
        soon, yeah?

Jack and Elliot get off the couch and walk out
the door. The valet is left sitting in a trance.

42    INT. ELLIOT'S CAR - MOMENTS LATER            42

        The boys are both sitting inside the car, still
        parked across the road from the valet's house.

                    JACK
        Well, that went good, ay?

                    ELLIOT
        Yeah. I guess.

                    JACK
        Come on. Went great. That's one thing
        off the list of things we've gotta
        do.

                    ELLIOT
        Yeah, yeah. What next though?

                    JACK
        Gotta get a crew somehow. And guns
        as well. No idea how we do either of
        those things.

Elliot puts his seatbelt on and turns on the car.

                    ELLIOT
          Yeah, nah, me neither. Maybe the
          psycho-girl will know some people; I
          dunno.

                                        CUT TO:

43    EXT. SHOPPING CENTER PARKING LOT - EVENING        43

The sky is orangish-yellow, the late sun frames
the edges of the clouds. The majesty of the
evening sky contrasts harshly with the dullness
of the shopping strip parking lot outside
the party goods store. There are only two or
three cars in the lot, all parked apart. Kelly
Pieterson gets out of one of them.

44    INT. PARTY STORE - MOMENTS LATER        44

There are two main differences at the party
store this time around. First: the monotonous
whites, greys and beiges that make up basically
every feature in the store are awash with that
same rich orange hue, pouring in from the
windows.

Second: Kelly isn't the cashier. That role falls
to GRACE HALFPENNY, 25. Pale skin and dark
brown hair.

                    GRACE
          Kelly? You're not rostered 'till
          Friday, I thought. Or are you
          actually going to buy something?
          Christmas decorations, or...

                    KELLY
          Nah, I'm here to talk to you 'bout
          something.

                    GRACE
          Yeah?

                    KELLY
          Yeah. Just you in here, or...?

                    GRACE
          Yeah, as usual.

                    KELLY
          I'm gonna rob the Platinum. Me and a
          couple guys. So...

A pause.

That was... I said it a bit fast,
didn't I. So, do you wanna be in on
it?

                    GRACE
Are you actually serious? Rob the
Platinum, how, why?

                    KELLY
Why is the easier part. 'Coz I don't
wanna have to come here anymore,
and I've got nothing else to do in
my life. It's the same thing every
day otherwise. How? That's what we're
working on, and, well, we've got a
pretty solid plan, but we need more
people.

                    GRACE
So you want me... to help you rob a
huge casino.

                    KELLY
Who else was I gonna ask? Anyways, I
trust you. Worst that could happen

would be you saying no. I know you
won't turn me in.

                    GRACE
Yeah, well, you've just turned this
into an unusual day.

                    KELLY
So? Every day is usual. Unusual is
good. Everyone does the same thing
every day. Do most people think to
pull a heist? No. Why not?

                    GRACE
Because they aren't stupid...

                    KELLY
Whatever. Look, sorry I dragged
you into this, dunno what I was
thinking. If you don't want to be a
part of it, all good, I don't blame
you.

                    GRACE
Nah, nah, I... I kinda get you.

                    KELLY
Really?

                    GRACE
          Yeah, just a bit. It's crazy. A bit
          stupid. But, then again, you were
          kinda right.

                    KELLY
          Kinda right how?

                    GRACE
          In that most people don't ever think
          of robbing a casino. Especially not
          in Perth. It's so unexpected, so out
          of the blue, 'reckon it could work,
          if you guys had a good enough plan.

                    KELLY
          So, you're in?

                    GRACE
          No. Maybe... nah. I guess, I'll see.
          I'm tired, can't think over this all
          now. And I'll have to see the plan
          and all. When you've got some stuff,
          then text me and I'll come over.

                    KELLY
          Can't believe it.

                    GRACE
          Don't get your hopes up, Kelly.

45    INT. VACANT WAREHOUSE: OFFICE - DAY            45

     The warehouse office has changed since we last
     saw it: The floorplans of the casino have been
     stuck to the wall; a small whiteboard has been
     brought in and is standing in the corner of the
     room.

     Jack and Elliot are the only ones in the room
     at first but that changes when Kelly enters,
     followed by Grace.

                    JACK
          Damn, alright. Kelly's managed to
          drag someone else into this thing.

                    GRACE
          Maybe. She hasn't yet fully convinced
          me.

                    ELLIOT
          Well, we're gonna need you anyways.
          Maybe some more people as well, but

we can cross that bridge when we get there.

(to Kelly)

> We've done the valet thing, by the way. Once we're there we can just take some keys.

               KELLY
Nice stuff. Um - this is Grace. Hopefully newest member of our crew.

               GRACE
Yeah. So, do you guys have a plan of some sort, or anything?

               JACK
Um, yeah. Not entirely 100 percent done, but it's mostly there.

A wave of SILENCE comes over the room as Grace awaits Jack's response. Jack looks at Elliot.

               JACK

(To Elliot)

> You wanna...

               ELLIOT
No. You can.

               JACK
Alright then. Um...

Jack moves over to the white board and, with a marker, attempts to DRAW the plan out as he speaks.

               JACK (CONT'D)
Basically, we have two teams. One goes in first, that's the team we need you for. That team is gonna go straight in the front door with big scary-looking guns and go over to the casino, try get all of the money that the croupier has. Won't be shooting anyone.

At the same time the other team, maybe a bit smaller, will be getting into the underground parking garage. We've got the valet on our side, so, he's gonna go away for a sec and in that time, we will get keys for a

big, fast SUV. Should be plenty of
them. We'll find it and get down to
the second underground floor which,

(He points to underground floorplan)

is only separated from the cash room
by a little brick wall. By now, by
the way, hopefully all the guards
will be busy, so we can get in, grab
the cash, get out.

By now the 'plan' that has been scribbled on
the whiteboard is incomprehensible. Jack CHUCKS
the pen away.

                    JACK
I'll fix that up.

                    GRACE
Alright, well, I guess that sounds
good. Do you have guns yet?

                    KELLY
Nah, we still are working on that.

                    GRACE
Right, well, my uncle has a heap on
his farm. I could ask him. I don't
know him super well but he's kind of
a crackpot. That's why I don't know
him super well, I guess. Anyways, I'm
sure he could, like, lend us some.

                    ELLIOT
Really? You sure he's chill with it?

                    GRACE
I - feel like he would be. He's, um,
he doesn't like the cops very much,
so I guess...

                    ELLIOT
Only if you're sure.

                    GRACE
Yeah, I reckon.

                    JACK
Does that mean you're in with the
heist, too?

                    GRACE
Um... Guess so. But one more thing.
How are we gonna escape?

                    JACK
          Once we've got the car, well, it'll
          be right there, so we were just
          gonna speed off in that and pick the
          other crew up in it at the entrance.

                    GRACE
          Would be pretty recognisable, though.
          Smashed up back end. If you're gonna
          be at the valet, why not just take an
          extra set of keys for a getaway car?
          Something inconspicuous.

                    ELLIOT
          Yeah. Good one. We could even get a
          driver to keep it ready for us while
          we're inside and getting rich.

Jack clasps his hands together and sets them on
the desk.

                    JACK
          Good ideas. Plan is coming along
          well, I think.

(To Grace)

          You, ask your uncle in whatever way
          you think'll work. We're gonna need
          probably three guns. Two for the
          crew who goes upstairs cos they'll
          need to be scary. One for one of us
          who does the cash room, just in case
          and guards or cops are down there
          still. Type of gun doesn't matter;
          we've got no intention of killing
          or hurting anyone. Just make sure
          they're big and scary-looking.

(To Kelly)

          Kelly, can you try get us masks and
          gloves and stuff? Shouldn't be hard,
          just take 'em from your work somehow.
          Five - four for all of us, one for
          the driver. Me and Elliot know a good
          guy for that.

                    ELLIOT
          Who, Cole?

                    JACK
          Yeah. Anyways, once that's all done,

we can find a day when the valet's on
shift and it's good for us to go.

CUT TO:

46      EXT. FARMHOUSE - MORNING                    46

A battered hatchback makes its way down an
empty dirt road. There's a thin wall of foliage
separating the road from a large expanse
of yellow grass. At the end of the road: a
FARMHOUSE, somewhat rundown: corrugated iron
roof, exposed brick, surrounded by native
vegetation. The car pulls to a halt in front of
the house. Grace gets out.

47      INT. FARMHOUSE - MOMENTS LATER              47

Inside, the house is more 50s rural
architecture. There's a fireplace, but it seems
not to have been used for years.

Above, a ceiling fan WHIRS. Pictures of classic
Fords adorn the wall. Grace is sitting on a
couch, somewhat nervous.

Opposite her: her uncle, BRAD HALFPENNY - late
forties, balding, specs of grey in his scruffy
beard. He speaks with a thick, deep Aussie
accent.

                    GRACE
          Thanks for having me, um, Uncle Brad.

                    BRAD
          No worries, darl, it's been ages!
          Were you down this way and popped
          in, or...?

                    GRACE
          Yeah, I was going to Busselton and
          um, yeah, I was down this way. But I
          also wanted to ask you something.

                    BRAD
          Yeah? Hit me.

                    GRACE
          Well, it's um... me and some friends
          kinda need, uh, if we could borrow
          some guns. It's kinda hard to
          explain, but, just, me and my friends
          are gonna need some and I thought of
          you.

> BRAD
> How many 'you need?

> GRACE
> 3, if that was ok.

> BRAD
> Right. Well, I'll need you to tell me what you're using them for.

> GRACE
> Um... hunting.

Brad shakes his head.

> BRAD
> Grace, look, you know me, I don't care. I won't tell your parents or anyone either. Just want you to be honest with me, can you do that?

Grace is about to speak...

CUT TO:

48    INT. PARTY STORE - DAY                          48

The cashier this time is neither Kelly nor Grace. The former, however, is in the store, in the back corner. There are piles of low-quality latex masks, many of them Christmas-themed.

Kelly, not particularly worried about what items she selects, GRABS 5 identical Santa Claus masks, and then some comparatively benign basic black gloves.

She approaches the CASHIER and places the items in front of him for him to scan. They know each other - that much is given away by the strange look he gives her - but not a word is spoken and she picks her purchases back up and exits the store.

CUT TO:

49    EXT./INT. ELLIOT'S HOUSE - DAY                  49

Around the same time, Jack is standing outside Elliot's house while he unlocks the door. They head in.

> COLE
> (Upon hearing door open, calling out)
> Hey, Elliot.

                    ELLIOT
          It's me and Jack. We wanna ask you
          'bout an, um, idea we have.

Cole is sprawled out on the loungeroom couch.
He's playing a racing game, which he promptly
pauses and turns to address the pair.

                    COLE
          Yeah, what?

                    ELLIOT
          You're good at driving cars, yeah? Me
          and Jack have a plan. We need you to
          drive.

                    COLE
          Robbing somewhere?

                    ELLIOT
          Yep.

                    COLE
          Damn. I dunno, I don't have to use
          my own car, right?

                    JACK
          Nah, bro. You'll have the whole
          Platinum Casino carpark to choose
          from.

                    COLE
          Seriously? You're robbing the
          Platinum? That's crazy!

                    ELLIOT
          It's... We've got a good plan, and a
          crew. We just need a driver, now.

                    COLE
          Alright, well, what do I have to do?

                    JACK
          We paid off the valet so you can just
          grab whatever keys you reckon - and
          then you pick us up and take us away
          once we're done.

          Obviously, there's more to it than
          that, just, we'll lay that out if you
          agree.

                    ELLIOT
          Yeah. Car has to be a five-seater

and not too obvious, though, so,
don't get your hopes up for any
Lamborghinis.

A pause.

                    COLE
Alright, that's fine.

                    JACK
That mean you're in?

                    COLE
Yeah. So long as the plan's not
stupid. And, Elliot, I mean, you're
not stupid, so...

                    COLE (CONT'D)
Not saying you aren't, Jack, just, I
know Elliot's pretty smart. Anyways,
anyways, just, tell me the plan
sometime, tell me where and when,
and we're good to go.

50    INT. JACK'S CAR - MOMENTS LATER                   50

Still parked outside Elliot's place. Engine on,
but they aren't going anywhere yet.

                    JACK
Almost like he wanted to be getaway
driver. So much easier than like, the
valet. And he doesn't even have a big
job, just has to, y'know, piss off
for a bit.

                    ELLIOT
Cole's chill. Likes cars, and money.
Anyways: we still gotta get the
valet, find a date we can do this
thing.

They buckle up their seat belts.

                              CUT TO:

51    EXT. VALET'S HOUSE - AFTERNOON                   51

It is early afternoon. Once again, the boys
have parked across the road from the valet's
residence, and once again they walk over the
road and knock on the door. The valet begins
to FLING open the door carelessly, but his eyes
make contact with Jack's and his demeanour
shifts.

                    VALET
          Go away. I already said, I don't want
          to help you.

He SLAMS the door closed.

                    JACK
(Speaking through the door)

          C'mon, man! Giving you an opportunity
          here!

A pause.

                    ELLIOT
          Don't make us get the bat. Open up.

There's another pause, this one longer.
Eventually, though, the valet hesitantly opens
the door and motions for the pair to enter.

52    INT. VALET'S HOUSE - CONTINUOUS                52

     Back inside, the valet looks less fearful and
     more defeated.

                    JACK
          We just wanna know when you're
          working, for the next week or so.

                    VALET
          Wha- why?

                    ELLIOT
          You know why. We're not asking much
          of you.

                    VALET
          Alright, sorry, I'm just...

          I'm working, um, tomorrow, 21st and
          22nd then a break on the 23rd and
          then an overnighter from the 24th to
          Christmas, then--

                    JACK
(Interrupting)

          An overnighter?

                    VALET
          Yeah, um... from eight at night
          on the 24th to four-thirty in the
          morning on Christmas day.

Jack looks at Elliot, who nods in approval.

                         JACK
               Here is what's gonna happen:

**TITLE CARD:**
**'12:00 AM, DECEMBER 25 - DAY OF THE HEIST'**

                                        CUT TO BLACK:

                                           CUT TO:

53      **EXT. VACANT WAREHOUSE: PARKING LOT - NIGHT**      53

        The parking lot outside the vacant warehouse
        turned planning-room is fuller than ever.
        Jack's grey sportscar, Elliot's red SUV, the
        battered, and now dusty hatchback owned by
        Grace, alongside two other cars owned by Kelly
        and Cole. The sky is dark, starless; the moon
        is large and is the only thing illumining the
        scene.

54      **INT. VACANT WAREHOUSE: OFFICE - SAME TIME**      54

        The office is fuller than ever. The room is lit
        only by an LED camping lantern placed on the
        desk. The rough scribblings on the whiteboard
        have now been replaced with a more coherent
        map:

        There are three main areas drawn on the map -
        One marked with an A, another marked with a B
        and lastly, one marked with a C.

        On either side of the whiteboard: Jack and
        Elliot. Sitting on the desk is Kelly, and Grace
        next to her, and Cole - only familiarised with
        Jack and Elliot - stands in the corner of the
        room. Next to him, three black hunting rifles
        are leaning on the wall. Thrown on the office
        chair are the masks and gloves supplied by
        Kelly, still in their original packaging.

                         JACK
               Alright, we've got everything done,
               and we're here. All on time. Merry
               Christmas, everybody.

               Just wanna say, like, we're in deep
               now. No backing out. Be confident in
               yourselves, and in each other, and we
               can do this thing real good, yeah?

                         GRACE
               Alright.

                    COLE
          Yeah.

Jack picks up a whiteboard marker and turns to
face the board.

                    JACK
          Gonna run through the whole plan,
          just so we're all fresh.

          It's twelve-ish now, maybe a couple
          minutes after. We're all gonna be
          here, this big A, by fifteen to one.
          It's a little parking lot thing, but
          it's always empty. Cole's driving.
          He drops us all off - we don't have
          masks on yet, by the way, but he'll
          chuck one on once we're dropped off
          and make his way down to the B.

(Jack is tracing a line from the 'A' to the 'B'
as he speaks.)

          That's the underground parking
          garage. In there, Cole, you park up,
          and go to the valet.

Cole raises his hand, like a student asking
a question, but doesn't wait for Jack's
acknowledgement to start speaking.

                    COLE
          Ay, so, you said I didn't have to use
          my car as a getaway car, right?

                    JACK
          Yeah, I was thinking you could just
          leave it there and grab a different
          car to escape in, or...

                    COLE
          No way, mate. It's only a little 2
          door anyway, 4 seat. Can't fit all of
          us in there.

                    GRACE
          Drive mine there. It's battered
          anyway, and once I've done this, I'm
          getting something new.

                    JACK
          Right, well, that's sorted out.
          Anyways, so, once you've done that,

get to the valet booth at exactly 12:55. There shouldn't be anyone there. You're gonna have a look through keys and get two; first's gonna be something big, like a ute, cos me and Elliot are gonna run that through a wall. Keep that in mind.

The other one's gotta have space for all of us, and the guns and money, and be fast, but not too obvious.

                    ELLIOT
That's a very specific kinda car.

                    COLE
Nah, nah. There's plenty of fast sporty SUV's driven by rich soccer mums. And I bet you there will be plenty at the platinum.

                    JACK
Yeah, so, once you've got both sets of keys, drive back to the carpark – the other one, A, in the getaway car. There, you're gonna pick up Crew One. That's me and Elliot. Cole drives us back to the underground parking garage, gives us the keys to the other car and we get in and wait. Ideally this'll be done by five past one.

Then you're gonna go back to A and pick up Kelly and Grace, crew two.

They'll have a gun each, by the way, either me or Elliot will have one as well.

Anyways, Cole picks them up and this time, drives 'em to site C this time, right outside the door to the casino floor. Once they're out, Cole, park up just outside – where they keep all the Maserati's and supercars. If you get too many cops around you, drive underground, hopefully that won't happen.

(Jack moves his hands to the Casino Floorplans, pointing as he speaks.)

Crew two: rush into the casino, fire
a couple shots. Yeah, your goal is to
get money from the chip cashier, but
more than that it's to get all the
security that would be underground
in the cash room to respond to you.
Don't shoot anyone and don't get
shot. At one-fifteen-ish, me and
Elliot are going in, that gives you
just enough time for you to get there
and draw out all the guards, but not
long enough for cops to be there,
hopefully. So, Elliot is pretty well
aware of the plan, but I'll tell you
basically what we're doing so you're
filled in. On level minus-2 of the
Platinum carpark, it's connected to
the cash room. We'll be in a big
beefy car, we ram into the wall once
we're in there, we should have free
reign to fill up two duffels with
cash.

Jack looks at Elliot.

                    ELLIOT
          We're all going at 1:15. Gives
          Crew One, that's us, enough time
          to quickly get in and up to Cole,
          waiting. Crew Two, you should be
          able to see out to where Cole is
          parked from the casino floor, there's
          big glass floor to ceiling windows
          looking out onto the street. So, keep
          an eye out for Jack and I running
          out into the car, once that's done
          you can get out of there.

                    KELLY
          The driver - um, Cole - takes us
          back here once we're done.

They all nod heads in agreement.

55    INT./EXT. GRACE'S CAR / PERTH STREETS - LATER      55

          Inside Grace's little hatchback, there's a
          distinct lack of conversation, of noise in
          general apart from that of the road and the
          wind. Cole is driving, his mask on the dash.
          Elliot is riding shotgun. Kelly is crammed

between Jack and Grace in the back row.

Cole twists on the radio. Begins to flick through them:

> RADIO
> ...a very hot and dry Christmas—

(flick)

> I gave you my heart, and—

(flick)

> ...distinctly new take on the decades old Christmas tradition—

(flick)

> ...you-oo-oo, baby—

Disappointed, he flicks the radio back off.

> COLE
> Does this thing have bluetooth?

> GRACE
> No, course not.

> COLE
> Yeah, just thought maybe you bought something for it...

Grace shakes her head, and silence comes over the car once again. Eventually, it's punctuated by:

> ELLIOT
> Turn up here.

Cole does as instructed. As they drive up the road that leads to the casino, their faces are cast in harsh yellows from the streetlights above. Not far up the road and Cole is once again given instructions.

> JACK
> This is the carpark we wait at here, the A that I drew.

> COLE
> Right. It's twelve-forty-two, you wanna get out now, or?

> ELLIOT
> We'll get out now. Take the extra minutes to look for the perfect two

cars, don't wanna rush you in that.
Don't worry about the valet, just

make sure you've got the mask on,
and he'll get out of there.

                    COLE
          Alright. Seeya, then.

                    JACK
          Good luck, Cole.

The four of them get out, leaving Cole alone in
the car. It pulls off down the road.

56      EXT. EMPTY CARPARK - CONTINUOUS                56

Jack, Elliot, Kelly and Grace make their way
over the street and into the all but empty
carpark. Jack, Kelly, and Grace sit down on the
asphalt, and Elliot leans on a streetlamp.

                    JACK
          Can't believe we've got here.

                    KELLY
          Wouldn't have been if I didn't
          blackmail you.

                    ELLIOT
          Yeah, thanks for that.

                    GRACE
          Feel like I missed something.

                    JACK
          Don't worry about it. We're all here
          now — gonna make beaucoup bills.

It's strangely peaceful here. Apart from the
distant noise of cars on the highway, silence.
The calm before the storm.

A calm that is interrupted by the blaring noise
of sirens.

                    KELLY
          Shut up, everyone. Listen.

Through a gap in the bushes, we see onto the
highways. A convoy of police cars, driving fast,
ducking and weaving through traffic-

But they drive straight by the road to the
casino.

> ELLIOT
> Well, that's good, then. They'll be
> preoccupied.

> JACK
> Hopefully.

BACK TO:

57    INT. GRACE'S CAR - IMMEDIATELY AFTER    57

Further down the road, Cole has pulled to
a halt outside the entrance to the Platinum
Casino underground parking lot. He grabs the
latex Santa mask off the dashboard, RIPS it out
of the plastic packaging and slips it on. The
gloves are already on.

58    INT. UNDERGROUND PARKING GARAGE - CONTINUOUS    58

Cole puts his foot down, turning the car down
the ramp into the underground carpark. He
passes the valet booth and parks Grace's car in
a space not far from it. He looks at the time
on the dashboard: 12:54. Close enough. Cole
turns off the car, gets out, and begins walking
towards the valet.

The valet is scared stiff, knowing what's
coming. He looks at his watch: 12:55. He quickly
walks through a door at the back of the valet
booth.

59    INT. TOILET STALL - MOMENTS LATER    59

The valet runs into a toilet stall and locks
the door. He sits on the toilet lid and runs his
hand through his hair.

BACK TO:

60    INT. UNDERGROUND PARKING GARAGE - SAME TIME    60

Cole is outside the valet booth, so he hops over
the bench, pulls open a drawer. He rummages
around, picking out two keys. He presses down
on the first set of keys, and in a space not
far from where he parked Grace's hatchback:
the lights flash on a large ute with a sturdy-
looking bullbar on the front. He pockets the
first set and then presses down on the second
set of keys; this time the car is in the far
corner of the carpark. A luxury German saloon
car, matte black. He chuckles, excited to be...

61    INT. GETAWAY CAR - MOMENTS LATER                    61

    Behind the wheel of the German saloon car.
    The interior is finished in a rich burgundy
    leather. Cole RUNS HIS HANDS up and down the
    steering wheel, then presses the push to start.
    The throaty ROAR of a V8 echoes throughout the
    parking lot. He pushes down on the accelerator,
    and it swerves out of the parking lot.

    Back on the road by the river, the same way he
    came up here. This time, it's a lot faster.

62    EXT. EMPTY CARPARK - LATER                          62

    The four soon-to-be robbers eye Cole as he
    approaches the empty carpark. The car pulls
    into the empty carpark and Jack hops to his
    feet; Elliot follows.

    They clamber into the back seats as Kelly and
    Grace look on. The car turns around once again
    and gets back on the road to the casino/carpark.

                               BACK TO:

63    INT. GETAWAY CAR - CONTINUOUS                       63

    Elliot pushes his back into the seat. Jack looks
    out of the windows.

                  JACK
          There were all these cop cars we
          saw.

                  COLE
          Yeah?

                  JACK
          They all rushed past, though.

                  COLE
          That's good then. They'll be
          preoccupied, hopefully.

                ELLIOT
          That's what I said.

                  COLE
          Yeah, well, great minds think alike.

    The drive continues. Closer to the underground
    parking garage, Elliot and Jack put on their own
    masks.

The getaway car is underground. It stops in front of the ute that Cole selected for Jack and Elliot.

> JACK
> This it? Bullbar, that's smart. Nice, good job.

Cole reaches back and hands Jack the keys.

> ELLIOT
> Thanks, Cole. Timing is good so far, so, we'll see you at quarter past.

> COLE
> Yeah. Seeya.

Elliot and Jack get out, the latter holding a rifle, and Cole turns around, heading back to the empty carpark to pick up Crew Two - Kelly and Grace. Jack unlocks the ute and the two climb inside. They switch it on; Elliot adjusts the air-con, and then we move back to:

65      INT.  GETAWAY CAR - MOMENTS LATER      65

Now it's Grace and Kelly's turn to get in, and this time, they won't need to come back to this carpark. Once inside, they slip on their Santa Claus masks. The two rifles are resting behind their headrests.

> GRACE
> I'm so getting a new car after this.

The drive continues, mostly in silence. This time, Cole drives straight past the entrance to the underground parking garage, instead pulling into the glamourous, palm-lined road into the Casino complex proper.

Outside, it is as glitzy as would be expected. Luxurious Bentleys and exotic supercars are parked outside the entrance, and there are scores of valets dressed in the same uniform as the one 'bribed' by Jack and Elliot. Kelly and Grace, masks still on, grab the guns from behind their heads, Grace also grabbing a duffel bag.

> COLE
> Good luck.

Grace and Kelly get out of the car as valets and guests outside either watch on in bewilderment

or are oblivious. Cole drives off, parking a
short way from the door, and we move to:

66   **INT. CASINO FLOOR - CONTINUOUS**   66

Kelly and Grace half-walk, half-run inside, not
really knowing what exactly to do. Gamblers
inside are beginning to notice their presence,
and so--

BANG, BANG, BANG...

The two let off shots into the roof. Panic
ensues. Wild SCREAMING and hysteria envelop the
room. The two move over to the chip cashier,
aiming the gun at his head.

                    KELLY
          Whatever money you have, into the
          bag.

Grace presents the duffel bag to the cashier,
while Kelly scans the room.

                    CHIP CASHIER
          I-- there's...

                    GRACE
          Just-- Shut up, money in the bag.

The cashier, fumbling around with his hands,
eventually opens the till and scoops out bills,
coins, whatever, chucking them all in the bag.

By now, security guards have begun to show up
around the casino floor, pistols in hand. Kelly,
not wanting to shoot anyone or get shot herself,
runs up to a cowering gambler and takes him as
a human shield, gun to his head.

                    GRACE
          (shouting, to Kelly)

          Time?

                    KELLY
          One-ten, gotta give it longer.

                    GRACE
          Get behind here.

          (To the chip cashier)

          You, open up the door.

The chip cashier nervously obliges, opening
the door to the small room he's in. As Grace,
Kelly, and the hostage walk in, the chip cashier
attempts to run out.

                              KELLY
                    No! In here, with us!

He turns back around and cowers beneath the
bench he had stood behind previously.

                                            BACK TO:

67    INT. UTE / UNDERGROUND PARKING GARAGE - SAME TIME   67

      Back inside, things are less tense. Jack and
      Elliot have been sitting, contemplating. Jack
      looks at the clock in the dashboard.

                              JACK
                    Ten:ten. Time to move, yeah?

                              ELLIOT
                    Yeah.

      The ute pulls out of the parking bay, driving
      round the underground parking lot and going
      down the ramp into the level minus two.

      They pull to a stop. On the other end of the
      parking garage, straight in front of them, is a
      large brick wall.

                              JACK
                    The bit we had to hit was right lined
                    up with this ramp, right?

                              ELLIOT
                    Right.

                              JACK
                    If we hit the wrong bit...

                              ELLIOT
                    We won't. Put your seat all the way
                    back, though. Don't want the airbag
                    to explode in your face.

                              JACK
                    Jeez.

      They both move their seats as far back as they
      can. Jack looks over at Elliot and then back
      at the wall in front of him, and pushes the
      accelerator down, hard...

68    INT. CASINO: CASH ROOM - CONTINUOUS                 68

      They SMASH through the brick wall into the cash
      room. The airbags pop off, and the car's cabin
      is filled with smoke, but Jack and Elliot are
      ok, just. They jump out of the ute. There are

lockboxes everywhere, and bricks and rubble on the floor. No guards though - or anyone - so Kelly and Grace's diversion worked. Both grab a duffel bag and Elliot a gun as well. He stands guard at the door, while Jack opens whatever lockboxes aren't locked, as well as grabbing cash left on the counting table. Soon, the first bag is full, and so he slides it across the floor to Elliot who in exchange chucks him the second duffel bag. Like before Jack fills up the bag, this time slinging it round his back. Elliot does likewise with his duffel bag, and goes to inspect the Ute, to see if they can drive out in it.

> JACK
> Look at the wheels, Elliot.
> Suspension on the front end has
> totally lost it. Couple bricks have
> gotten through to the radiator, too.
> We're gonna have to run out.

> > BACK TO:

69    **INT. CASINO FLOOR - SAME TIME**    69

Kelly and Grace are getting desperate now. The chip-cashier turned hostage has broken down into tears, while the other hostage seems more acceptant, and is sitting down in a corner.

> GRACE
> Time now?

> KELLY
> Thirteen past. I reckon we leave now.

Grace aims the gun at the chip-cashier, and Kelly grabs the other hostage. They all stand up and exit the small chip cashing booth, making their way across the casino floor. A number of security guards have their guns pointed at them as they do so - some of them suited, with small police-issue revolvers - these are the guards that stand around the casino floor; other guards are armoured and aim either revolvers or larger shotguns at the pair - these guards are the ones lured from the cash room.

> KELLY
> Nobody shoots. We don't want anyone
> to get hurt, yeah?

70    EXT. CASINO GROUNDS - CONTINUOUS                70

          Kelly and Grace, still firmly grabbing their
          hostages, back towards the door outside. They
          look around, eying Cole in the getaway car.
          Once they step outside the doors, they DITCH the
          hostages on the ground and run towards Cole.
          Grace, who was carrying the duffel bag complete
          with a small fortune in coins and notes, drops
          it onto the floor as shots ring and both her
          and Kelly break into a sprint towards the
          getaway car.

71    INT. GETAWAY CAR - CONTINUOUS                   71

          They both enter through the nearest-side rear
          door, chucking the two rifles in the footwell.
          BANG -- a bullet rips into the rear-quarter
          window, narrowly missing Grace's head who
          has instinctively ducked. Cole steps on the
          accelerator, and the car tears down the road.

                        COLE
          Go ok in there?

                        GRACE
          What does it look like?

                        KELLY
          Went ok. The guards from underground
          came up, I think, that was the plan
          in the first place.

                        COLE
          We'll wait outside the underground
          carpark for Jack and Elliot.

          Cole turns off the short Casino road and back
          onto the main riverside one, and we go back
          to...

72    INT. UNDERGROUND PARKING GARAGE - MOMENTS LATER   72

          Jack and Elliot are jogging up the ramp to
          street-level; masks on, bags on back, Elliot
          holding his gun in one hand. Suddenly, the
          getaway car pulls to a stop right in front of
          the ramp exit. The boys break into a sprint;
          Elliot gets in the front seat and puts the
          duffel bag in the footwell, fumbling around with
          his gun and resting it between the footwell and
          his lap. Jack gets in through the rear door,
          forcing Grace to slide to the middle. He chucks
          the duffel bag on top of one of the rifles in

the rear footwell, and slams the door closed.
Cole floors it.

                                            CUT TO:

73    INT./EXT. GETAWAY CAR / PERTH STREETS - LATER    73

On a highway, now, everyone's mood has changed
from stressed to celebratory. Police cruisers
rush past in the opposite direction, as the
occupants of the getaway car try to get comfy
in their squashed surroundings. Jack PICKS his
duffel bag up and rests it in his lap.

                    GRACE
          Turn the radio on.

Cole obliges, turning it up.

                    RADIO DJ (V.O.)
          Hope you're all having a wonderful -
          very early - Christmas morning. This
          one's for Caroline in Morley.

A Christmas song begins to play. They continue
their drive down the highway, and police cars
continue to rush by them in the opposite
direction.

                    JACK
          Took ages to respond. Must really
          have been preoccupied with something
          else.

                    ELLIOT
          How lucky's that?!

                    COLE
          A Christmas miracle.

74    EXT. VACANT WAREHOUSE: PARKING LOT - LATER    74

The getaway car pulls into the parking lot,
parking up next to their cars - and probably
costing more than all of them combined. They
all get out, and head into the vacant warehouse.

75    INT. VACANT WAREHOUSE: OFFICE - MOMENTS LATER    75

All of them are gathered around the desk,
excited. Jack and Elliot both throw their duffel
bags on the desk and unzip them: inside, stacks
and stacks of bills.

                    JACK
          I'm sweaty as. Dunno what just
          happened, but we're rich now.

                              KELLY
                    Cheers to that.

                              JACK
                    But-- it's Christmas day, we're all
                    tired, a lot of us have to see our
                    families in a couple hours. How about
                    we leave it all here, lock it all up
                    nice and good. We can come back on
                    the twenty-sixth fresh and dole it
                    all out.

          Some of them nod their heads in agreement -
          others, like Elliot and Kelly look less certain.
          A pause--

                              ELLIOT
                    Fine. We can all trust each other,
                    yeah?

                              JACK
                    Course we can.

                              GRACE
                    We're all rich. I can't believe it.
                    Actually worked.

          Jack zips both bags up, and 'hides' them under
          the desk.

                              JACK
                    In the off chance someone comes into
                    an abandoned warehouse on Christmas
                    day.

          The robbers run their hands through their hair,
          or wipe sweat off their face. They've just done
          the impossible, and tomorrow will reap the
          rewards.

                              ELLIOT
                    See you all at twelve on boxing day.

76   TITLE CARD:                                            76

     '10:27, DECEMBER 26'

                                        DIP TO BLACK:

                                        CUT TO:

77   INT. GRACE'S HOUSE - DAY                               77

                    It's a picturesque morning. Grace Halfpenny lies
                    on her bed, half-conscious, unfettered by any
                    future commitments or responsibilities. Shafts
                    of sun light flood through venetians. Birds
                    CHIRP. Then--

Someone is POUNDING on the front door. Grace, annoyed, gets up.

> GRACE
> (Calling out)

One second!

She slips a T-Shirt over her pyjamas, and the pounding continues. She walks over to the door and opens it. It's Brad, her uncle.

> GRACE
> Uncle Brad? Ah, the guns, right?

> BRAD
> Forget about them, Grace - did you only just get up? Doesn't matter. Grace, honey, you've made me a very rich man.

Grace says nothing, not entirely sure what Brad is on about.

> BRAD
> Come out here, I wanna show you something.

78     **EXT. GRACE'S DRIVEWAY - CONTINUOUS**          78

In the carpark - a shiny, new, luxury crossover. White, with black wheels.

> GRACE
> You - what?

> BRAD
> Yours. It's not totally new, was a demo, they had none like it new in the showroom.

> GRACE
> How did you do this?

> BRAD
> Not all me. You as well. It was the least I could do. That, and, well, I had to make sure it all went well.

> GRACE
> What are you saying...?

> BRAD
> Come back inside and I'll explain.

> BACK TO:

Both Grace and Brad are sat on a couch.

                    BRAD
          Knew when you asked for the guns,
          you were up to something. I reckon
          you knew I knew — didn't expect me
          to do anything. Mum tell you the
          stories 'bout me?

                    GRACE
          Kinda, yeah.

                    BRAD
          Well, I got myself into a fair bit of
          trouble back in the day, your age or
          a bit younger. So I thought I'd help
          you out a bit. Followed you around
          a bit, heard you talking to your
          friends about the Platinum. So, I
          thought, why not, and I. You know the
          Orelium, place by the ocean?

Grace nods, encouraging her uncle to continue.

                    BRAD (CONT'D)
          Their stocks have been piss poor as
          of late, so I thought maybe, just
          maybe, if you rob the Platinum then
          Orelium stocks will go way up. Turns
          out, my gamble was right. Up heaps in
          the past two days. Haven't sold yet,
          so, bought the car in my name and
          I'll pay it off soon enough. Oh, and,
          had to make sure the robbery went
          ahead. Filled some cars in the city
          with ammonium fertiliser and made
          them go up in flames a bit before
          you guys hit the casino. I thought
          it might divert the cop's attention a
          bit.

                    GRACE
          Yeah, it...really helped.

                    BRAD
          After that, still had some fertiliser
          and a bit of fuel left. I figured
          you guys would do something stupid,
          leave evidence, so I followed you
          back to that planning room type
          place. Hung back till you all left,

then I torched the getaway car and
warehouse, too.

> GRACE
> That's amaz... The warehouse?

                              CUT TO:


80      EXT. VACANT WAREHOUSE: PARKING LOT - DAY          80

It's noon. Jack, Elliot, Kelly, and Cole are
all gathered around. Opposite, cordoned off
by police and firefighters - the smouldering
remains of the warehouse turned planning room,
and with it, the fruits of their hard labour.

No one speaks. Jack kicks a charred brick, and
it rolls along the asphalt.

> COLE
> Where's Grace?

Amongst the ash and rubble, there is a single,
half-burnt one-hundred-dollar bill. Kelly
reaches down and picks it up. The camera
focuses on it.

                        MATCH CUT TO:

81      INT. FAST FOOD RESTAURANT - MORNING               81

A police officer holds a one-hundred-dollar bill
bill in his hand.

> OFFICER
> Sorry, I don't have any change.

> JACK
> Nah, that's alright.

He pops open the till, and rummages around for
a fifty, two twenties, and two dollars fifty
worth in coins. He reaches out and places them
in the police officer's hand.

> JACK
> Shouldn't be too long.

> OFFICER
> Thanks, mate.

Jack closes the till.


**END CREDITS ROLL**

# STAG NATION

**RAFAEL S.W.**   MELBOURNE, VIC, AUSTRALIA

Having beaten my tactless retreat, moved
back home for a resentful rebirth,

I'd forgotten the howling. Hot summer
roar. Young bucks on night streets

with new money burning cars
like rubber, stealing bins, stealing

lovers. Pretending at a confidence
that knew no priors. Relentlessly restless.

I'd returned to ruminate on a childhood
I thought I'd outgrown. Fallow to the bone.

My mother turned docile, spine curled,
shoved her heart into her soles and walks

like she intends to keep it there.
Tells me off for growing taller

than her. For leaving socks on the floor,
spoor on the door. I ache every evening

to cut my own head off. Mount
it on the wall. Run wild. Grow horns.

But I had my time, I'm twenty-five.
Too old for a hart, still can't drive.

Outside the sky's bright. It's stag night.
And I'd punch holes in the darkness

if it would help me sleep tonight.
But I stay home. Bed early and alone.

Pass out to the sound of heels clopping
past my door, draped in velvet dreams.

Wake to the deer on my lawn and gaze,
amazed at their clumsy grace, long

for those lashes, to stroke their face.
The bravery of tranquillity. Their poise.

Both of us watching each other through mist,
waiting for maybe gunshots. Or a kiss.

# DISTORTED LENS

**AOIFE McFADDEN**   MORPHETVILLE, SA, AUST

Annie raises the camera lens to her eye and waits for the perfect moment. Click. A pause and a breath. Click. Click. Then the moment is gone. She smiles and lowers the camera. Another moment will appear, so long as she waits.

There's a light tug on her jeans.

'What are you doing?' A small voice asks.

Annie smiles down at her little cousin, Mia. 'Taking photos,' she says, crouching down to show Mia her camera.

Mia looks through the lens and takes a close-up photo of Annie. Click. Mia giggles. Click. Click.

'How do you see the photos?' Mia asks, turning the heavy, old camera in her little hands, looking for the screen that isn't there.

'You can't. Not yet anyway,' Annie says, taking the camera back. 'This camera takes film, so I have to develop the photos later.'

'What's film?'

Annie smiles and wonders how one explains film to a four-year-old raised with an iPhone in her hand. She is saved from the task, however, when they are called inside for lunch. Mia races off without a backwards glance, leaving Annie alone in the garden. She raises the camera lens to her eye and finds that perfect moment waiting for her. Click. Click. Click.

Faye stands at the window, arms folded over her chest and a full wine glass held delicately between her fingers. She stares mutely out at her daughter. Annie has that old camera glued to her eye as usual. Faye takes a gulp of her wine. It is sour on her tongue.

Annie is the last to arrive at the table and slides into a chair beside her cousin Ella. The camera still hangs around her neck.

Faye ignores her daughter and smiles broadly across the table at Ella. 'I hear uni is going well for you, Ella?'

Ella nods enthusiastically, her mouth full of food. 'Mmm, it's fun! So many cool people.'

Faye glances sidelong at Annie, but her daughter's eyes are intent on the tomato she is pushing around the plate with her fork.

'And what are you studying, Ella?' Faye continues.

Ella scrunches up her face. 'Economics, at the moment, but I don't think it's for me. Too much math, so I'm probably going to swap into arts.'

Faye frowns. Annie smirks into her salad.

Annie flicks on the red light in the back shed and starts the process of developing her latest photos. The shed door creaks open, startling her, and a moment later, Faye pushes through the black curtains.

'Is everything alright?' Annie asks her mother.

Faye frowns. 'Of course. Am I not allowed to visit the studio?'

Annie shrugs. 'It's just you never come out here.'

Faye shrugs in reply and perches on a stool, looking at the photos pegged on the string to dry. Annie shuffles uncomfortably on the spot.

'I thought it was just a phase, and you'd get over it,' Faye says softly to the photos on the wall. 'This photography,' she continues, still not looking at her daughter, 'it's a waste, Annie. You're wasting your life inside a dark shed.' She sighs. 'Kids your age should be out... living. Not hiding in the dark. You finish high school this year, and you need a career. Something that pays the bills, Annie.'

Annie stares at her grubby shoes. Faye sighs again.

'Just think about it OK Annie,' Faye says, getting to her feet. 'Because this' she flicks a photo of Mia, 'this won't cut it.'

Annie watches her mother slip out between the black curtains. Annie doesn't move until the shed door bangs closed. Then slowly, deliberately, numbly, she turns back to her task.

Mrs Jenkins draws deftly on the blackboard, her hand fluid and steady in its flight. The lines come together in such simplicity; it is beauty personified on the coarsest of canvas. Annie stares with a mixture of awe and jealousy.

'Careful, or you'll catch flies like that,' Georgie whispers, clapping her hand beneath Annie's chin and pushing her mouth closed.

Annie smiles, embarrassed.

'Shut up,' she hisses back.

Mrs Jenkins' eyes fall on the pair of them, and her hands come to her hips. Annie and Georgie duck their heads, giggling, then resume their attempts to imitate the master. The bell saves them from further trouble. Georgie jumps up and bolts toward the door. 'Gotta go!' she calls back to Annie.

Annie shoves her things into her bag. She stares up at the blackboard, and when everyone is gone from the room, she lifts her heavy camera from her bag. Click. Click.

Mrs Jenkins watches Annie disappear from the art studio. She half turns back to her office, but something catches her eye on the floor beneath Annie's chair. Mrs Jenkins crouches and lifts the shiny paper, a large print photograph. Her eyes widen at the image captured there, and she smiles to herself with a mixture of awe and jealousy.

Annie clomps down the stairs in annoyance and hauls open her front door. Her mother is ignoring the doorbell again. She blinks in surprise to find Mrs Jenkins on the doorstep.

'Hi, Annie. Are your parents home?' Mrs Jenkins asks.

Annie goes pale but nods. 'Mum's here.' She opens the door wider to allow her teacher in.

'Don't worry, Annie,' Mrs Jenkins says, 'you're not in trouble.'

She follows Annie into the neat kitchen. Faye is perched at the breakfast bench, a magazine is open in one hand and a glass of wine poised in the other.

'Mum, this is Mrs Jenkins from school. She wants to talk to you,' Annie says.

Faye comes to her feet slowly. 'Since when do you make house calls?' she asks, then glares at Annie. 'What have you done?'

Annie shrugs and backs out of the room.

'She's not in trouble at all,' Mrs Jenkins says. 'Quite the opposite in fact.'

But Annie is already gone. Mrs Jenkins pulls the photograph out of her bag and sets it on the kitchen bench. Faye looks down at it, and then back up at the teacher.

'Yeah, what of it?'

'Annie is brilliant,' Mrs Jenkins says softly. 'She has an incredible eye.'

Faye snorts. 'Brilliant?' She picks up the photo. 'It's rubbish. The sooner she learns that the better.' Faye's eyes narrow, and her voice hardens. 'Don't you dare mislead her into following some foolish artist's dream. Annie is going to university next year, not some backwater art school.'

Faye shoves the photo back into Mrs Jenkins' hands and resumes her seat.

'Please don't come here again,' Faye says, picking up her magazine and making a show of burying her head in it.

Mrs Jenkins stares open-mouthed at her for a moment, but when Faye doesn't look up, she turns and goes quietly back the way she came.

Annie catches her on the doorstep.

'Sorry about Mum,' she says softly.

Then she spots her photograph in Mrs Jenkins' hands. A gentle flush creeps up her neck and spreads out across her face.

'It's brilliant, Annie,' Mrs Jenkins says, holding the photo out to her. 'You've got an incredible eye for it.'

Annie blinks in surprise. Brilliant? The word echoes around in her brain uncomfortably.

'Mum says it's a waste of time,' Annie says, shaking her head. 'You keep it.'

She turns and disappears back into the house.

Annie keeps her head down in art class the next day. Mrs Jenkins doesn't pay her any heed. When the bell sounds Annie jumps up fast, gathers her books and legs it toward the door.

'Annie?' Mrs Jenkins calls out to her before she can escape.

Annie's shoulders slump, and she turns back slowly. Mrs Jenkins waits for everyone else to leave before she speaks.

'Annie, I took your photo to a friend of mine. He's an art dealer in town,' she says with a smile.

Annie stares at her blankly.

He really liked your work. He said a collection of that quality would sell easily.' Mrs Jenkins continues.

She hands Annie a business card. Annie takes it slowly, reading the name. She knows the gallery; she has stared at the works in the window many times, but she's never gone in.

'Just think about it, Annie,' Mrs Jenkins says softly, sounding like an echo of Faye.

Annie frowns at her feet and shakes her head, trying to get the conflicting voices out of her mind.

'Why can't you all just mind your own business?' Annie whispers, backing away from Mrs Jenkins.

Annie turns and runs. She pauses only to drop the business card into the bin beside the door and then she is gone. Mrs. Jenkins sighs.

'What did Mrs Artistic Genius want?' Georgie asks Annie when she catches up.

Annie shrugs. 'Nothing.'

Georgie raises an eyebrow sidelong at Annie as they trudge towards their next class.

Annie relents under Georgie's gaze and rolls her eyes. 'She thinks I should show my photographs to some art dealer.'

'What?!' Georgie squeals, pulling Annie to a halt in the middle of the corridor. 'That's amazing. Where? When are you going? Can I come?'

Annie frowns. 'You think I should do it?'

Georgie puts a hand on each of Annie's shoulders. 'Annie, of course I think you should do it! You'd be mad not to.' She tilts her head a little to the side, as though contemplating her friend for the first time. 'You do *want* to be a photographer, right?'

Annie wakes early and dresses for school, but as she's leaving, she ducks around to the back of the house and sneaks into the shed. In the bottom drawer of her photography-supplies chest is an album bound in black leather. She draws it out reverentially and runs her hand across it. But she doesn't open it. She gently places it into her empty bag and creeps out of the shed.

Town is busy on a weekday. Annie feels out of place, but she clutches her bag close and pushes open the door to the gallery. The reception is unattended. Annie hovers in the foyer for a minute, but her eye is drawn to the works displayed in the gallery off to her left. She drifts toward them, mesmerised.

'You can't be in here!' A voice startles Annie.

She jumps and spins around to find the receptionist standing behind her. The woman has her hands on her hips, and her lip is curled up with indignation.

'I'm sorry,' Annie stammers.

'Shouldn't you be at school?' The woman continues, 'You'd best get out of here before I report you.'

When Annie doesn't move, the woman repeats herself, tapping her foot impatiently. 'I said, get out of here.'

Annie gulps back all she came to say and runs for the door. She crosses over the street and slumps down on a bench, drops her head into her hands and breathes deeply. Her heart hammers in her chest for several minutes before she calms down.

Annie draws her album out of her bag. She runs her hand across the leather cover and then opens it. She looks at the photos one at a time, turning the pages slowly.

'Beautiful,' a voice comes softly behind her.

Annie slams the album shut, then jumps to her feet as the stranger steps toward her. He smiles at her and sits on the bench.

'May I?' he asks, pointing at the album in her hand.

Annie nods slowly and resumes her seat. She opens the album once more, and for the first time, shows someone all her work.

'You must be Annie,' the man says when the last page has turned.

Annie nods. 'You're Mrs Jenkins' friend.'

'Call me Harry,' he says, extending his hand to shake.

Annie takes it reluctantly, uncomfortable with the gesture.

'Your work is very good, Annie,' Harry tells her. 'I'm glad you came. Perhaps you'd like to come into the gallery and have a look at what we do?'

Annie glances over at the gallery. The receptionist is staring at them. Annie gulps and nods.


Annie arrives at art class early the next day. She stares at her shoes as she apologises to Mrs Jenkins, her face red as a beet. Mrs Jenkins smiles and tells her she has nothing to apologise for. Annie tells her about the gallery, awe in her voice. She explains that Harry is going to help her put together an exhibition for one night only.

'I'm glad you went, Annie. You have a talent; it would be a waste to hide it away,' Mrs Jenkins tells her happily.

Annie frowns, worry knitting lines onto her forehead.

'Mum says I'm wasting my life with photography,' Annie half-whispers.

'I know, Annie,' Mrs Jenkins says softly. 'Your mother is afraid.'

Annie blinks in surprise. 'Afraid?' she asks. 'Afraid of what?'

Mrs Jenkins shrugs. 'Only she knows the answer to that, Annie.'


Faye flips the magazine pages without seeing them. She sips her wine without tasting it. The house is quiet when Annie is out. She glances at the cabinet across the living room. The doors are closed, but something within is calling to her. She uncrosses her legs, and for a moment, she is about to rise, but something seizes her inside, and instead she tucks her legs up beneath her and takes a gulp of wine. It soothes her momentarily. But minutes later, her eyes drift across the room once more.

'Ridiculous,' Faye whispers to herself and launches to her feet.

She crouches down as she pulls open one door on the far left of the cabinet. She reaches in without looking, groping for something way at the back. The box is heavier than she remembers, but she lifts it with one hand out onto the carpet.

Faye sits back, pulling her knees to her chest like a child, and stares at the small wooden box. It is old; the varnish is faded, and the metal clasps are beginning to rust. But they come open easily at Faye's touch. The lid creaks as she lifts it, but she cannot bring herself to lift out the contents. Tears well in her eyes, and anger rises in her chest. She slams the box closed and shoves it back into the cabinet.

The wine slides easily down her raw throat, soothing and cool.

Annie opens her bedroom window and clambers out quietly. She tiptoes across the back lawn and creeps into the shed, wincing at every sound. Photos hang everywhere in the shed. Annie has never developed so many before, certainly none so large. Harry had wanted her to have her photos professionally printed, but Annie refused. This is her process, her art, and she will do it her way. Although she is beginning to worry that she has made a mistake. The exhibition is only a week away, and she has a lot of work to do. Not to mention school. Annie yawns and gets to work.

When she clambers back in the window, Faye is sitting at her desk. Annie's heart begins to race.

'I know what you're up to,' Faye says softly. 'All those photos. You think if you get into some fancy art school, you've made it? No portfolio will ever make you successful enough, Annie.'

Annie stares at her shoes.

'My grades are good,' she whispers, daring to defy her mother. 'What does it matter if I make photos too?'

Faye glares at her daughter. 'What does it matter?' she hisses. 'What does it matter?' she repeats, glancing about the room as though searching for an answer. Faye stands up, 'I'm trying to protect you, Annie,' she says. 'You'll thank me one day.'

Faye walks out of the room before Annie can reply.

Georgie's eyes are wide as Annie reaches into the back of the cabinet in the living room. Annie glances over at her and hisses, 'You're supposed to be keeping an eye out for Mum!'

'Oops,' Georgie whispers and turns back to stare out the front window.

'You don't have to whisper,' Annie whispers.

Georgie looks back at her, and the two of them dissolve into giggles. Annie pulls the wooden box out and sets it on the carpet. She opens the lid carefully. Georgie moves towards her, the watch post forgotten.

'What's in it?' Georgie asks.

Annie lifts out an old photo in a tarnished, old frame. A ballerina is pictured in mid-flight.

'That was Mum,' Annie says, tapping the photo.

'Your Mum was a ballerina?!'

Annie nods. 'She won't ever talk about it. Something bad happened, and she stopped. I don't know what though. She won't say. This box of things is all she has left from back then.'

'Won't your mum be mad that we've opened the box?' Georgie asks, concerned.

Annie nods. 'Yes.'

'Oh.'

Georgie resumes her post by the window.


Mrs Jenkins stares down at the invitation in her hand. An invitation to Annie's exhibition. It is tonight. Mrs Jenkins sits in her car for a long time before she gets out. Her last visit here didn't go so well. She suspects this one won't either.

Mrs Jenkins rings the doorbell. The house is quiet, but Faye opens the door. She frowns instantly.

'I thought I told you not to come back here?' Faye snaps.

Mrs Jenkins nods. 'You did, but I wanted to give you this.' She holds out the invitation to Faye.

Faye takes it, still frowning. She reads it slowly, then re-reads it.

'It's Annie's,' Mrs Jenkins explains in the awkward silence. 'Annie's exhibition.'

Faye continues to stare at the paper.

'I hope you'll be able to come along to support your daughter,' Mrs Jenkins says softly.

Faye says nothing, so Mrs Jenkins walks back to her car and drives away.

Annie bites her fingernails as the guests arrive. Some are dressed in suits and gowns that make her jaw drop. Others are more eccentric, their clothes hideous or outrageous. Others appear almost normal, except for the pink or blue hair and a piercing here and there. Annie feels out of place. She has avoided going into the gallery, but now Harry is beckoning her.

Faye steps through the gallery doors alone, her eyes searching for her daughter. She drifts along with the crowd. There are more people here than she had expected.

Annie's photographs adorn the walls. Some are familiar, some Faye has never seen before. All are larger than the usual prints. Murmurs fill the space, and glasses clink. Faye lifts a champagne glass from a passing waiter's tray.

'It's very good,' a subdued voice comes from behind her. 'Never heard of the artist before.'

'Hmm, neither, but I would love this one.' Another voice comes.

'Harry tells me they're not for sale.'

'Not for sale?' comes the indignant reply.

Faye drifts away from the voices. She raises her glass to take a sip but stops and lowers it again before the liquid can touch her lips. The colour drains from her face.

A single piece hangs on the far wall. Different from the rest. A photograph of a photograph. All in black and white. A ballerina in mid-flight, captured so long ago. Her image propped up against an old wooden box, and beside it, a pair of worn ballet shoes.

Tears well in Faye's eyes, and for the first time in a long time, they slip delicately down her cheek.

Annie sees the moment her mother sees the photograph. Faye stares at it for a long time, and when she turns, Annie's eyes meet hers. Faye sets her untouched champagne on a surprised waiter's tray and moves slowly towards her daughter.

Annie stares down at her high heels, but unexpectedly, her mother wraps her up in a hug. Her tears are wet on Annie's cheek.

'They're beautiful,' Faye whispers.

She releases Annie, nods to Mrs Jenkins and walks out. Wide-eyed, Annie stares after her.

Faye has the box sitting on the kitchen bench when Annie arrives home. The lid is open, but the contents remain untouched. Annie opens her mouth to apologise, but Faye speaks first as she lifts the old photograph from its tomb.

'I was told my whole life that I would succeed at whatever I did,' Faye whispers. 'That I could not fail.'

Annie sits down on the stool beside her mother.

'You don't know what that's like, Annie, to believe failure is impossible. To be admitted to the best schools, to be told how brilliant you are. Only to have every door slammed in your face until there is nothing left of you; because that was all you ever were.' She taps her finger on the ballerina—on her own image.

'I'm trying to protect you, Annie. You don't know what it's like,' Faye says quietly, a pleading note in her voice.

Annie nods slowly. 'You're right,' she half-whispers. 'I don't know what that's like. I've been told my whole life that I will fail, that success is impossible.' Annie goes on, 'I'm well prepared to fail—I've always expected it.'

She looks up at her mother and a tear slides down her cheek. 'But now I'm here, faced with success...'

She falters, and the words seem to catch in her throat. But she has come this far. She wipes the tears from her cheek.

"Will you help me?' Annie chokes out.

Faye takes in a breath and ever so slowly nods once. She sets the photograph face down on the bench.

'Even though I might fail?' Annie whispers, more tears cascading down her face.

Faye nods again and wraps her daughter up in a hug. Then she sees, from the corner of her eye, scrawled in her own faded handwriting on the back of her photograph, words she had long ago forgotten: *If you don't try, you've already failed.*

Faye squeezes Annie tighter. 'If you don't try, you've already failed,' she whispers.

# NIGHT OWL

**DREW GRANT**  BRIGHTON-LE-SANDS, NSW, AUST

A subtle tick,
drawing circles
passing time.
half mug of water
perched upon the bedside.
Silence adorns a lively home
with peaceful sighs,
freed from my lungs
I can exist
no games in mind.

A gentle breeze escapes a crack within the drapes to stroke my face,
A dim lit salt lamp sits alone in the same place.
Ruffled blankets
and worn-in sheets
Cosy warmth encases me.
The moving box of words and colours lay brick and cold.
These tiny moments
fail to hide
the complete solace in my soul.

In the early hours before dawn
hours past a midnight born.
A much simpler time,
when the whole world seems to sleep.
Thoughts come minimal
breathing deep.
Glaring at ceilings
deemed not so bleak
Where I allow myself the time
 to bleed out on a page

Where I find rest
in my true form.
When I'm not poked at, lost or torn.
In the early hours
before daylight breaks
All my accomplishments, my mistakes.
 A call rings through some higher power
The spirit answers
in the witching hour.
When the owls are the only ones awake.

# TRUMPET

## EVE NUCIFORA    TURNER, ACT, AUSTRALIA

A woman. Alone at the bar asks, 'Is this your trumpet?'

The bartender says, 'It isn't.'

Her client arrives. He speaks of his children. His wife is away.

His apartment is white. Carpet. Walls. Furniture. The windows are enormous. Inside, the woman feels she's in a diorama. Too colourful a piece to belong. There's money for her in an envelope. It's white. There's no name on it.

The woman returns to the bar. She gets as close as she can to the trumpet. She smells verdigris. Whiskey and tobacco breath pushed through its metal tubes. Or does she? She looks at the trumpet for so long that all the ice in her drink has melted.

She returns to the client. He has cooked for her. He talks of his children. He talks of his mother's death. He talks of his wife's sense of guilt over his mother's death. She's away on business. She works abroad a lot. The children are too often with the babysitter.

The woman asks (or does she?) if he, too, feels guilt. Perhaps his own guilt makes him say these things. Perhaps he, too, could parent the children.

The man lights a joint. Closes his eyes. He appreciates her candour. He keeps talking.

She isn't listening anymore. She hears the horns on the stereo. Competing for space with the organ, the drums, the ecstatic voices. If she listens hard enough, she can hear the trumpets.

She catches the bus to the library. The librarian knows right away she doesn't own a trumpet. That she cannot play. He tells her where to find the books on jazz, and she reads A Trumpet Around the Corner on the bus ride home.

The woman returns to the bar. She watches a man swirl his whiskey before sniffing it. She tells him that he shouldn't. Or does she? She's so close to the trumpet now. Her bag is large. She slips it in. Slips out without paying the bill.

In her own house, which isn't white, she carefully inspects the instrument. She releases the water key, hoping for even the tiniest drop of moisture. She presses the valves. One sticks. She unscrews it. Lubricates it. The metal turns her fingers black-blue. She smells them. Tastes the metal. The instrument has warmed in her hands. She presses her lips to the mouthpiece.

# DEBARKED

**DIANA STOICESCU**   BUCHAREST, ROMANIA

Debarked from my mother's womb
I came to be in this world
Of flashes of light and cars in the street
Of loud honking horns and heavy concrete
Where lives have a price and can be bought
Where mankind got lost in its structures of thought
So,
I either debarked at the wrong stopping station
Or here I have something to be and to do

# MUDGEE RAILWAY STATION

**PETER FITZGERALD**   MUDGEE, NSW, AUSTRALIA

Ginger glow of dawn smears hillcrest.

Decrees a new day. Births light.

Seeps over sleepy railway station building.

Steel tracks.

Standard gauge four feet eight and a half inches.

Rusted.

Overgrown with tufted weeds and faded grasses.

Tis a timeless Mudgee dawn. Bleached-blue violet sky.

Chasms of soundlessness.

Till— Bird life awakens.

Magpies warbling.

Chink and chirrup of a new day.

But here at Mudgee Railway Station— Modified Day?

Memories of bygone ways.

Black and white photographs.

Passé scenes.

Sizable engines of yesteryear.

Hissing. Billowing smoke and steam.

Past veiled women in long dark dresses.

Suited men with hats.

Folk, *we'll* never know.

Coming. Homecoming. Becoming.

Going. Unknowing. Kisses throwing.

Seamless days. No mobile phones— can you believe?

No electronics or digital deliverance.

Tractile time to ponder or wander.

Walk within one's own wooded wilds.

Find meaning. Relevance. Reason perhaps.

Without pressures and erasures of logins, user names and passwords.

So here we stand on Mudgee Railway Station platform in February 2022.

Regal building.
Layered rooftops.
Broad of chest.
Wry silver-roofed smile.
Gaze up a lengthy strip of tar. Past brown brickwork.
Bearing up. Beige archways. Brother coloured poles.
Criss-crossed brown doors bolted shut.
Rustic drinking fountain.
Disengaged. Decades dry.
Ladies Waiting Room.
Now time's tomb.

Mudgee Railway Station.
Once First Nation People's land.
Wiradjuri country. Strip of earth with growth.
Wattle. Willows. Wallaby. Weeping grass.
Later grit. Now grout.

Mudgee Railway Station designed by engineer John Whitton.
Father of NSW railways. Planner of 3494 kilometres of railway tracks.
Designer of— *Devastation of First People country? Some* could certainly say.
But progress happens eh?
*Who* dares stand in *its* way?

So here *we* stand.

                                                    To think—
                                                    To hear—
Railway station footfall of one hundred and thirty eight years.
Of people scribed on Mudgee rolls.
Long-gone time.
Once—

Waiting for trains. Boarding trains. Exiting trains.

F-folk. Free settlers. Families. Farmers. Friends. Fire fighters.

Callers, companion— citizens one and all.

Newcomers to nurture lives.

Who faced challenges beyond bias—

Bushfires. Wars. Droughts. Floods. Plagues.

Yes pandemics too.

Folk with courage and foresight who built community.

Mudgee— Ageless Mudgee.

Once Moothi. Nest in the hills.

Mudgee Railway Station. Track to connect— parallel lines of steel,

To crisscross sixty thousand year old county.

Parliament endorsed extension of railway line August of 1879.

A momentous month— Wallerawang to Mudgee.

Top hats tilted, news of approval reached Mudgee at midnight.

Town band played till dawn.

So Mudgee Railway Station was built.

Townsfolk greeted first steam train Wednesday 10th September 1884.

Mixed goods and mail.

Brought one penny newspapers— I imagine—

Big-smoke news.

Smells of coal and oil.

Smoke hues.

Next day six trains arrived in Mudgee town.

Carried celebratory official party for grand opening.

Feasted in 'Market Square'.

Picnicked in 'now' Robertson Park.

Joyful townsfolk and visitors mingled as one.

Feasted on roast bullock.

Hundreds of loaves of oven baked bread.
Ten gallon casks of crusty beer heartily consumed.
Musically inspired.
No more Cobb & Co coaches though.
Horse pulled. Bumpy.
Once daylong rides for Mudgee people, soon grand-folk tales.
Time saw extension line to Gulgong open 1909.
Not to mention notable 'Mudgee Refreshment Room'.
Opened 5th Dec 1911 to cater for traveller's needs.
Less than three years later, served King and Country's inevitabilities.
Transported bold young men, perhaps benighted—
To war.

Years rolled by.
Drifting clouds.
Over Moothi.
Good times more.
Bad times sure.

Mudgee Railway Station classified by National Trust in 1977.
Categorized with trust.
Maybe— now needs tender loving care?

> Paintwork peeling.
> Pinhead graffiti.
> Purged by punks.

Who do not know—
Or bestow.
Mudgee Railway Station's

> Sweeping.
> If not fragile.
> If not fervent.
> If not fascinating life journey.

Brown and beige 2022 model.
Which 96.3% of 2017 folk wanted restored for Sydney trips.
Still look'n good though.
'Art and Crafts Mudgee' opens for visitors.
Vintage car club office.
Valiant veteran's drop in centre.
But— as of this day—
No more Mudgee folk train travelling.
Off to war.

Trains departing, tears destroy.

Trains arriving— tears of joy.

Or journeying to the opening of the Sydney Harbour Bridge.
Or to the 1956 Melbourne Olympic Games.
Or places of family, love or dreams proclaim.

Mudgee Railway Station heart still beating with confidence.
History of souls.
Long may Mudgee folk console—
By day, from heaven's height—
Silver roofed ski slopes shining.
By night, wonderland of flaxen lights.
Palace of peace and paranormal.
Mudgee Railway Station, a photographer's delight.
Now seen in wistful light.
For well-being, in testing times we now live.

Mudgee Railway Station awoken by birds day after day.
Passing traffic.

Still standing strong.

Nothing really changes.

Oblivious to pandemic.

What *it* is.
Who *we* are.
No mask for Mudgee Railway Station.
No Eureka Stockade here.
Just stillness and serenity.
Daily awakenings by Mudgee town fringe.
Town's verandah sits sentry—

Sunrises.
Soft sunsets.
Sequestered.

Moothi—nest in the hills. Orange glow.
Reminisce steam'n'smoke days.
Now smeared eternal.
Smells of oil and coal.

Train sounds.
Whistle.
Long lonely horn.
Forever warns—
That Mudgee train leaves at dawn.

*Acknowledgement of factual information such as names and dates of events from research sources.*

# THE LINE OF TREES

## OLGA PAVLINOVA OLENICH CASTLEMAINE, VIC AUSTRALIA

You do not ask.
The road is full of silent holes
and we bump along deep
in our own thoughts.
But I am compelled to surface
and to tell you.
I believe in the solid line of trees
standing tall against those sudden winds
that slap us in the face with our misgivings.
I believe in their resilience and confidence
the generous reach of their embracing limbs
their whispering and reassuring leaves
making sense of the wind's real purpose.
In the noise of blasted news
I isolate the quiet rustle in my head and I know
there's got to be belief in something
and nothing but the line of trees
keeps the shape of things together.
I think of trees I think of growing up
and those new leaves veined with life
transparent in spring's hopeful light.
In the dead of summer's crazy heat
another bolt of madness
cuts through the bluish screens
and there is blood
cut rubies on the polished floor.
I make myself a cup of bitter coffee
but somewhere in the sipping
my throat constricts
and fills with desert dust.

I choke and scrape on words
and I must spit them out to someone
perhaps again only to you.
Our shattered understanding
leaves a legacy in never ending stories
repeated over breakfast when the news tastes fresh
and the warm cup doesn't tremble on the table.
While you are renovating your next house
and fixing the garden so that it knows its place
I break away into a field of dreams
and walk under the line of trees
surer of my footing with every secret step.

# SOMEWHERE: 2021

## HEATHER COMPTON   PRESTON, VIC, AUSTRALIA

Homemade banana bread,
An unprecedented frown.
Not everything's rising,
In my lockdown town.

Out of the window,
Kites scuff clouds in July.
There's only a shadow of normal,
As the sun withers goodbye.

Losing confidence in the globe—
Contact tracers needed.
But there just aren't enough staff,
Hope has receded.

I didn't want to make bread,
I didn't order mistrust.
I crave politicians with conviction,
That don't leave us in the dust.

It can never be the same,
But with losses we grow.
A slice of hope with my coffee,
As a new day waves hello.

# POACHED

**LESLEY DAY**  UPPER STURT, SA, AUSTRALIA

Minute bubbles rose slowly from the base of the pan, making their way up to the pop on the surface. The girl watched them intently. It was time. One by one, she cracked the eggs into the simmering water, pausing only to delicately lift each one to prevent it sticking to the bottom of the pan. The slotted spoon trembled in her grasp.

The seconds ticked by. After one minute she whirled around and slammed the lever down on the toaster. Timing was crucial. With a quick glance out the window, she hurried back to the stove. Through a cloud of thickening white strands she could see the yolks, still entrapped in a translucent coat. One more minute.

She jumped as the toast popped loudly from the other side of the kitchen. Wielding the butter knife like a clumsy sword, she fumbled to spread an even layer of pale gold on each slice.

The rustling of paper from outside sent her into a frenzy. Armed with the two slices of toast, she retreated once more to the stove, collecting the slotted spoon on the way. Her heart sank when she saw that one of the prized eggs had drifted to the very bottom of the pan, attaching itself with infinite white tentacles to the heavy steel base.

Thudding echoed in her ears. Her heartbeat.

Like a mother cradling her child, the girl removed the lone free-floating egg from the pan and placed it gingerly on the toast. She held her breath as she went back for the second, trapped victim, shuddering when its golden yellow blood spurted into the simmering water.

Thudding again. Footsteps this time.

'For god's sake! How dumb are you? Lift the goddamn eggs off the bottom when you put them in.' His fist struck her in the chest—almost as hard as the words pounded into her soul.

He grabbed his breakfast and went back to his newspaper.

The woman cradled two perfectly poached eggs in a slotted spoon and placed them delicately on the crisp, buttery toast. Deftly, she twisted the pepper and the salt in quick succession and whisked the plate away to the kitchen table with the confidence of a professional chef. Her husband glanced up from the paper, shuddered in disgust and went back to the cryptic crossword.

The woman laughed in delight and kissed him on the head. 'I'm so glad I married a man who doesn't eat eggs!'

# THE CURRAWONG

**AMELIA CARTER**   BRADDON, ACT, AUSTRALIA

Cycling has reopened the world for me. Not professional, lycra-layered cycling. Just regular cycling. Ambient cycling. Scenic cycling. As lockdown unravelled, and summer slowly crept in, I thought it would be a good idea to buy a bike, and what an idea it was.

Cruising along on my purple Repco wheels brought the perfect compromise: walking was too boring, running was too much of an effort, but God I had to get out of the house. I had sat stagnant for so long, commuting two metres each day: bed-desk, desk-bed. Repeat till fin. Repeat till mad. I was like a bottle of orange juice sitting for too long in the fridge: staring at the white walls and glowing screen, all my pulp sunk to the bottom for lack of movement. But the bike shook my pulp, raised my pulse, and sent buzzing all those little molecules inside me that had been in suspended animation for so long.

As I cycled over the bridge, an arc in the sky, crossing the highway, I felt the life breathe back into me. Hell, I felt the life breathe back into the whole city. Where had all this activity come from? All this lakeside chatter, bright colours, and picnic perfect sunshine. As I breathed more air into my lungs, so too did the circumference of the lake. In my loose shirt, I felt like I was flying as the wind flapped beneath it.

On one particular day, I returned from a swim, brimming with endorphins and the sweet green smell of chlorine, invincible. As I circled past the park, I spied a currawong perched on the fence, its black body and talons blending in with the pickets.

Most people mistake currawongs for crows or magpies, but I've always known better. In fact, I'm a little smug about my relationship with birds. I've never been swooped, by any bird, ever. Full stop. It's like we have a mutual understanding, I don't fear them. I joke with my friends that I'm the bird whisperer. I take a look at this bird as I get closer to it, and I seem to catch its attention too. As I hone in, I get a clear look into its dark yellow eyes, punctuated by a defiant black dot. I humour myself and briefly shift my body towards it. Startled, it shuffles back.

I chuckle to myself and cycle past, looking to the roof of green leaves above me, thinking myself a cheeky—

THUD.

Scream. Something hits me hard on the left of my face. Was it a ball from the kids in the park? Can't have been– they're on the right.

As I wait at the lights I look up and see a black silhouette looming in the greenness above me. I cycle home faster, more panicked, vigilant of a trio of magpies which later fly near me, but do not swoop.

Once I get home, I still feel a tiny, sharp, warmth on my ear, and the mirror reveals a thin red line from the beak of my victim. A reminder of what I had done. So stupid of me.

I thought back to my trip on the light rail the other night, and how a man got off at the same stop as me. I thought he'd been watching me on the tram. But we walked off to different streets and I knew I'd been paranoid. Still, I have every reason to be. Hyper vigilance serves me more than obliviousness, and no matter the man, if any trail behind me at night, my heart rate rises. I wondered how I'd react if he had tried to scare me, even as a joke, and regret sank through my chest like a stone in a river.

Now I'm on the other side of that vigilance and am just a little more aware than I normally would be when passing birds. I even pay more attention to pigeons, with their pathetically flailing feathers, as I cycle past them. I don't call myself the bird whisperer anymore.

# PARROT PEOPLE

## JANEEN SAMUEL   MORGIANA, VIC, AUSTRALIA

They're the ones who feather themselves
in flaunting colours —
        scarlet and yellow,
        purple, viridian —
cock their crests and cry
'Who cares what anyone thinks?'

They're the loud jolly bunch
who'll give you a good time,
tumble and clown,
swing on fortune's wheel,
hang upside down and shout
 'Hey! Look at me!'

They're the smart ones:
clever with their hands,
they can take apart
anything, leaving you the fun
of trying to make it whole
again; clever with their tongues,
they can talk
even when there's nothing to say,
say it loud and strong,
never quaver or flag.

They are not quite smart enough to understand
that sometimes you would rather be
silent
and sad.

# BARRED ROCK

**SUE HALL**  KERIKERI, NORTHLAND, NZ

'It's alright Mum. I know you had to do it.'

Two days before, Ben had arrived in the kitchen before breakfast. 'Mum,' he said, 'Barred Rock doesn't look very well. Could you come and have a look?' Ben didn't usually show much emotion, but I knew he was deeply upset.

'Jess,' I called, 'Ben and I are going down to the hen run. I'll finish breakfast when I get back.'

'OK Mum.'

We picked up the food scraps and walked down the path together with our arms linked.

Ben opened the gate and a flurry of red, white and black feathery bodies grabbled and seethed around us. They battled with each other for supremacy, squawking and pecking, poking and pushing. There's no warmth in a hen's eyes, I thought, when it wants something. Ben scattered the scraps and the melee settled.

Barred Rock, however, hadn't joined the rabble. She stood at a distance, her back arched, feathers hanging awkwardly. Usually the most elegant, stately and splendid creature in the run, her regularly-spaced alternating dark and light plumage set her apart from the others. Ben loved her because she walked tall and with self-assurance. But she had changed dramatically. Her strength had gone, her poise diminished.

Ben offered her a piece of apple he had saved for her, but she just stared at it. He stared at her in disbelief. I could see him deflating. His hens were his pride and joy. They always had been, and were even more important to him now that he was dealing with loss.

'Maybe she's got mites,' I said, scrabbling for a positive response. 'Let's get the powder and see if that will help.'

I held her while Ben gently rubbed the powder deep into her feathers. Afterwards, he placed her carefully behind the coop where the roof overhang would provide shade during the day. She stood immobile. Worrying about her pitiful demeanour, I promised to keep an eye on her during the day while Ben was at school.

Where was Tim when I needed him?

After school, Jess, Ben and I went together to check on Barred Rock.

She was crouched in the same position she had been in all day. The apple, of course, had been eaten by the others.

Ben's eyes were distraught, but he bravely made plans. 'Jess, will you help me make a fence around her. I'll have to put her somewhere where the other hens won't take her food or annoy her.' Jess was keen to help her brother, and they got to work.

I ambled slowly back to the house, thinking of the time last year that Tim had gone with the kids to deal with a sick hen. How stroppy I had been then, refusing to go anywhere near the murderous operation. How horrified I had been when the kids arrived at the back door, each holding a hen leg, each of them pulling on tendons to make the toes move, fascinated and laughing.

'How could you?' I choked.

'It's just biology,' said Tim.

Looking back, I was surprised to find myself smiling, remembering his cavalier attitude, his candour, and the energy he always found in dealing with awkward situations. Nothing was insurmountable for him. The next day's sun was always on the rise. How we all missed him. How I wished that he could find a way of pulling someone's leg again now.

Later that evening, Ben went down to the run again and carefully placed Barred Rock on a perch alongside the other hens. She needed to be up high and safe.

'Mum, I think she's really sick,' he said in the morning. 'She's on the ground under the perch and she's not moving. I think she's dying.'

'OK Ben. I'll see what I can do.'

Alone later that morning, I knew what had to be done. Quiet panic gripped me and stopped me thinking clearly. A hole in the ground yawed into my consciousness; a hole much bigger than needed for a hen. I was falling into it, weighted down with memories. Dark walls of earth started slipping uncontrollably.

'Pick up the shovel. Get on with the job. You've got a job to do.'

Expending some energy helped me on my way. I shovelled furiously, focussing my intention. Hole dug, I got the axe from the shed and went to find Barred Rock. She was limp as I cradled her in my forearms. Her third eyelid slipped sideways, white across her eye. She was too sick to respond and she lay torpid when I placed her on the log.

I lifted the axe and closed my eyes. Tim tapped me on the shoulder. 'When you've got livestock, you have dead stock,' he said.

'It's alright Mum. I know you have to do it,' said Ben at my other shoulder. I let the axe fall.

I picked up the two pieces, put them in the hole and shovelled relief in on top.

I had grown as a mother, that day in the hen run.

# JOINT WINNER, POETRY

## KEVIN DYER

DENBIGHSHIRE, WALES, UNITED KINGDOM

Kevin lives in North Wales in the UK. He is a professional playwright and recently won the Writers' Guild of Great Britain's 'Best Play' Award with 'The Syrian Baker'. He thinks of poetry as a form of playing—with words, ideas and people's expectations.

# DAHLIAS

I think we need Dahlias this year.

Brash antidotes to all our stressing;
as big as dinner plates in colours your mother
wouldn't be seen dead in.
The ones the taste-police at the National Trust would
if they could
confiscate. Incinerate. Obliterate. Exterminate.

Plant the pinks next to the reds
and the blues and lilac next to the yellow, like Velasquez
on acid,
and don't give a damn what Costa Georgiadis says.
Break the colour wheel,
do what you feel, don't give a damn what is juxtaposed,
make the neighbours squeal and pull their curtains closed,
plant the glorious gaudy blobs and knobs of hallucination
in every bed, in pots and old cracked sinks and discarded toilet pans.

I think I'll paint the shed pink this year, and the dog's kennel,
and the kids' swing—not because I'm doing the gay politics thing,
but because I no longer have the timorous feel for Quantum Butternut
    and Forest Green.
I'm just not keen. In my life from now on pastel colours
will not be seen. Magnolia will not, this year, cut the mustard.

And talking of mustard, I'll slap it on everything—my pork pies,
    my porridge, my fingers,
and lick it off in dollops and swallow it down like gobbets of
    yellow phlegm
until my eyes pop and the heat lingers
and I have to rush to the bath and douche my head under cold water.

I think I'll swim in lakes this year—cut a hole in the ice and plunge in
    to minus-5 degrees
till my testicles freeze into balls of ice and my skin is pimpled like purple
turkey flesh.

With a pompon dahlia in my button-hole, I'll handbrake turn
my Crimson Subaru in car parks,
race it to a skiddy halt across the parent and toddler space;
I'll go giddy and date people thrice my age;
I'll take illegal pills and go insane and rage and throw dollar bills
off the top of tall buildings
and laugh like a drain;
I'll kiss policemen hiding behind their riot shields;
I'll get tattoos of cats on my eyelids;
I'll shag in fields; I'll vote Conservative.
Well maybe not; that's going a bit far.

As the dahlias bloom and fill vases in every room
I'll tell people I love them this year—those that don't expect it,
but also those that need it:
sad men called Sid
and those who have hid
away, and the people on the supermarket tills, the folk behind masks,
and the ones who are desperate to be touched and held.
And if they don't want my love, when asked,
my attempts to make the bad world stop and spin the other way,
to pull the distant moon down from the sky, to Canute the waves,
to scream and scream until the tarmac cracks...
if they don't want all that

fuck 'em.

# TOWNSCAPES

**SCOTT HALLARN**  TORONTO, CANADA

We follow the long black car ahead of us. My mom nervously clutches the steering wheel of our rusted station wagon, her head bent forward as she peers through a large spiderweb crack in the windshield. Beside her in the front seat is my sister Beth, fifteen years old though most think she looks older, especially on a day like today when she's all dressed up. Her face is caked in makeup, with lots of pinkish-red on her cheeks and light blue under her eyes, just like the old woman who reads palms at the summer fair. Rarely does Beth talk to me anymore. When she does, she scowls and tells me how sick she is of having a kid brother who doesn't know anything. Today, though, both she and my mom are unusually quiet as I gaze out the backseat window, wondering how much longer we have to follow the black car.

Shifting my body so my mom can't glance at me in the rearview mirror, I undo the top button of my white shirt and loosen the tie, which feels like a python tightly coiled around my neck. It's the first time I've ever had to wear a suit. My mom said she didn't have the time or money to buy me one, so my cousin Jimmy lent me one for the day, a dark one with thin stripes. I told her I didn't want to wear it because of the blazing heat outside and because it's too big on me, especially the pants that need to be cuffed so I don't trip. Still, she insisted I had no choice because of what happened.

'It's only for one day,' she said this morning in the kitchen. Her voice creaked a little and she kept dabbing at her eyes with a tissue. 'Everyone dresses up for things like this.'

Things like this.

Kind of a strange way to put it, I thought. Maybe she thinks I'm too young to understand what really happened, or maybe she's trying to protect me from what my teacher Mr. Higgins calls, 'the evil in the world.' I know exactly what happened and have enough confidence in myself to deal with it, not like my mom and sister who've been crying a lot the past couple of days. If my dad was around, he'd say whatever was on his mind, no matter who he was talking to. That's just how he was. Sometimes he'd swear and say mean things about people, mostly about the handful of black people living in our small town. He usually did this when he was drunk—and he was drunk a lot. My mom always said he had a good side to him, but he didn't seem to show it much, at least not when I was around. I've never told anyone what he used to do to me.

I stick my head out the window to look back at the cars behind us. The warm breeze messes up my hair, but it feels good compared to the heavy air in the car. Like us, the cars move slowly through town with their headlights on, even though it's the afternoon. Saturday afternoon, the busiest day for the shops along Front St. That is, those shops that aren't boarded up because there's not enough business. My mom said it's because people don't have enough money to buy things ever since the mill closed and people lost their jobs. My dad was one of them.

Nobody on the street takes much notice of the stream of cars going by. To them it's just another day, though for us it's a big deal. Beth didn't think I understood how serious it was, how our lives would never be the same. Of course, she said it like she was spitting venom at me.

'Don't you get it? You're so bloody thick in the head! Everything's going to be different from now on, so start cleaning up and get ready for tomorrow.'

She said this last night when I was sorting through my baseball cards. The truth is, I do get it. I'm just dealing with it in my own way.

As we pass through the outskirts of town, there's mostly black people outside. Some of the houses look even worse than ours, small and run-down with dirt driveways and weeds sprouting up through patches of brown grass and between the front steps. We stop at a red light. I look to my left and notice two black men shingling a garage roof with the scorching sun beating down on them. When they see the car in front of us and the long line of cars behind us, they put down their hammers and take off their hats, each of them wearing a solemn expression. None of the white people did that when we drove through town.

'Look, they're showing respect,' I say.

Beth and my mom don't buy it. 'No, they're not,' Beth sneers. 'They don't know anything about respect.'

My mom tightens her jaw and says, 'You're right. They should mind their own goddamn business.'

Just like my dad.

Beth and my mom appear ugly and devil-like as I stare at them in profile from the back seat.

Then I look to my right and see Hayden standing on the sidewalk, the only black student in our class. Everyone ignores him, including me. Even Mr. Higgins treats him like he's not even there. When the light turns green and the car begins to move, Hayden raises his arm and shyly waves at me. I pop my head out the window and look back at him. When I wave back, he opens his mouth and says something. I can't hear it, but I think he said, 'I'm sorry.'

When we arrive at our destination, I'm not thinking about who's in the black car in front of us. I'm thinking about Hayden. He won't be by himself at school any longer.

# MABEL

**ANNA RODWAY**   WAGGA WAGGA, NSW, AUST

Mabel was sitting on the second step of a boarded-up bungalow on the corner of Main Street and Third Street when she first felt the kick inside: urgent and unmistakable, a joyous, miraculous hello.

She inhaled gently. Her neck was clammy and her eyes were closed. Her two hands smoothed their way across her stomach, meeting in the middle and lacing themselves together in perfect symmetry. She wasn't the praying type but found herself murmuring a gentle, 'Thank you' to whoever might be listening right now from their place on high.

Third Street wasn't much to rave about; a handful of small shops with faded signage offered a hairdresser, a butcher, a pharmacy and further down the road, a gated retirement facility. The town itself had a population of 3,323—a 'thoroughfare' as it was often unkindly called. It was near a major highway and between two vibrant epicentres so wore its points of pride in its World-Famous Pie and Tidiest Town awards from earlier times.

If the townsfolk had cared to peek through their windows they would have observed that small, private moment between mother and child at the old Mason place. They would've seen a slight woman with the wide-eyed giddiness of a child perched on that step, nodding anxiously as though to a song she couldn't place and tapping her dainty foot with a frenetic beat. She was about thirty-three. Possibly twenty-eight. It was difficult to tell—she had often been told she had 'one of those faces.' She wore a crumpled blue dress that did little to hide her fluctuating figure. Dark haired. Not conventionally pretty, whatever that meant. A touch of the exotic about her, like a hummingbird poised on a wire. She must have caught the bus from two streets over as she didn't appear to own a parked car. At one point she pulled a cigarette out from a comically small purse which seemed to fit no more than a few coins. She didn't light it, but toyed with it between her fingertips; with a distracted sleight of hand motion. Without moving from the step for almost an hour, she continued gazing at one place and one place only.

*Roy's. No Vacancy. Air conditioning. Now with colour television.*

The motel with all its innocuous small-world charm was single storey, offering twelve double rooms, humble breakfast options, a twenty-four-hour concierge and a surprisingly clean pool. There were even two sun lounges and a BBQ grill, astro turf and a single flamingo. Local children were known to gape longingly through the security fence during their summer holidays, drooping around with their swimmers hidden under their shirts. Yet Roy Jr. had made it clear he certainly didn't want to be fishing band-aids and coins out of the chlorinated water unless it was for paying customers thank you very much. The children would plead, jibe, make promises they couldn't keep, then eventually drift off, reduced to lying in the shade or spraying each other with a hose until they were scolded by their mothers for *wilfully ignoring restrictions*. And so the pool, in this thoroughfare town, for the most part, lay unenjoyed.

From her vantage point Mabel had a clear view across the street to the doors of Roy's rooms 1 to 7. It was nearly four o'clock and the sun cast a shimmering glare across a cracked car window. Mabel opened her purse and swapped the cigarette for a stick of chewing gum. She slowly unwrapped it and placed the mint strip in her mouth. She crinkled the paper into a teeny ball and tossed it towards the footpath. The afternoon carried the scent of burnt rubber and rotting lemons. Inhaling deeply Mabel again placed her hands sacredly on her stomach.

*Hi, hello Sonny. It's me.*
The corner of her mouth creased with a smile.
*I wish my ear could reach all the way to my tummy so I could hear what you're saying in there.*
She lightly drummed her fingers, one by one.
*I'm gonna sing to you. When we get home it'll be lullabies all night. OK?*
A young boy with torn shorts rode past on a bicycle. He flew by with his head down, on a gleeful, sweaty mission.
*Some day I'm gonna teach you how to ride a bike. All kinds of things. Just wait and see.*
Mabel scooped up her coin purse and gently rose to her feet. She rolled her right ankle to wake it up and smoothed her dress.
Wandering up the Mason's front path, she stepped out into the wide road, still adjusting to the dull twinge in her lower back. She took it as another sign from Sonny so she wasn't bothered. *He's so keen to meet his mama.* She knew it was true. Shading her eyes from the glare, she noticed a barefoot woman carrying a shopping bag on the other side of the street,

who seemed to be regretting her lack of footwear. She cursed as a prickle stuck to her heel and waved Mabel over.

'Hiya.' The woman winced; her weathered brow furrowed. 'Ouch. Why's it always the tiny pricks that kill the most?' She laughed hollowly.

'Like knocking a funny bone. Awful,' Mabel offered, eager to please. She tucked her dark hair behind one ear.

'Yeah. Exactly.'

The woman was rake thin, drowning in her denim jeans. She adjusted the plastic bag to her other side, twisting the handles as if by nervous habit. Tasting the full force of the sun bouncing off the hot pavement, Mabel nodded kindly and stepped up the curb towards the motel. A jolt of hunger came upon her and she wished for the third time that day, that she hadn't washed her uneaten breakfast down the sink.

'You're not Sal's kid, are you?'

The words rang out: earnest, urgent. The thin woman moved closer, scanning Mabel's face.

'Saw you sitting there for an hour—wasn't spying—but wondered if you were her kid. Finally come home.'

'Who's kid?'

Mabel followed the woman's scrawny finger back to the lonely house across the street. She surveyed the place from this new angle: the broken leadlight, the lonely bronze water feature; sucked dry and shaped like a fish.

'Oh sorry. I didn't think anyone lived there. It seemed very quiet.'

'They don't. One day they just vanished. Didn't take everything. That was weird. Just special stuff, I guess. Cat. Toothbrush. Made us think they were coming back, just left town for the weekend. But they never came back.'

The woman blinked in the oppressive light as she scratched at her foot with the other toe, awkwardly balancing on one leg. Mabel noticed that despite her waifish size and smoker's teeth, she had a surprisingly deep voice. It was musical almost, like the lingering strum of a guitar.

'I couldn't believe it.'

'Why not?' Mabel asked, though her concern rang false in her ears.

'Well,' the woman softened. 'I knew they were broke. But I always thought they looked happy.'

Mabel placed her hands over her stomach as the thin woman squinted painfully off into the middle distance. She felt irreverent with the constant chewing of her tasteless gum so seized the moment to quickly swallow it.

'I'm sorry. I wish I could be of more help.' The formality of the words caught in her throat. She glanced away from the bungalow which now hummed with added meaning—a prickly reminder of past pains and a pair who slipped through the cracks one day and never returned.

The woman fidgeted, rubbing her eye distractedly, not yet finished. 'What was weird though was the mail kept being delivered. Like when there was clearly no one home. Their post box exploded. In the end. Just imagine.'

She paused and Mabel did imagine. In her mind the postie was short, with a regrettable tattoo and a tendency towards the theatrical—hundreds of scraps of paper scattered across the overgrown lawn around him like a hailstorm in spring. She knew she ought to offer a word of condolence but marvelled sometimes at how rarely the right words flew to her mind.

She instead raised her hands apologetically. 'I'm sorry, I– I think you've confused me with someone else.'

The thin woman bit her lip. 'Right-o.'

A momentary pause.

'She never talked about the kid. But Sal—she told me when we were having a knock-off one night—celebrating a fundraiser for the art room—made quite a bit, you wouldn't bloody believe it—she said it had all happened so fast—she knew she couldn't keep it to herself, there was no father around—jeez, it's always the –' the thin woman trailed off as another car passed, this one slowing almost to a halt as the window ominously rolled down.

Mabel inadvertently stepped back yet the thin woman broke into a grin and leaned right inside.

'No, you'll break it—I'll show you—gimme a sec!' She turned back to Mabel, a twinkle in her eye, gesturing through the window with a cock of her head. 'This is my locksmith.'

Mabel heard a roar of laughter from the driver's seat.

'I've got a front door problem. Better get on it.' She gave Mabel a large, overly suggestive wink and snuck into the car, feline-like. Before she wound the window up, she called, 'You need to be somewhere?'

Mabel shook her head—'Just passing through.' She'd heard that in a film once. It seemed a fitting and innocent response, though far from the truth.

The thin woman waved with the same encouraging salute she had given Mabel earlier and the car growled off up the quiet road, grinding the painful Mason memories into the dust.

The serenade of the first cicadas warmed Mabel's ears. As she turned to make her way towards Roy's, the patio light outside the reception desk stuttered on, almost as though it knew she was there. She reached the door, pushed it open and slid inside with as much composure as she could muster.

It was as though she'd tipped straight into a refrigerator, the door smacking tightly shut behind her. She immediately covered her stomach, yet was relieved by the momentary respite, the chilly air and the pristine, quiet room. There were a couple of fake pot plants by the window and a certificate of authentication smartly propped up by the counter bell. Against the other wall was a small table with a stack of brochures advertising local walking routes and a balloon expedition that had been rated five stars by someone called Larry.

Mabel hovered on the linoleum floor, opening and closing her coin purse. She was enchanted by the black and white photo of the horses over the desk, tilting her head to one side. She'd always held on to a girlhood dream of owning a horse of her own someday. A curvy woman in her forties emerged from the tiny back room, holding a tall glass of orange juice. She had bright eyes and her hair was twisted up in a style that reminded Mabel of a jazz singer. The woman bustled forwards and placed the glass surreptitiously out of the way.

'Oh I am sorry, I didn't hear you.' She beamed and smoothly pulled a registration book to her chest, flashing perfectly buffed red nails. 'You have a reservation?'

Mabel stepped to the desk and gingerly ran a finger along its shiny top.

'I should have rang the bell—sorry.' She shyly touched it and a merry 'ping' rang out. The woman giggled awkwardly, her name badge gleaming.

'Not to worry. Who is the reservation under?'

'John Junior, my boyfriend?' She glanced away, the thrill of saying his name aloud, making her blush.

'Cynthia' flicked the page and smiled. 'Here we are. Lovely. Yes, he checked in last week didn't he? It's the smaller room with a view to the pool.' She handed Mabel the secondary key to Room 8 proudly, leaving the hook empty. 'The mini fridge remains stocked and billed on departure. There is a guest lounge over there—and the gate to the pool will be unlocked until ten o'clock. Roy's a real stickler,' she winked. 'We have a light dinner available as there aren't many joints close by or I'm on standby if you need anything else. Sheets and towels should be fresh as housekeeping went through this afternoon.'

Mabel swallowed; the fear of small talk biting at her tongue. 'John—is working on a film—they're on location and he's been so busy doing that—so I've come to visit him.'

'Oh aren't you lucky!' Cynthia's eyes widened and she seemed to stand a little taller. 'It's been a wild week for us—not complaining one bit. I admit I haven't met one of the stars yet—it's only some of the crew who are staying here as they couldn't get a hotel closer. Would you believe it!' she laughed gaily. 'Which one's your beau?'

Mabel leaned on the counter, her head starting to feel cloudy. 'He's tall. Brown hair. He's just an assistant but he could be in the film himself, he's so beautiful. He has the softest hands. They're too soft for a man, really.' She felt Sonny move again and a laugh tumbled out of her.

Cynthia sighed, indicating her wedding ring with a good-humoured eye roll. 'I knock off at seven so I haven't seen him. Drat. I'll keep an eye out though—who knows, maybe I'll have to work late tonight.' She giggled again and Mabel joined in. The sisterly enthusiasm was rubbing off on her. As Mabel turned towards the door, Cynthia called through her perfect teeth: 'I wish they'd whisk me away. I'm quite the artist myself.'

Mabel tipped the last few peanuts out of the plastic packet and slurped down her third can of lemonade. The box of chocolates lay by her side, half empty. She didn't really have a sweet tooth but she'd unwrapped them with a fervor. It was growing darker outside, the silence of the town evident in the hum of cicadas, the occasional call of wildlife or the odd creak of car tyres. She'd set the television on mute, in case she couldn't hear footsteps at the door, flicking around past the garish infomercials and the nightly sitcoms.

She had already made an indent on much of the room. She'd opened the door, pulled off her shoes and landed straight on the bed with her feet up. Mortified by her dirty toes on the white duvet, she had dunked them in the bath and dried them on one of the many fluffy white towels. Disappointingly, there was little evidence of Johnny in the room at all except for his watch on the nightstand and his locked case in the corner. She'd sniffed the pillows, hoping to catch a whiff of his expensive sandalwood, but they were, as Cynthia had said, freshly laundered.

Roy's motel room, number 8, was clean and simple, a picture cutout of so many other motel rooms dotted around the country: the easily cleanable lines and textures, the tiny complimentary soaps and carpeted floor, the oil painting of a bunch of roses, the tub smelling of bleach. She did like the view of the pool and the dainty lights that had flicked on in the courtyard. A short man with a sandy moustache, presumably Roy, was marching about in shorts, cleaning down the grill. He greeted an older man carrying a stack of papers, who pulled up in a large van with two tall women. The man stuck a finger under the brunette woman's skirt, before they all disappeared into Room 3.

Mabel stood in the shower, massaging her jaw, her hair shampooed and her back tooth aching. She expected she had her wisdom teeth pushing through but knew that wasn't a pain she could afford to fix. She ran the yellow square of soap over her thighs in thoughtful, circular motions. She slowly drew an 'S' on her stomach, watching the streak of foam appear then vanish under the soft water pressure. She stood in front of the mirror and examined her pointed chin, using her index finger to wash her teeth with Johnny's toothpaste. She plucked a stray hair from her eyebrow then dropped her towel and returned to the bedroom, sliding naked into the stiff sheets.

She awoke some time later to the shatter of glass followed by a laddish call of male voices. Through the window, she saw Cynthia, managing to remain the professional hostess and Roy, red-faced, running about with a dustpan and broom. Mabel peeked at the clock on the bedside. It was half past eight, so she assumed Roy had asked Cynthia to stay longer than her shift after all. Three men were talking animatedly out the front of Room 4, drinking wine in short glasses and leaning over the edge of the pool fence where the two women from earlier were draped on the lounges. They wore striking two pieces and despite the 'No Smoking' sign, Mabel saw a silver ashtray by their feet. Her heart lurched and she quickly scanned the well-lit area for a tall, brown haired, soft handed figure, but he was nowhere to be seen. She guessed he must be among them somewhere – this group were clearly not country types with their logo shirts and fancy words. They talked loudly and spoke to each other with a brash intensity that Mabel recognised from Mrs Aberman, the mother who she had nannied for last year in a ritzy suburb of the city, and her circle. It was all flowing champagne, nights to the theatre, promotional dinners and loaded conversations at the Aberman home. For Mabel, it was easy work and pleasant enough—the children had usually been asleep, a girl and a boy who seemed to enjoy reading books more than any other glittery distraction. Mabel had admired them for that.

It was at that time that she'd met Johnny. She'd been catching the bus back to her tiny apartment in the west, a paperthin shoebox with a a melancholy view of a concrete wall from her bedroom window. She had stared out the bus window at the slick skyscrapers, wrapped up in Mrs Aberman's barely stained coat that would otherwise have met its fate in the rubbish bin. He sat behind her, leaned in close and whispered gently that she had a neck to die for. He confidently moved to sit next to her, chatting to her all the while in a sweet, careful hush. They had slunk off at a busy stop and seen a film, in an art deco beauty of marble and gold trim. She had kept her eyes on him, this figure, who held her hand brazenly and pulled her away early, before the final credits danced. They had caught an elevator to the twenty-third floor, to a room with plush surroundings and French white wine. She'd sculled her glass, a smile stretching on her face so wide she thought she would tear. He'd held on to her all through the night; his silky palms on her trembling waist. She'd awoken in the highrise hotel, his face in her hair, to a horizon of clouds and the dawn of a red sky. That was the first time. Then there was a second and a third time. Until he slipped away to the north, after an urgent call from a producer he couldn't resist.

The poolside group guffawed and one of the women lit up a cigarette, fanning her face. Neither of the women seemed to want to swim, their hair bone-dry and their movements sluggish. Mabel craned her neck around the other side of the window and saw Cynthia march inside, shaking her head. Another van had rolled up with two women with clipboards and a leather case, who rushed into Room 10 without stopping. Mabel felt a wave of nausea and knew she should ask for dinner before the kitchen closed. She crossed to the cupboard to put on her dress, pushing back the other wooden door and was surprised to find Johnny's bathrobe. She traced her finger along the gold 'J.J.' sewn over the breast pocket, before carefully pulling it out and slinging it on. She heard a jovial hooting of laughter and crossed quickly to the window, pressing her nose against the glass.

There he was, at last—the figure from her memory—cutting a tall silhouette as he emerged from Room 2. Mabel lifted her hand instinctively then with unexpected abandon, rushed to the door and opened it so swiftly that she nearly forgot her key. She padded down the corridor with the dressing gown dragging on the vacuumed floor, and followed the lit sign to the exit. Beaming, she walked straight out into the garden, crossed to the pool fence and called out—'Johnny!' to the figure from her memory, who was stroking the arm of a petite girl with huge, bashful eyes. He looked up, confused, and Mabel nearly tripped on the corners of the robe, her heart thumping in her mouth. The circle of men looked over, enjoying the sudden spectacle.

'Well, hello there,' one called, staring at her fixedly over his horn-rimmed glasses. 'Coming to join us?'

Mabel, her head spinning, gazed at Johnny and said plainly—'I've been waiting for you.' She saw a flash of embarrassment as he crossed the courtyard towards her. She squirmed, feeling bedraggled, as the chaise-lounge women smirked in amusement.

'How did you know where I was?' he whispered urgently, his ordinarily slick hair ruffled. 'I haven't seen you in months.'

Mabel flinched. 'You left your business card, and I called the number last week and they said you were here.'

He looked stunned.

'I had to pretend I was your sister, then they told me about Roy's. I thought I would surprise you.' She smiled anxiously, gently reaching for his hand. He let her but it hung limp between her calloused palms. His brow was glistening and he smelt of tobacco and sweat.

'You must have travelled all day to get here.' It didn't sound like a compliment.

Mabel nodded slowly. 'Shall we go back to your room?'

'You can't take our boy, yet,' called the older man childishly. 'Come and join us. We're all celebrating.'

'John. What's going on?' the bug-eyed woman asked.

Mabel looked at him expectantly, keeping the robe wrapped tightly around her middle. He met her gaze squarely and said, 'Go back to the room. I'll be there in a moment. Promise.' He patted her arm and turned back to the crew, scratching his head, his long legs striding away from her.

Mabel sat on the bed, back in Room 8, in the darkness with the curtains drawn. She raided the rest of the mini-fridge but the food just sat in her stomach, heavy and liquified. She lay back on the bed, feeling for another kick inside. There he was, loyal and true.

She awoke at dawn, still in the robe, with crumbs in her tangled hair. The room was empty. Mabel felt her stomach, unable to imagine a baby without the soft hands of his father.

She sat up slowly and made her way out the door to the dusty heat of a new day in this tiny town. She creaked open the pool gate and plonked on the chaise, the remnants of butts underfoot. The old Mason place across the road radiated such a pensive sadness she couldn't look too long. *I hope you're OK, wherever you are*, she prayed into the swollen, silent, emptiness.

One of the doors creaked open nearby and she heard the scratching and husky voices of the crew preparing for another work day. She peered out of the corner of her eye and saw Room 2 had opened. There he was, on the other side of the gate, watching her, a helpless look on his face and his hands raised blankly.

Mabel stood up slowly and looked at him for a moment. She undid the robe and let it fall, revealing her naked, blooming body. She heard him murmur but she didn't hesitate—she turned and jumped into the pool, just her and Sonny, in perfect, radiant, free-fall.

# WHEN THE SEA TAKES YOU, I WON'T COME

**MOROUJE SHERIF**   WATERLOO, CANADA

I

In this grim valley of iron festering
must accentuate the viridescence,
wreathing a derelict hand through twitching
eyes, unveiling
                    in synchronous ambuscade.
Moments hang nowhere and hazy
in words of cunning cripples;
The trees reach for their apples.

If it were any spring but in this, the
skull stagnant in wonder's antics may miss
The magical seven, of love or three
yearns for what it means to live.

Yet, in this valley Spring may never come,
Only the tempest ruin in which we call home

II

Remember summer's embrace            Despair
beyond the easy solution awaits still to flourish
when those and I are dead
I can walk you through grass blades stabbing the bloodless
snow. On the placid winter touching earth and what you will
most desire is to

III

Free this indistinguishable death: gaunt tree,
hopeless giraffe, reach for your
apples
Your individual breath has the flank of the wind.
So, see the year fall back on tide. Hide your head in
the candle's distorted gloom, reach
the night where wolves prowl, embrace the land seeking
what love or pity may exist
All dreamers are free until they wake: in this insomnia
the lake we saw was all sky, neither buoyant, ever blue?

To walk into the valley, watch the rat or the
deer, in hopes of summer.
Sea on bare arms: dismiss the park in which every perfect tree holds a
new home, where all hills lie carnally in the marsh.
Your impossible November wish,
reach for
the apples.

# SOVEREIGN

## REGINA DE BÚRCA DUBLIN, IRELAND

Our guide is Dr Kinsella, the first woman in Ireland to earn a PhD. She bats it off when I mention it in front of Steve, but I wanted to make him aware. He does not acknowledge it, instead opening the map he picked up at reception. We stand at the gates of the council's golf course, just as rain starts to drizzle. We look at odds to the people around us, who are wearing mud-splattered golf clothes, wheeling equipment in their wake. Their laughter hangs in the air as they pass us by.

'I like to think of it as a seminal moment, meeting your first Sheela na Gig,' our guide says. 'Hers is a symbol upon which different meanings have been imposed and superimposed for centuries, but I believe that it's only when you visit one that you can really understand her. An experience one remembers forever.'

I smile. Our guide doesn't offer many tours. It is kind of her to invite me, considering I'm not in her research group anymore.

'Ireland has the greatest number of surviving carvings of Sheela na Gigs, or in Irish, *Síle ina Giob*, meaning "fairy woman on her hunker".' She continues, before being interrupted.

'Jørgen Andersen wrote that the name was originally *Sighle na gCíoch*, meaning "the old hag of the breasts".' Steve puts away the map as its edges start to curl in the rain.

'That's true. He did write that.' A shadow passes over our guide's face. 'Now, we need to be quiet; quick, fit in and look like we know where we are going,' she says.

I muffle a snort as I pull up my hood. We could never fit in this place. Our clothes are achingly modest and clean, though second hand. We are not as happy as those who surround us make themselves out to be.

Our guide starts off, marching past the 'Do Not Cross' sign as a club-brandishing golfer tips a ball that careens inches past her head.

'You're not supposed to be here!' he shouts, his pose frozen, holding his dripping club in front of himself, angled, at waist level.

Our guide smiles and waves at him while marching on.

The golfer's mouth gapes—he is struck dumb.

Steve splutters an apology on our behalf, then turns to me.

'We could have simply seen a Sheela na Gig in the museum's stacks,' he hisses. 'I told you this trip was unnecessary. It's even dangerous!'

I ignore him and follow our guide who is waiting for us beside a copse of Sitka spruce trees at the edge of the golf course.

'What would a pilgrimage to see a Pagan deity be without a guardian of the threshold?' Our guide smirks.

'Pagan? Hardly. Academics have dated them. They are medieval. Law of superposition and all that,' says Steve in the didactic tone he seems to favour in the company of women. 'Since I got tenure, my office has been in the Arts Building next to the History Department. I attended one of their panel discussions about this very subject, during a recent symposium.'

I look at my watch. We met up with our guide not twenty minutes ago. Usually, he mentioned his promotion much earlier in conversation.

'There *are* Norman versions of the Sheela na Gigs, but they are copies of the original pre-Christian examples, like the Sheela we are about to see.' A knowing smile lights up Dr Kinsella's face.

'Hmm. The latest research—' Steve seems to inflate as he embarks on another robust debate.

'The symbolism is wildly different depending on historical context,' I protest, despite knowing that Steve will tell me later I am being over-emotional. 'Pre-Christian, she's a symbol of sovereignty, a fertility goddess and a protective talisman. Post-Christian, she's a dire warning of the dangers of lust and moral corruption, an interpretation that led to many Sheela na Gigs being hidden or destroyed.'

'Of course the historical context changes the symbolism. That's blindingly obvious. But Sheela na Gigs are medieval architectural gro-tesques. End of.' Steve is about to say more but pauses to assess my expression, in the same way he does whenever my medication protocol changes. Whatever he sees in me makes him wary, and he stops speaking.

'The Sheela here is Pagan. This is a hill I will quite happily die on,' says our guide.

'We will all die on this hill if we don't move it,' mutters Steve. 'There are balls flying everywhere.'

Our guide shrugs and marches onward.

'Be more careful on the driving range!' Steve advises, voice raising.

Our guide does not pick up her pace or cower as balls sail past. We are now too far away from the golfers to hear what they are shouting, but their contorted expressions convey indignation, outrage, disbelief.

Our guide stops with no warning. We are now standing in what must be the middle of the golf course. It is too late for the golfers to stop shooting. It is too late for us to take shelter.

'What is she standing here for?' Steve throws me a murderous glance, as though I am her keeper. I stand beside our guide, as a familiar sense of solidarity pins me in place.

'Don't look at me like that. I am doing my best.' Steve shrugs and jogs to a tree-lined grove.

Our guide links my arm, a smile animating her face just as the sun makes an appearance. A shaft of light illuminates her white clothes and silver hair.

'Not too far now,' she says, before setting off once again. 'I like to think that...'

A ball narrowly misses the top of my head, a whooshing noise drowning out the rest of her words. I speed up, half-dragging her with me.

We join Steve, who is clenching his map, beside a large plane tree. Its bark has flaked off in patches. Its scant leaves are perforated and crumbly.

'Why didn't we just come before the golf course was open?' He directs his question to me, even though it is my first time here too.

'It's impossible to enter when the place is locked up,' says our guide. 'You're not seriously afraid, are you? I can assure you, we are quite safe.'

Steve glowers. His cheeks are flushed. 'Are you sure we are in the right place?' he asks. 'I don't see a Sheela na Gig marked on the map?'

'That's because they call her the cross,' says our guide.

'Really?' he says. 'I don't see a cross marked here either.'

'Dr Kinsella first published her research on this site thirty years ago. Of course she knows where it is,' I snap, swallowing the rest of my argument.

A brown-and-white striped feather floats in front of our guide. She holds out her hand as it glides and gently lands in her palm.

'It's an owl feather,' says Steve.

'How do you know that?' I ask him. Not many owls in the Arts Building.

'I've taken an interest in owls since the nature museum in Jutland.' he says.

'What were you doing in Denmark?' asks our guide.

'Conference,' I reply. 'One of the panels took place in the function room of a nature museum—'

'It was wonderful,' says Steve. 'They had a resident owl. Every afternoon at 3pm, there was a demo, where the owl would circle around our heads—'

'Within a small space, seeing how her leg was on a leash. She had been imported from Africa, as it's illegal to keep Danish birds in captivity,' I speak quickly to fit my words into the shrinking space before the next interruption.

Our guide snorts. 'Figures.'

Steve side-eyes me. 'Anyway, is this Sheela much farther away now or what? I have assignments to grade this weekend.'

'No.' Our guide turns and walks in the direction of a sprawling thicket. We follow her until we reach the forgotten part of the golf course. The grass is longer here. Its glistening blades hide stray balls, beer cans and fast-food wrappers that reveal themselves as we venture deeper. A stone wall lies ahead, in front of it, a mound of what looks like compost.

'This isn't good,' mutters our guide as she stands before it, hands on hips, surveying the land. She bends down and begins to tear away clumps of earth and stones.

I don't see what she sees.

'Is this the place? I really don't have much time today...' says Steve.

Our guide straightens and sighs. 'Fair enough.' She slaps the earth from her hands and moves to the right of the mound.

We follow. Our guide stands at the entrance to a round hollow, crowned with a canopy of willow trees. Their branches sweep the ground in a swaying movement, forming an undulating tunnel.

'You need to find her for yourselves,' says our guide.

Steve rolls his eyes as he lunges forward.

Refracted light through the branches sends shimmers through the leaves as I step inside, frantically glancing left and right; above and below. I have seen pictures in books and journal articles of this Sheela, and all who meet her say she is hard to find.

'Ahhhh,' says Steve, making a sighing sound, not unlike the one he makes when he climaxes. I march over to match him stride for stride, to experience what he has. Why should he be the one to get there first?

I do not see what he sees. Nothing but trees and soil and stones. Being the last of our group to find Sheela feels like a personal failing. I take a step away from Steve, about to ask our guide for a hint when—

Peeping behind a mound of torn branches and clumps of earth is the uneven edge of golden stone. I step closer. No branches above her, she is spotlit by the midday sun, dead centre in the sky above us. I am cold despite the light. It is quieter in our tunnel of trees than moments earlier.

'What do you see when you look at her?' asks our guide, who now stands behind us.

I hesitate, reluctant to have a Jungian analysis of my interpretation revealed in front of Steve. From experience, I know it to be wiser not to answer my guide when she asks these types of questions.

'It looks like an alien,' says Steve, probing the Sheela with his fingers. 'I see why they call it the cross. We can see the remains of a stone cross that contained this specimen. Most certainly medieval. Reminds me of that field trip to Kilpeck. Do you remember, Morgan?'

He turns to me and blanches when he sees my horrified expression. 'Oh. I forgot that trip took place after you dropped out,' he whispers as his gaze drops to the ground.

My stomach lurches with a shame I had never been able to reconcile. The thick and blurry three months of inpatient treatment began just as I was due to submit my final revisions. I blanch and pull my phone from my pocket in a clumsy reflex; the device becomes a remote control initiating a protective force field. Ignoring Steve always makes him seek attention elsewhere, and, sure enough, he turns to face our guide, his back to me.

My phone compels me to engage, dangling the promise of relief. Scrolling past message notifications, I click on the LinkedIn icon to browse for new listings. A job would solve most of my problems. I scan through posts by women I studied with, who are tailgating a popular meme. The posts show glossy, professional-looking images of themselves side by side with their seven-year-old selves. One had been overweight. One had been born with a cleft palette. Another had been much taller than her peers. All had been bullied. But look at them now.

My life's trajectory had been the reverse.

Deflated, I plunge my phone back into my pocket, unworthiness amplified.

Steve and our guide argue again about Sheela's provenance.

This time, I don't get involved. Instead, I seize the moment to study Sheela in private. She is unbounded and wild. Sovereign. Self-possessed. Embodies true confidence. Enduring, despite the patriarchy and its wretched golf courses. Hers is a burning history, fearsome and unapologetic. Mine contrasts pitifully.

'Take a picture of us.' Steve stands behind Sheela and gestures for our guide to join him. He puts his arm around Dr Kinsella, who smiles weakly as I click. 'Send it on to me, will you? One for Instagram. My students will be amused.'

I message them the photo. Neither of my companions suggest taking a photo of me, and I don't ask them to take one either. I don't want this experience captured for posterity after all.

# MOVE

**JESSICA KILKENNY**   SURREY HILLS, VIC, AUST

The sound of the tyres on the bitumen was a constant murmur, and she felt it in her body. For hours she had felt the warmth of the friction, her liver, lungs and heart jostling around inside her with every bump and erratic squiggle of tar. Behind her, the back seat and trailer she towed was full of cardboard boxes. Boxes bought, sourced from the backs of shops, given by friends with meal box subscriptions. They, too, quivered with movement. She whipped past the paddocks and gumtrees. The occasional herd of cows underneath the shade of glittering poplar trees lifted their lashed eyes, and the thin branches of dead and dying trees cast shadows like long witchy fingers across the road. Through all of this, the woman drove. Next to her on the passenger seat was his little black notebook. Its gravity pulled a taut line straight to her, and despite its smallness, it carried the weight of a real person. Someone giving her the cold shoulder, the silent treatment, flipping her off behind her back as she drove away.

The world spun past, and the woman thought about the second last night in Brisbane before she left. Her friend Sophia had thrown her a leaving party at the wine bar around the corner from the local primary school. All their friends came. She participated in the conversations; people asking her how work's been and saying she looked great, and telling her what a great party and how it was good to catch up and they'd miss her. When she arrived, no-one asked her where her husband was. Everyone was very careful. Before she had left for the party, she dressed attentively; sheer stockings, heels, a wine-red dress. Her styled hair was sticking to the back of her damp neck, and she felt sweat trickling between her shoulder blades, but she took a coat anyway. Before the taxi arrived, she had slipped the little black notebook into the pocket of the coat, and as she mingled, she fingered its soft cover and ran her fingers along the edge of the cool paper. Someone handed her a glass of champagne. As she took a sip, she noticed that the glass was smeared with blood, turning the wine inside a soft pink. Sophia shrieked and fluttered for a bandaid, a tissue. It's OK, the woman said. It's just a paper cut.

It got dark on the highway, and the light from her headlights threw out towards the edges of the road, smudged and uneven. The staccato lines of white paint flashed in and out, and there was nothing in the world but the road. The woman pulled the car over at a truckstop; unpacked the cooler bag from the boot of the car and pulled out the tent and sleeping bag. Quietly, she ate the egg and lettuce sandwich she had bought at the last petrol station. For a long time, she sat still, her head tilted back to watch the slow-moving satellites, tracing their paths. Just after midnight, a semi rolled in. The woman watched as a man got out, lit a cigarette, unpacked his things from the cabin of the truck. He was very tall, and for a moment she was scared as he approached her tiny tent on the side of the highway.

He peered over her head into her car.

'On the move, are ya?'

The woman nodded, said nothing. He took a drag of his cigarette.

'Hey, you got an old newspaper or something? I need to get a fire going to cook these snags. I'll cook ya one if you like.' He held up a packet of raw supermarket sausages, the three red health-rating stars bright as blood on the label. The woman started to shake her head, but then stopped, got up. Going to the passenger seat, she unlocked the car, took out the little black notebook, and handed it over. She watched the man's retreating shape, and kept watching until she saw the little spark and then the bigger flames, a small black rectangle becoming a shapeless ball of heat and wood and light.

Back on the Hume, the morning was grey and soft. The shadows that apostrophised the road and the flashes of white light were gone, and now when she passed through paddocks and past groves, the landscape was bucolic. A horse galloped alongside the car. Towards the left, an eagle hovered low and then dove to the ground. The woman's body vibrated with the energy of the car on the road, and she thought of nothing, nothing at all.

She pulled into the driveway, and for the first time, she saw the house. Its face was open; the blue weatherboards were peeling, but the windows were candent in the glow of the streetlamp. At home, the streets were lit up with high, white rods, maybe not quite fluorescent but still severe. Fat-bodied moths beat into those lights relentlessly. At sundown the sound of them punctuated her dinners on the verandah, where she would eat on the nights her husband didn't come home. Here, in this little bent street, the night was still and cold and muted. She turned around in the car, searching for the keys she'd had sent up to Brisbane and her shoes. She slipped them on, took her small backpack from the passenger seat and got out and moved towards the porch. A stout, grey cat sat on the bottom step up, and as she reached down to scratch its head, an old woman poked her head over the front fence.

'That's Alistair. That house you've got there has been empty so long he thinks it's his. You might find it hard to get rid of him.'

The woman straightened up and smiled at the face over the fence.

'That's OK, I'll be glad of the company'.

The old woman ran her eyes over her clothes, the car, the boxes in the back.

'Is it just you moving in then?'

Inside her pocket, the woman slipped off her ring, feeling the grooves it left behind in her skin.

'Just me.' She slipped off her coat and went inside.

In the morning, she sat at the kitchen table the last tenants had left behind. The legs were unlacquered but smooth against her bare calves, and she leaned her elbows into the little dents and grooves on its surface. The sunshine filtering through a leadlight daffodil in the window made the table look like a stick of butter, the room wide like a dish around it. Against the wall, the cardboard boxes glowed, sealed tight and ready for unpacking. Taking a knife, she dragged one of the boxes towards her and sliced through the packing tape. The stale Brisbane air rushed out of it, and she smelled her old house—mildew and heat. The woman watched the flecks of dust spin up and out of the box, mingling with the motes stirred up by her movements in the old house. Moving through them, into them, marrying, golden, shimmering and gone in the air.

# DRAGONS DON'T SMOKE

**SHOSHANNA ROCKMAN**   ELSTERNWICK,
AUSTRALIA

I draw a cruel lungful of fresh air
and when I let go
a whooooooooshh sounds out.
With scales iridescent,
I unlatch my great jaws. This time
words pour forth
and bounce between cliff walls—
my meaning is hot,
unwavering and still. I watch

as its glowing end
smoulders and shrinks.
The sudden clarity—
no cigarette lasts forever.
As barriers go,
it's too flimsy to install between
fears and their sources.
As for procrastination—when craving
eons, mere minutes spill
madly as that most notorious milk.
I could soon be cramped again
in that dank lair, behind boulders—
in airlessness.

So, after packets,
entire cartons smoked to ash,
I put this out
half smoked, and grind it under
a yellowing claw.

I exhale like the dragon I've always
wanted to love—
purple plumes shoot from my mouth
to rival the stratosphere.
I watch as my dense breaths mingle
with storm clouds.
I watch until smoke and vapour merge;
until there's no distinction between
that of my lungs, and that of the sky.

# VICTORY MEMORIAL

**EVELYN MENARY**  OTTAWA, CANADA

Holding her breath as much as possible, given her tickly throat, Rose peered around the corner of the staircase where she perched on the bottom step. A rogue piece of tinsel rope from the bannister crept down her neck and scratched at her skin. The light was on in the kitchen at the end of the dark hallway, but no one seemed to be there.

Rose exhaled and disentangled herself carefully from the prickly golden tinsel rope. She surveyed the ascending length of the wooden bannister, inhaling the fragrance of the woven evergreen branches, and twinkling her eyes back at the friendly goldy-white lights among them.

In the dark, she groped in the hall closet and pulled out a bulky, lined, long wool jacket and put it on. It was impossibly wide in the shoulders and she could feel it touching just above her knees. Maybe it was Ma's or even Papa's. In the closet, all of the coats had an intermingled smell of pipe smoke and perfume. Well—no one would miss the coat. Surely no one in the house would be going out tonight—they never did. Once Papa came home on a Friday night, he sat with his bottle of amber liquid and poured it into a cut-crystal glass, suckling at it until he fell asleep. Ma spent most of her time in the kitchen, reading the newspaper in the evening.

When Rose leaned way back and hauled on the glass knob of the heavy wooden door, the holly wreath hanging from the glass outside swung from side to side. Her small figure inside the huge coat crept out onto the snow-crunchy porch. The inrushing December night air caught in her throat and she nearly choked to stifle a cough. As she made it down the front stairs to the street, the Northwest wind assaulted her cheeks. The ice fog created by her warm breath obscured her view. Luckily, the church wasn't far.

On her way to the concert, Rose passed her new school—*Victory Memorial School*; a very grand name, she thought. Her mind went back to earlier in the day, when her class was practising for the concert. Her cheeks were reddening and burning now, even more from the memory than from the cold. She started to dwell inwardly on the events of the day as she picked up her pace on the night bound street.

It was bad enough to have to change schools in mid-December. Papa's job moved them here. She missed her old friends, every moment of every day. Rose did well in her first week of new classes for the most part: English grammar, science, geography. The other kids said things like: '*Browner!*' when she put up her hand to answer too many questions.

No one walked to school or home with her. They stayed behind her in a rollicking clutch of misery-makers. As cars approached, they laughed and shouted and pushed one another off the sidewalk. They did slides along the greasy wet piles of leaves mixed with snow. At one point, she felt a *whap* on the side of her head. She put up her hand to feel a cold clot of sopping, decaying leaves in her hair. Hoots of derision followed.

Friday afternoon's schedule had her class going into a different room. There were odd musical instruments all around the perimeter on the yellowed grey linoleum floor. This was a bit scary, as her old school had no instruments; they just sang. It was her favourite thing to do—to sing. When no one picked up any of the instruments, she was relieved. This was going to be okay.

When Mr. Brewster swept into the room, the students' clamour stopped. Above his furrowed brow, a long narrow shock of red hair atop his hairline tossed and lifted eerily, as though full of static electricity. His grey suit looked well-worn and shiny in spots. Without looking at anyone, *Rooster*, as the bolder students derisively called him behind his back, took a thick sheaf of paper out of his brown leather briefcase, also well-worn and shiny in spots.

'Rickard!' Mr. Brewster called out, 'hand these out.'

The clown complied, slouching and sashaying up to the desk, making faces to his fellow jokesters as he gave everyone a package of pages. At the last moment, he brushed by Rose's desk, scattering her loose papers to the floor. She hastened to pick them up, head down.

'Right!' boomed Mr. Brewster, 'tonight will be the Christmas concert. This is our last practice! *Today*, we need to *nail down* the final carol! Turn to page eight.'

The fluttering sound of shuffling pages filled the room. Rose's eyes fell on the first page in front of her. A sudden weakness flooded her body, as she stared at the unfamiliar lines and squiggly shapes. The title at the top of the page, she knew: *The First Noel*. Rose knew perfectly well how to sing it... but, that was page five. Glancing from side to side, to see what others were doing, she found page eight, the last page.

'*O Holy Night*,' it said. Her breath became fast and shallow. She did not know this one.

'Who can start us off now?' demanded Mr. Brewster. Hands went up, but he ignored them.

'Miss Bell,' he boomed, looking at the class list in his hand, 'you're new here. You can start us off. Stand up!'

Rose's tongue was devoid of all moisture and the insides of her lips clung to her teeth. 'I don't know this one,' she whispered.

'Read the music!' Mr. Brewster demanded, looking up sharply.

When she did not reply, Mr. Brewster picked up a pointer and whacked it on a symbol above the blackboard.

'What is this?' he wanted to know, staring at her. Rose said nothing.

'Anyone?' he asked, scanning the room imperiously.

'A treble clef, Sir,' said everyone else in unison.

'Exactly,' said Mr. Brewster.

'Miss Bell,' he intoned, 'it seems that rural schools don't see fit to teach music.'

Snickers rounded the room.

'Take a seat at the back of the class, Bell. You can work on your homework. You need not attend the concert tonight. I'll phone your mother to let her know. We'll figure you out in the New Year.'

It was a relief to have the spotlight off her at the back of the class. She stared at her homework while the class practised O Holy Night over and over and over and over.

Rose shuddered now, dispelling the memory, as she reached the front door of the church. The snow was coming thickly now and hers were the only tracks on the path. She had timed her journey so that everyone would already be well inside; she planned to stand just inside the vestibule to hear the concert, and to leave before anyone else saw her.

Her thin fingers stuck to the cold metal door handle and she tugged, without success. As she looked down instinctively to see if something was blocking the door from opening, she was distracted by a dreadful sight. On her feet were her fuzzy, faux fur, pink bedroom slippers!

Agonized with embarrassment, Rose slid away from the door. Maybe there was a side door and she could wait inside there, where no one would see her. There seemed to be no lights emanating from the church. Oh— yes—she recalled now, hearing that this was to be a candlelight service. How beautiful that would be! How lucky everyone was to be inside there— it just wasn't fair!

At the side of the church, she found no door. In a little protected grove of evergreens, Rose sheltered and listened. Nothing. Her slippered feet were getting damp now from the deeper snow. Then—there it was! On the night air rode the notes she loved so well. Her eyes adjusted to the darkness and the hollow she was in seemed to hold her in a sacred way.

*Good King Wenceslas* floated out to her. She hummed along at first and then gently sang some of the words.

'In his master's steps he trod, where the snow lay dinted;
Heat was in the very sod, which the saint had printed...'

*We Three Kings* followed next.

'Field and fountain, moor and mountain,
Following yonder star.
Ooo O—star of wonder, star of night...'

Rose looked up and a star winked at her through the branches. It didn't matter any longer about not being invited inside—or rather, being dis-invited! This, outside, was heavenly.

Rose began to shiver as other wonderful songs floated toward her and she sang quietly along.

'Glo Ooo o o O ooo O oooo O ria, in excelsis Deo....'

She couldn't much feel her face any more. She could feel her fingers and toes, which were crying for warmth.

'While fields and floods, rocks, hills and plains,
Repeat the sounding joy, repeat the sounding joy,
Repeat, repeat the sounding joy.'

Rose was now truly suffering with the cold that had entered her bones. She was just about to give up and go home when the final carol broke the silence.

'O holy night! The stars are brightly shining...'

Rose's voice joined this most holy of songs she had ever heard. She sang every note and every word faithfully, having learned it earlier in the day when Mr. Brewster made the class practise it.

'Long lay the world, in sin and error pining,
'Til He appeared and the soul felt its worth...'

No longer bothered by the cold, Rose eased her full voice into the hymn.

'A thrill of hope, the weary world rejoices,
For yonder breaks a new and glorious morn...
Faaaaall on your knees....'

Rose did just that. She fell to her knees, partly from weakness and partly in prayerful gratitude. The long jacket collapsed around her legs like a tent, as she sank down on the frozen ground.

When Rose awoke, she was lying under the snow-laden branches; she couldn't feel or move any of her body. It was dark, but bright red lights were flashing on the snow.

'Her door was a bit open when I went by,' a woman's puzzled voice was saying.

'Don't tell Papa, Ma,' Rose murmured.

'She always lived with her parents until they died,' the woman's voice continued. 'She's lived alone in the house forever. I help out when I can. I went to decorate her place for Christmas earlier today. I don't know what she was thinking to come out here. This church closed a while back. Someone bought it to renovate it for a house. It's so sad how many of the churches are closing,' the woman said, digressing.

'Bring the stretcher,' a man's voice directed, cutting across the woman's voice impatiently, 'She may have broken a hip.'

'*Just* what we *need*,' another man's voice replied, 'another *bed blocker.*'

'What do you *mean?*' asked the woman, wary now of the man's dismissive tone.

'The hospitals are full of old ladies like this one here,' he replied, guiding the stretcher beside Rose. 'Can't go home again. No space in long term care. She could still be in the hospital months from now, using up a bed somebody really needs.'

Rose couldn't fathom what anyone was talking about. She did know one thing though.

'I sang it, *Rooster*,' she thought triumphantly, as she felt her sparrow-light body being lifted toward the starry sky. 'I *did* it!'

# THE KINGDOM OF THE OVER-WORLD

**JERICHO ELLAO**  ALBURY, NSW, AUSTRALIA

Beyond the light-polluted cities,
Amongst the stormy skies
Slumbers ceaseless voids of perilous realms,
And within, a kingdom lies;
Fields of stardust, and cloudy plains,
Stars in perpetual bloom,
Amongst the foreboding side of the eclipse
Encased by folds of twilight gloom

The kingdom lies upon a cloud
With a gold and silver whirl,
Seas of air, do I dare
To venture within the kingdom of the over-world.
I was lost, in the tumult, the eastward lands of earth
Which sundered far from my home
I needed to return, before the collapse of dusk
Before the armies of Gourmou grew

The sun had journeyed beyond the edge of the world,
And obscurations arose from light,
A melodious breeze hummed a hollow song,
And I perceived the first-star aflight;
A vertiginous illusion formed within the wind-swept fogs,
Thither, sundered the star from the cloud
Tulmult beat thunders amidst the eastward lands
And the world amid elvish wars did enshroud

Distant roars from the looming clouds
Subdued the everfalling flame of bloodshed
As squamous creatures soared beyond
The clouds nevermore a fiery red;
And from the haar arose a creature,
Clamouring among a silver breast,
Ere could I flee, I plummeted on its back,
And a white dragon commenced its quest

My cold ears like a flute for the piercing wind,
My hands gripping its ivory horns,
The lightning like emerging trees,
And beyond the downpour, a dark cloud mourns;
The storm is unleashed, it convulses with sheets of rain,
It heavens with a sob and a sigh,
For within the dark there is a light,
And so we continue to fly

Fuming tempests of dark clouds, gyre and writhe,
crying amidst the skies caterwauling tone
The light of the skies was vexed within a crestfallen nightmare
And within the evenfall ether, we rome
The storm is pierced by beams of the sun,
And casts of blues replace the greys,
The sky is clear, and something appears
Within the heavens of this dire day;

I've ne'er a glimpse within this part of the ether,
But I am curious as to what lies within the skies,
The dragon alights on the nearest cloud;
But I am caused to agonise

In this dismal dimension of vast voided seas,
I lied in vexation above a canyon of astrality
But something arises in the form of a palace
Which paused my sorrowful agony;
I drag my gaze to a kingdom white,
With a gold and silver whirl,
For now my days immortal
Within the kingdom of the over-world

Beyond the light-polluted cities,
Amongst the stormy skies
Slumbers ceaseless voids of perilous realms,
And within, a kingdom lies;
Fields of stardust, and cloudy plains,
Stars in perpetual bloom,
Amongst the foreboding side of the eclipse
Encased by folds of twilight gloom

The kingdom lies upon a cloud
With a gold and silver whirl,
Seas of air, My kingdom fair;
My kingdom, of the over-world.

# OF MACHINE AND LOVE

**LEE A BAGLIN**   JANE BROOK, WA, AUSTRALIA

The machine is near perfect ; As light beckons darkness

Extensive wiring meticulously spread ; Pain insists to be felt.

Cogs ever turning ; As the waves are unrelenting

But what is its purpose? ; This love will not surrender.

This is my design ; As my heart breaks

Organic yet construct ; Shattering into the quantum void.

Constricting blueprints ; As I interrogate my soul

To an existence of machination ; Will you be the one to help find my pieces?

As you are the light, and my darkness.

# GONE SOUTH

**STEVE FENDT**  CLIFTON SPRINGS, VIC, AUST

It was shortly after losing her that he began to lose himself.

Just little things at first. He lost words for days at a time, only for them to return unbidden. Familiar faces became difficult to pin a name to.

Speaking of pins: he stumbled over a PIN while accessing his bank account, and then all at once forgot the bloody lot. They just fell out of his head.

One day he couldn't even open his phone. The fucking thing wouldn't recognise his face after restarting and wanted a passcode. 'I don't KNOW!' he roared, then sat in his armchair sobbing, desolate, for an hour.

The odds and ends of knowledge generally came back, at least the ones that he remembered forgetting. As for any others, who knew? He started to dread fresh lapses. Words, dates, numbers—they were no longer reliable, constant.

More terrible, his sense of self started to fade. His inner voice became disordered at times. No longer a steady monologue: a babble of strange voices that had no business being in his head.

He wasn't going into that place. The one that they took her to in the end. When he could no longer look after her. When he failed, shamefully, in his duty as a man and a husband. *What was her name?*

The place that stank of shit and disinfectant. Some of the warders were nice, friendly, if a little condescending. Some were sour faced, passive aggressive.

*They're called nurses, carers, Old Son, not warders.*

He had a line of poetry rattling around in his head: something he read in his youth, about old men becoming explorers, 'cause they had little to lose. It had seemed a fine sentiment back then.

*What you don't yet realise, Sonny Jim, smart-arse kid, is the less life you have left, the more precious your little becomes.*

There was something in it, though. You couldn't hoard life: you had to spend it freely. He had become miserly with life over the years: an insipid cook, a frugal shopper, a tepid lover—while he still had someone to love. A timid, inshore sailor.

*You can't take it with you, Matey Boy, and you're sure as hell going.*

Isolated, with only a few acquaintances and half-friendly neighbours to keep him in touch with reality, his mind turned inward. He started to plot and scheme, half in jest, half in earnest.

*What about sailing off into the wide blue yonder? Literally?*

She was a good little boat. Seaworthy, although the forehatch was dodgy and the crazed portlights wouldn't take much of a beating. But she had nearly a tonne of lead in the keel and she was strong. He'd sailed her for thirty years and knew every inch of her.

The VHF radio would only work for the first 20 miles out into Bass Strait and he didn't have an HF set. But what did that matter?

*Who are you going to call? God? Neptune? Helena? Ah, that's her name. That was her name. See—not completely doolally yet, Sonny Jim. Still got some marbles.*

He'd never seen the Ice. What a wondrous thing it must be! He knew that it was out there, tantalisingly out of reach. Just steer east of Flinders Island, then keep heading south. Keep an eye on the GPS so as not to bump into Tasmania, and even a small boat could get there, surely?

O'Donnell of the Antarctic. What an adventure! What a laugh!

The prospect of the voyage gave him new focus and energy. Passage plan, provisioning, everything had to be written down meticulously, or he would forget.

*That's all part of seamanship, Sonny Jim. Meticulous record keeping.*

Then one fine afternoon in late October, he put his insane plan into action. His marina neighbour shrugged at the garbled description of a voyage to 'see the penguins.' At St Kilda Pier, maybe? You never knew quite where you were, with old Jim.

With extra jerry cans of fuel and water lashed to the rail, the lockers stuffed with random provisions and warm clothing, he cast off the lines of his marina pen for the last time and gave Geelong a wave farewell.

Overnight he anchored off St Leonards, watching the lights of the town reflected on the inky water as he broached the first of his stash of rum. *Gout be damned.*

At eleven the next morning, he sailed out of the Heads, timing his passage through the feared Rip to perfection. The little yacht sailed out on smooth seas and a fair tide, popping out of Port Phillip like a cork out of a bottle. Out into Bass Strait, where he had never ventured alone before.

The short chop of the Bay gave way to the long rolling swell of the Strait. Still not quite the regular rhythm of the Southern Ocean: too many islands and shoals in the way, giving the yacht an odd, lolloping gait. A blocking high over the Tasman kept the wind steady from the north at 15–20 knots. No need to shorten sail. He made superb progress. Noon the next day saw him 120 miles southeast of the Heads, rounding the Prom.

Off the east coast of Tasmania, the weather turned ugly as a deep low moved in from the west. He scampered around the deck like a young man, laughed and swore into the teeth of the storm. A portlight was stove in by a rogue wave; he swore some more, patched it with scrap timber and duct tape, bailed out the cabin with a bucket.

Without fear and without hope, in old age Jim O'Donnell became the sailor he never had the courage to be in his youth.

After the storm abated, he slept for 30 hours, exhausted, while the trusty autohelm struggled to keep the boat on course. When he woke, he ran the engine for 12 hours to recharge the depleted battery.

Ten days after leaving Geelong, he cleared the southern tip of Tasmania. Battered, bruised and bone-tired, with salt-cracked lips and reddened eyes, but determined.

It was as if the Screaming Fifties granted the little yacht safe passage on her final voyage. A steady breeze from the north east, a gentle swell and sunny, clear skies sped her onward. At night, the Aurora Australis shone down in its majesty. The air grew cold, and colder still. Snow fell.

At dawn on day 25, he huddled in the cockpit swaddled in blankets, gloved hands clamped on the tiller, the last rum bottle empty at his feet. His dying eyes registered a milky glow in the southern sky, then, as the chill sun rose, a glitter on the horizon.

The Ice.

NOTE: The quotation that Jim could not quite remember is to be found in T.S. Eliot's 'East Coker', the second of the Four Quartets. It's a poem that I hadn't read for many years, probably half a lifetime. Rereading it felt like coming home.

This story is dedicated to the memory of Dr Jim Watts, GP in Hopetoun, Victoria. He would have approved of Jim O'Donnell's plan, I think.

# CONFIDENCE IN HEALING

**HANNAH SMALL**   MIDDLE PARK, VIC, AUST

Light sifts through the snow gums, ricocheting off the impenetrable earth below. A crow caws, piercing the still air. The wind descends from the skeletal limbs of the trees to wrap itself around the Person, whispering faintly as it does.

*Unburden yourself to me.*

A tempting thought, and something the Person would have done without hesitation just two years ago. Twenty-three annual trips to the Victorian alps made those mountains their true home. Do they not say home is where the heart is?

In those mountains, they unburden their emotions from the latest year to their surrounds. The sun glares down, admonishing the Person's moments of indiscretion. Luscious grass ripples in amusement at their latest anecdotes. Meanwhile, the trees bear silent witness, with their warm bodies emanating comfort. The landscape is mapped with 23 years of their deepest desires and darkest fears.

Once the Person leaves, Autumn begins and so too does the falling of the leaves. As the trees shed their ashy green foliage, the leaf matter falls upon the previous year's remains. In doing so, that year's emotional landscape is cemented into the mountain's topography. The leaves eagerly decompose, taking to the earth as water to a parched mouth. Memories of the Person's life can be found through rifling amongst the years' worth of drying leaves and crumbling soil. That crushing rock layer deep below the surface; the year of the family breakdown. The fine sand reminiscent of troubled youth, and the worry that it could all slip away. Rich dirt after the drought, consistent with those later years of passion and wonder once thought to have been lost forever. The landscape knew all this of the Person, and withheld judgement.

Two years ago today the bushfires struck and feasted on the mountains' offerings. Ash blanketed everything and no hint of green remained. Smoke curled in towering columns and bore down on witnesses, oppressing the mind and throat. It's voice mimicked the winds of the past, merciless.

*Do you not trust me anymore? I thought you wanted someone to talk to.*

But it was not the same voice the Person knew so well. Then, more than ever, they required a return to their past self, to a place of comfort and familiarity. Years of love and heartbreak had not prepared the Person for the devastating loss of their job. Peculiar that this loss could be more detrimental to the mind than anything else so far, but the Person prided themselves on their work. They liked making people smile, even if those moments were as fleeting nowadays as flashes of sunlight in a tropical rainstorm. Their internal demons were kept at bay. To the Person, their work was how they could justify their existence.

So it was the visit during the bushfires which burnt a hole in the Person's soul. They watched in shock as their past, present and future went up in flames. This sacred place had become tainted, with the smoke simultaneously acting to blind and choke. Tracks of tears down hollowed cheeks, a tightening in the chest. It was a long drive home that day, and one that they did not make again for two years. The Person sunk into themselves, hiding their demons in the dark recesses of their mind, unable to find a release. When they most needed the place which knew them so well, it had forsaken them.

Today, looking around at the landscape the trees were still burnt, their white skeletons in stark contrast to the blue-bird sky. Agonised, the Person cried out, echoing the lone crow. They wondered why they came back at all as this only hurt more, seeing their former life remaining in tatters.

*Have confidence in me.*

The wind had unravelled itself from the swaying limbs and trickled down to the Person. Humiliation swelled in the Person. Despite the courage it had taken for them to return, this voice was still haunting to them. A shadow of former glory.

And yet, as the Person made to leave, their attuned tastebuds detected a hint of sweetness in the air. A crow cawed again, softly this time, and it filled their throat with warmth. Out of the corner of their eye, the Person saw a hint of green. Upon inspection, it was a shoot of grass.

Just the one.

And yet that seemed enough to the Person. Maybe they had to have belief in life. Trust that things will return to their natural order. Confidence in oneself, that they can bring themselves back from the brink of destruction, just as their landscape had done.

# TREE OF KNOWLEDGE

**JENNIFER HURLEY**   PORTARLINGTON, VIC

Eva leaned her head back against the stack of pillows that Marg, the personal care attendant, had fashioned for her to take in the view from her window.

'Beautiful day out there, Eva,' said Marg cheerfully, placing the breakfast tray on Eva's overbed table.

'Mmm, looks nice now, but is it going to rain?' asked Eva.

'Nope, no rain. It's going to be one of those glorious winter days today. Cold, but sunny,' Marg replied with a bright smile as she quietly closed Eva's door behind her.

Looking through the window, Eva's gaze whizzed past the low-maintenance succulents straight to the distant sea. Such a deep blue today and glittering like sapphires. Was it really more than seventy years ago that she and her mother had boarded that ship to take them from post-war Europe to a new life in Australia? Looking at the sea invariably brought her back to that moment so long ago when she had embarked on her new life. Such an adventure, and now here she was—alone—and at the end of her life. As she distractedly ate her breakfast, her thoughts drifted...

*Come on, Eva!* Her mother had beckoned when it was time to disembark in Melbourne. Surprisingly, Eva had enjoyed the weeks-long voyage, making friends with other children whose parents were also seeking a better life after the years of wartime chaos. She missed her old friends from home, and now she would probably never see these new friends again either. Startled to taste salt on her lips, she realised she was crying. Hastily using her sleeve to wipe away her tears and turning so her mother could not see her face, she mentally severed ties with her new shipboard friends and linked her arm through her mother's. It's just us now, she thought, and a wave of sadness hit her in the throat as the faces of her grandparents, aunts, uncles, cousins, friends—but not her father—rushed through her mind's eye. She was too young when her father died to remember him. Tilting her head up, she knew now why she had overheard her grandparents—Oma and Opa— say many times that her mother was so very, very brave. Squeezing her close, her mother urged Eva to stay by her side and reminded her to only speak English now. Eva nodded. No more Dutch and no more Holland.

Without waiting for her knock to be answered, a different personal care attendant marched into Eva's room, 'gums flapping' as her late husband would have said.

Brusquely sweeping away Eva's breakfast tray, she demanded, 'Are you going to stay there all day, lazybones?'

Eva grimaced a reply, 'Actually, no. I'm going out for a walk today.'

'Ha! Wouldn't that be nice, but you can barely walk from that bed to the bathroom, so I don't think you'll be going anywhere!'

Eva gritted her teeth, willing the gormless woman to leave her room. When she was finally alone, Eva slowly got up from her bed and locked the door. She went to her wardrobe, selecting some thick winter jeans and a warm jumper. She was glad she had let her daughter talk her into buying these new clothes a couple of years back. She noticed how loose her jeans now seemed around her waist and realised that she had lost weight. Her interest in the institutional fare was not great as she missed her own cooking. *Why would you want to go out?* her husband used to say about Eva's cooking. Eva smiled at the memory. Cyril had been dead for more than ten years. Ten years! The person that she had spent most of her life with, had built a family with, was all but dust now. And soon I will be too, she thought.

Slowly pulling on her dressing gown over her clothes, she tucked a favourite silk scarf and a tube of lipstick into her pocket and sat down to put on her runners. Wearing a dressing gown in the retirement home was a form of semiotic communication: *Hey, I'm not going anywhere! I'm staying in again today!* Conversely, being properly dressed (as Eva preferred to be) would often evoke questions: *Are you going out today, Eva?* And, *oh, Eva, don't you look nice—where are you off to?*

She hoped no-one would notice the incongruity of runners peeking out from below her dressing gown. Uppermost in her mind was getting out for a walk to the sea, to find the tree again. *Her* tree. No, *our* tree. The tree that she and Marion had climbed as teenagers, finding themselves a refuge and a dreaming spot all in one. The place from which she would first spot Cyril. But she was worried. Would the tree still be there? Would she be able to find it? After more than two years in the retirement home, and with her memory declining, she felt a good deal of trepidation about her escape.

It was the location of the retirement home that had finally cemented Eva's decision to accept her children's insistence that she could no longer live alone. 'You can't manage any more, Mum,' each of her three adult children had said to her at different times in the lead up to her eventual move to the institution. Just cooking a simple meal had become an ordeal for her. With fingers and hands lacking strength and prone to losing their grip, her once deft culinary skills seemed to decline each day. She had resorted to buying frozen meals that made eating no more than a necessary exercise of refuelling. 'Like a jet aircraft,' she had said aloud to nobody. And then, answering herself—as she was wont to do these days—she replied with a laugh, 'no, more like a slow coach!' Losing the joy of eating her own home cooking proved to be the final straw for Eva's independence.

She had decided one morning to make herself a simple omelette. It was on this dull, drizzly day that she finally capitulated to not only her children's pressure but also her own inner voice. Her 'fall' (from real life?) happened when she slipped on the wet concrete, having gone out to pick some herbs for her omelette. Her ridiculous non-slip slippers had stuck so much to the wet concrete that her foot had come out of its slipper, and she had fallen headfirst into her parsley patch. How dizzy she felt, lying there facedown, trying to roll onto her side and figure out how to get up again. At least it was a relatively soft landing. She even managed a wry smile as she imagined (heard?) Cyril saying, 'Strewth, old girl, what are you doing down there?' Suddenly feeling cold and shivery, her weak smile turned to a frown as she realised that her knee had twisted on the way down. Oh no, Eva thought, how am I going to hide this from the kids?

When she had finally made her way inside, crawling at first, then making it up to a limp, the acrid smell of burning egg hit her olfactory nerve. She painfully made her way to the stove, picked up the frypan and sent it hurtling into the sink. Fortuitously, she had turned on the stove exhaust fan before she went outside. The last thing she needed was the smoke alarm going off! She felt the temperature of her half-drunk coffee, still sitting next to the stove where she had been sipping it as she cooked. It was barely warm. Hobbling to the freezer she pulled out a packet of peas and retreated to her armchair.

Pulling up her trouser leg, she could see her knee was starting to swell. She winced as she applied the frozen peas. Sitting there, she looked around the immaculately clean lounge room and then gazed from her knobbly, arthritic fingers and hands to her elevated knee. Eva knew it was becoming impossible to live alone. She covered her legs with a blanket and reached for the television remote control. 'Nothing but rubbish,' she complained as she went through all the free to air channels. Eva flicked the TV off again and regretted not having turned on the radio instead.

'Mum?' Eva was startled awake, immediately aware that her legs were wet, and remembered that it was Saturday and that her daughter had a key! *Just for emergencies*, Nina had said, several months back, adding that she had also had keys cut for each of her brothers.

'What's happened?' demanded Nina, surveying the scene, from the elevated leg to the abandoned omelette still in the frypan.

'Nothing, darling! Nothing, nothing,' Eva insisted, seeing the concern on Nina's face. 'I just twisted my knee a bit when I was picking parsley. I'm fine, the peas have worked a treat, and now I'm OK.' Secretly, she was in pain and weak with hunger.

'OK, Mum, it's OK. Stay calm... lucky I had that key... I'll make us both some lunch, but let's get you out of these wet pants first.'

Eva felt like a child but didn't resist Nina's gentle support and guidance to change into dry trousers. Finding some ice in the freezer, Nina made a new icepack, this time placing it inside a plastic bag and wrapping it in a tea towel. Eva admired the way Nina quickly cleaned away the burnt omelette, started a new one, and then disappeared outside to pick parsley, oregano, and thyme. Within half an hour, Eva was enjoying her tray of omelette, with her favourite herbs, buttered toast, and a fresh cup of coffee.

Nina eyed her mother, noticing she still had patches of dried dirt on her face, and she smiled as she noticed a few green shoots in her still lovely hair. Eva, catching her daughter's gaze, simply said, 'OK, OK... I'll go.'

'Where?' asked Nina.

'To a bloody retirement place! But I'm only going to one in Flinders Bay, nowhere else!'

'Flinders Bay?' Nina asked in disbelief.

'Yes!' Eva said firmly.

'OK, Mum, I'll find out what's available there, but you won't have any of us visiting as often. It'll be further away for all of us. Is that really what you want?'

Eva nodded and said, 'Besides, how are you going to meet anyone new when you have to worry about me?' Nina had been divorced for almost five years now.

Nina laughed and said, 'That, Mum, is the least of my worries!'

At Eva's request, Nina had driven them to the tree when they had come to inspect the retirement home together, shortly after the omelette incident. They had stayed in the car, the weather being inclement and blowing a gale.

'I can see why you loved this spot, Mum,' Nina said, taking in the spectacular view.

'Marion and I were the "queens of the world" up there in that tree!' laughed Eva. 'We could see all the boats coming in, who was swimming at the beach in summer... who was out and about... and with whom! We used to get a couple of bob's worth of chips and snuggle in up there together... in all sorts of weather. And the conversations we used to hear... people didn't know we were up there... we'd hear—and see—a lot! I first spotted your dad from up in that tree. Now they're both gone... Cyril... and Marion.'

Nina reached for her mother's hand, 'Mum, I can see that you have a lot of memories here, but do you really want to live so far away from me and all the family? I won't be able to visit every week, not with the kids in their final years of school. I'm working all week, and the kids have their sports most weekends.'

Gripping her daughter's hand, Eva replied, 'Yes, this is where I want to go. It was my first home in Australia, and it's where I want to see out my life. And besides, I already know that house... the retirement home... it's the old Chisolm property. I knew the owners, many years ago.'

As Eva stealthily made her way from her room to the main entrance, she was glad she had insisted on the move to Flinders Bay. This town was the first place where she finally felt at home, after the war years and then arriving in Australia and spending two years at Bonegilla, the refugee camp. It was also where she had met Marion, and then Cyril.

Knowing the routine post-breakfast, she carefully avoided all routes that would bring her anywhere near other residents or staff as she made her way to the entrance lounge. It was uncanny, the way that she could remember her way around the Chisolm house, or Flinders Bay Retirement Home, as it was now called. She and Cyril had attended several glamorous parties there in their youth, when the house was still grand. Eventually, it fell into disrepair when old Mrs Chisolm lost her husband and the family's fortunes declined. Unable to maintain the property, Mrs Chisolm began her gradual descent into genteel poverty. The house was eventually sold to pay off her debts, and she became the home's first resident. Legend had it that Mrs Chisolm could be seen walking the halls at night, and though Eva had never seen her, she felt her presence everywhere.

Entering the ladies' toilets, she went into a cubicle, then shut and locked the door. She awkwardly pulled off her dressing gown, the confines of the cubicle and her physical limitations compounding to leave her panting as she reached up to hang the gown on the door hook. Sitting down on the closed toilet lid, recovering her breath, she reached into her pocket for her scarf and looped it a couple of times around her neck. She unlocked the cubicle door and checked her appearance in the mirror, adjusting her scarf. Eva took out her lipstick—blushing bloom—and applied it expertly, despite her arm's slight tremor. Nodding at the mirror with approval, she returned to the entrance lounge and waited in one of the large armchairs, careful to sit only on the edge of the seat. It would be too hard to get up quickly if she was comfortably settled in, she reasoned.

Within half an hour, Eva saw a young couple approaching the door. As swiftly as she could, she made her way to the door, smiling and saying 'thank you' to the young man with the gallant expression who unwittingly held the door for her. With a steady focus on the outside world, Eva made her way in the direction of the sea. Careful not to overexert herself, she looked for likely spots to rest. First, she sat in a bus stop shelter, examining the carved-in names and initials of local kids while trying not to read their curses and vulgarities. Another bout of walking, and she sat down at a park bench to catch her breath. Her knee ached, and she rubbed it soothingly. Can't be much further now, she told herself, getting up again, and when she finally glimpsed the dazzling sea, a deep, involuntary breath left her body. She drew the fresh sea air up through her nostrils, feeling its coolness fill her lungs. Her mind sharpened, and momentarily closing her eyes, she audibly exhaled again, 'Ahhh.'

Eva felt more relaxed than she had for a long time. Her worries had lifted, and in their place, a sense of tranquillity had descended. Finally, she had made it out of that room! She laughed out loud at the thought of being missed and the staff looking for her. *How did she know the code to get out of the building?* Eva imagined them saying. Let them look, she thought. She was so close to her destination now: *the tree of knowledge!* She smiled at how grandiose and pompous it sounded to call this tree—their tree—*the tree of knowledge.*

It was shortly after arriving in Flinders Bay that Marion had introduced her to the tree. Eva was thirteen. From a distance, it looked like one huge tree, but once upon it, it was revealed to be two cypress trees with gnarly bark; stiff, horizontal foliage of rough emerald green; and broad branches perfect for climbing and disappearing into. The name had come about after a religious instruction class at the local church. As Eva's mother couldn't afford to send her daughter to the Catholic school, she insisted Eva attend this weekly instruction before Mass each Sunday. Taught by a diminutive nun, Sister Ethel, the classes were made bearable only because Eva's new friend, Marion, also went along.

Eva had met Marion on her first day on the bus ride to her new school, and while some of the others looked unfavourably upon the 'refo kid' with the 'funny accent', Marion had warmed to her immediately. She went out of her way to make Eva feel welcome, including sharing her special tree with her. On the day that they named the tree, Sister Ethel had introduced the class to the concept of knowledge as a dangerous thing, referring to the tree from which Adam and Eve ate the forbidden fruit. Later that day, snugly ensconced in the shallow recess where branch and trunk met to form the ideal hidey-hole, the two friends had just enough room to lean back against the trunk with their legs bent and resting on the branch in front of them. The clifftop was the perfect observation spot. To their left, they could gaze down upon the swimming beach, and to their right, they could see local fishing boats and watch the big ships as they entered the bay from the vast ocean beyond. Being just off a well-worn walking path, the tree offered privacy yet also a bird's-eye view of their little seaside town—their own tree of knowledge, they joked.

With memories overwhelming her now as she got closer to her destination, Eva recalled that hot summer afternoon when she first saw Cyril. She had not long turned sixteen. She and Marion had been swimming all afternoon and had bought chips to take back to the tree. Reclining in their favourite position, savouring the salty crunch of deep-fried potato, they were watching a group of local teenage boys, gathered on the jetty's edge, dripping wet. They were engaged in one of their favourite summer activities: taking a running leap from the jetty into the water, often holding one knee into their chest to perform what was colloquially known as the 'can-opener'. The aim was to land with as huge a splash as possible. After landing in the water, they would swim to the jetty ladder and climb back up to do it again and again.

The arrival of a small, open boat, caught their attention. As it pulled up to the jetty, a young man, not much older than the leaping boys, with rope in hand, sprang lightly from boat to jetty, securing the boat's rope to a cleat. As the local boys looked on, a second young man in the boat manoeuvred it next to the jetty and tossed the boat's other rope to his friend.

'Who are those two?' asked Eva, entranced.

'Ooh, the blonde fellow is one of the Chisolm boys... not sure which one. They've got that enormous old holiday house up near the cemetery. They live in Melbourne. Not sure who his friend is though; never seen him before,' replied Marion.

'Well, come on, slowcoach,' teased Eva. 'Let's find out!' And she quickly shimmied her way down the tree, landing deftly on terra firma.

Within minutes, the girls had run from the clifftop down to the main street and spied the pair standing outside the fish and chip shop, perusing advertisements and handbills on the community noticeboard. The taller of the two, the Chisolm boy, cut a dashing figure with his fair hair cut severely short at the back, and a long, thick wave of hair sweeping across his forehead. It was while Eva was enquiring in a louder than usual voice about the family dance that the Chisolm boy's friend turned and noticed them. Nodding politely, the boy with dark, curly hair and vivid blue eyes, gestured with his hand at the noticeboard to 'take a look'.

All smiles, Eva announced the details that she and Marion were already well aware of, having memorised the summertime dance schedule weeks ago.

'They any good, these local dances?' the dark-haired boy asked Eva. 'Very... good,' replied Eva, beaming.

'Sounds like we'd better go then, Harry,' said the dark-haired boy, returning Eva's grin with a warm smile.

'I'm Cyril, and that's Harry,' he added with a thumb gesture to his friend.

'I'm Eva, and this is Marion,' replied Eva. 'See you at the dance then.'

And so it was that Eva and Cyril's story began at a summertime Flinders Bay Family Dance in 1953.

As she made her way closer to the tree, Eva thought she could see what looked like a pair of shoes dangling from mid-way up the trunk. She rubbed her eyes in disbelief. Getting closer now, she saw legs as well! Moving as fast as she could, Eva reached the bottom of the tree, and reaching out to hold onto the trunk and steady herself, she peered up and gasped.

'Marion? Is... is that... you?'

A cheeky face and grin peered down from above.

'Of course, it's me, silly! Come on, slowcoach! Here, give me your hand...'

And stretching up, Eva grasped Marion's extended hand. Her feet found the familiar and well-worn footholes of yesteryear. How easily she manoeuvred her way into the nook they had so often shared as girls. The view was mostly as she remembered it, except that there was now a view to the high-rise buildings of the city across the bay. Eva felt a great sense of tranquillity, her hand warm in Marion's clasp. The weather was no longer cold, and she loosened her scarf. Closing her eyes, she rested her head on Marion's shoulder.

In a very un-Nina style of packing, she threw random clothes and incongruous objects into her small overnight suitcase. Old, but surprisingly unbattered, this suitcase had been a constant travelling companion since Eva had bought it for her when she had left home at eighteen. *You need a good quality suitcase, darling,* Eva had said; *One that will last a lifetime.*

With dozens of thoughts rushing through her mind, Nina finished her frantic packing and commenced her drive to Flinders Bay. One moment she was regretful for not insisting that Eva find a closer place, the next she was chiding herself for not visiting often enough. Nina had intended to visit at least fortnightly, but sometimes it had been a month, or even two, between visits. Two years had flown by for Nina, but had they for Eva? The two-hour drive from Melbourne seemed to take forever! Agitated, she couldn't listen to the radio, and she struggled to find music to suit her mood. She kept a few classical music CDs in the car, mostly for Eva, which she flicked through, eyes darting between CD cases and the road ahead. Finally, she settled on Saint-Saens: soothing, yet suitably grave for the saddest day of her life.

Entering Eva's room, she was taken aback to see her mother, laid out on the bed. Nina had rarely seen a dead body, and although she was expecting to see Eva, it was still a shock to take in the sight of her lifeless mother; she who was the essence of life. Or had been. Becoming aware of what seemed like a sea of people in the small room, she made her way around, kissing and hugging her brothers, their partners, nieces and nephews, explaining that her own children were on their way.

'So, what happened?' Nina asked. 'They said she had a heart attack?'

'We're not sure of the details,' began John, the younger of her two brothers. 'We're waiting for the manager to fill us in.'

'I can't understand it,' said Peter. 'I wasn't aware she had heart issues... problems?'

As the three siblings wrestled with the possibilities, the manager entered and sympathetically greeted each of them. She asked them to prepare themselves for some shocking news: Eva had had a heart attack as the result of a fall. As she hesitated, Nina asked, 'Where did she fall from? Her bed?'

'No,' said the manager, eyes downcast, 'from a tree'.

In the shocked silence, the manager continued to explain that Eva had somehow managed to slip out of the home, unnoticed, and walk to the cliffs overlooking the beach. Once there, she had climbed a tree, tragically fallen, resulting in myocardial infarction and her death. Nina gasped, her hands involuntarily covering her mouth as she heard the word 'debacle' escape Peter's lips.

It had been three months since her mother's funeral, and Nina had been returning to Flinders Bay every weekend. At first, it was out of necessity, to finalise her mother's things and estate, but today it was simply out of habit and the desire to feel close to Eva. With both her children finished school, she was free to spend her weekends as she chose. She decided to have lunch at one of the many cafes that lined the main street. It was a splendid spring day, and Nina had opted for an outdoor table, on the footpath, basking in the sun and watching the world go by. Enjoying her final mouthful of mussel risotto, with a glass of Riesling, Nina was startled by an unfamiliar voice saying hello. She looked up and slowly recognised the friendly smile of Marg, the worker from Eva's retirement home.

'Hello, it's Nina, isn't it?'

'Yes, hello—Marg?'

'Yes, yes, it is,' said Marg, as she lingered by Nina's table. It was clear to Nina that Marg wanted to talk, so she gestured to the seat opposite, inviting Marg to sit down.

'How have you been, Nina? Such a difficult time, losing a parent.'

Nina was appalled to find her eyes filling with tears and that she was unable to form proper sentences, as she let go of months of pent-up sadness and regret.

'I'm sorry, I'm sorry,' Nina said.

Marg patted her arm and said, 'It's perfectly fine—in fact it's perfectly normal.'

'We loved Eva so much. Such a lovely soul, and she still had an alert mind. She didn't deserve to... I'm sorry, Nina... I feel like we let you down...' said Marg, teary-eyed.

'It's alright, Marg, it's not your fault. Mum was a very determined person. It's still hard for me to comprehend how it was possible for a frail eighty-five-year-old woman to have walked all that way to the clifftop, but she wanted to go back to her tree. It was part of her childhood, and I like to think it gave her the peace she was seeking.'

Marg listened thoughtfully and seemed to be relieved to hear Nina's words. After they had said their goodbyes, Nina knew it was time to do what she had been dreading for months.

She drove along the road that hugged the coastline, and when she spotted the tree which had started its life as two trees, she pulled up. The trunks had grown so closely together it was almost imperceptible where one finished and the other began. Nina recalled her mother saying how she and Marion preferred the tree on the left as it had the perfectly sized hollow for them to snuggle into together. She slowly ambled towards Eva's tree, admiring its magnificence. The trunk was vast and thick, and the low branches were just above the top of her head. Standing on the water-facing side of the tree, she stood with her back against the trunk, surveying the azure bay, and the furrow between her brows relaxed. Gazing up, she contemplated how to climb Eva's tree.

There was one branch low enough to grab hold of, and the aged and weathered trunk provided ample hand and footholds. Within minutes, Nina was squeezing herself into the nook, leaning back and resting her feet on the branch in front. She imagined Eva and Marion holed up here for hours, sharing their secrets and aspirations.

As she took in the view of the calm external world, Nina's thoughts were a maelstrom of unanswered questions. Closing her eyes, she heard her mother's voice, *Don't think too hard, darling—feel!* With her eyes closed, Nina felt the cosy protectiveness that the tree's hollow provided. She listened to the sound of the seagulls calling and felt the cool breeze on her face, drying the hot tears that had started to run down her cheeks. She thought she could hear murmured words and giggles.

Nina wasn't sure how long she spent like that with her eyes closed—perhaps she fell asleep? When she opened her eyes, she looked up into the branches above and spotted a beautiful swirl of colour. She gazed dreamily until her sense of recognition kicked in. That was her mother's scarf! Scrambling up to the branch above, Nina grabbed at the scarf, but it was snagged on a twig. She climbed higher until she could safely disentangle Eva's scarf without tearing it further. Returning carefully to the sanctuary of the nook, she wrapped the scarf around her neck, luxuriating in the feel of silk on her skin as though it was Eva's own hand caressing her one last time.

# A NORTHERN FLICKER

**KAREN LEE MILLS**   ECHUCA, VIC, AUSTRALIA

A flicker of hope
a twinkle of self-belief.

Foraging in visual perceptions
till the digging is complete
incubating words of courage
building an appealing platform.

Hear the call ringing in your soul
sometimes weak, sometimes bright
feel the rhythmic pounding
sensing the refreshing vibrations.

Generating confidence, amidst the complexities
enticing environment, luring the mind
spread your wings, shine with wavering light
watch the dazzling flight.

Flickering hope and twinkling self-belief
illuminating beautiful literature
across the Northern Skies.

# THE PEOPLE OF THE ART

**OLIVIA CAMPBELL**   MELBOURNE, AUSTRALIA

the art of living veils its own living art
yet we the people can tear both apart
but you are the artist of cultural matter
as well the paint brush and the splatter

as one body tunes on a solo basis
en masse they ensemble in homeostasis
mind then not only who now are we
if the symphony cares for what it may be

as sculpting hands shape the social space
digital buds stretch the human interface
gradually tweaking the artist's mould
while today's theatrics script lines to unfold

but our lines need not read tragedy
if the show is directed creatively
from one to another, in mutual giving
we can breathe the spirit of artful living

linking the marvel of a living cell
to a minded brain and its embodied shell
shimmers wisdom and wonder of infinite reflect
as a work in progress, beautifully imperfect

though it stands we don't have full sound
that feet can't always feel toes on the ground
with echoing senses of thought and choice
the people of the art are gaining voice

# WINNER, SHORT STORY

## ALEXANDRA SVOBODA
### ST KILDA, VICTORIA, AUSTRALIA

Alexandra Svoboda (she/her) is an emerging writer. Her short story, 'Jesse, Jessy and Me', won highly commended in the Mid-North Coast Writers' Centre Short Story Competition. She lives in Naarm with her silly white dog and is close to completing her second manuscript, an action-packed feminist historical zombie thriller. When Alexandra isn't demolishing fantasy novels or writing about zombies, she can be found covered in mud, chasing a funny shaped ball around a football field, for no other reason than the joy of it.

# ALL THE PAIN AND ALL THE JOY

'Westside Mutual Bank, Card Services, you're speaking with Gabrielle.'

'The ATM ate my card.' The voice at the end of the line belongs to an older man. He speaks too loudly, as if he doesn't know how to use a phone.

'I'm sorry to hear that, Mr Drew. Did you enter your PIN incorrectly?' Gabrielle keeps her voice light and pleasant.

'No. Had the same PIN all me life.' Gabrielle looks at his account and confirms this is true.

'I'm sorry, Mr Drew, but the system is telling me that you entered the incorrect PIN three times. When that happens, the ATM takes the card.'

'But I was entering the right PIN. You lot must have changed it.'

Gabrielle's gaze is dragged down to the bottom right-hand corner of the screen where the time is displayed. 9.48am. Dammit. She tries to avoid clock-watching until at least after morning tea to avoid the litany of calculating minutes and quarter hours too early in the day. On good days, she doesn't begin counting until after lunch.

Hearing her exasperated sigh, Gabrielle's supervisor Erin peers over the top of the faded blue plasterboard wall that divides their desks into cubicles. Gabrielle sits in a cluster with Erin and Nina. Three other clusters make up their department and four similarly sized departments are packed onto the floor. The place is clinically clean and the air is perpetually dry and cold. The bank is bereft of seasonal change, the lighting, temperature and atmosphere kept in a numbing state of stasis.

Erin and Gabrielle have been co-workers for five years, although Erin has only been her superior for the last 18 months. Since being promoted to supervisor, Erin has transformed from friendly colleague to supercilious master, loftily flaunting her new authority whenever the opportunity arises.

Gabrielle resists the urge to tell Erin to sod off.

'Mr Drew, Westside has nothing to gain by changing your PIN. The buttons on the machine must have been sticky. It happens a lot!' She looks up to Erin as she speaks, nodding to signal that she has the situation under control.

'Well then, you need to get some people out here to clean 'em regularly!'

'I'll pass that feedback on to management.'

Hearing mention of potential escalation, Erin frowns and Gabrielle rolls her eyes skywards to indicate that Erin won't actually be required to do her job. Satisfied, Erin's head disappears back below the divider and Gabrielle continues to talk through her script.

Gabrielle glances back down at the time. 9.53am. She's going to miss morning tea. A woman from insurance has made marble cake—Gabrielle's favourite.

The member cuts in. 'Hold on a sec. Can ya send the card express?'

Oh no.

'I can, but it's a five dollar fee.' Gabrielle winces.

'A fee?!'

*Here it comes.*

'I shouldn't have to pay a fee! This isn't my fault! You said yourself, the keys were sticky.'

'Let me talk to my supervisor.'

A crowd of workers is assembled around the tea table. Gabrielle approaches tentatively, hoping catch Erin's attention without the rest of the group noticing. Seeing that Gabrielle is still wearing her headset, Erin offers no such dignity.

'Oh wow. Still going?' Erin remains in the centre of a cluster of young grads. Conversation among the group is forced to cease and the grads looks on in interest.

'Um. Do you mind if I waive the express post fee?' Gabrielle keeps her voice quiet, hoping that Erin will follow suit.

'Gab, you know we only do that if we're at fault. Didn't he enter the wrong PIN?' Erin speaks loudly, relishing the opportunity to wield what small amount of authority she can.

'Sorry Erin, but he's being really difficult. He thinks we changed his PIN. You know the type.' Gabrielle hunches her shoulders, attempting to condense herself so that she won't stand out so much among this group of petite youths in trendy, bright clothing. The attempt is unsuccessful. Gabrielle is six foot three, wider than most and still dresses in the bank's dowdy old uniform of navy collared shirt and black cotton skirt that they began to phase out three years ago. Her clumsy attempt to blend in only makes her more awkwardly noticeable.

'Gab, I heard you tell him that the ATM had sticky buttons. If I waive the fee, you'll never learn how to manage customer expectations!'

'Aw, come on Ez, that's a bit rough.' One of the grads speaks up.

'Yeah, jeez, I'd say anything to placate them.' A second grad agrees. Erin flushes.

'Fine. Waive the fee.' She sounds angry and some of the grads frown. 'But you've got to stop using the sticky buttons excuse!' Erin tries to brush off her sudden sharp reaction with a joking laugh but her smile doesn't meet her eyes.

Before Gabrielle can return to her desk, Nina saunters from across the table, brandishing an unidentifiable lump of brown squishiness in a napkin. She holds it aloft, as if it might damage her perfectly manicured talons or the huge diamond on her finger. Nina looks at the mess in her hand the same way she looks at Gabrielle's life: with an upturned nose.

'Here, Gab!' Nina offers the napkin of mush toward her. 'What's that?' Gabrielle reflexively reaches out to take it.

'There's no more marble cake left, but I know how much you like it because last time you ate, like, three pieces! All that fat and sugar doesn't agree with me so you can have the rest of mine!' Nina smiles widely, her artificially whitened teeth contrasting brightly against her fake tan.

As Gabrielle takes the cake, Nina looks over her shoulder and calls back to her friend from EFT, loudly for all to hear, 'I told you Gab wouldn't mind eating my leftovers!'

Gabrielle opens the napkin to see that the cake has been massacred— picked apart and dissected—and is utterly inedible. She throws it in the bin. The group laughs and Gabrielle returns to her desk, face burning.

That afternoon, Gabrielle gets stuck on a long call that she answered at 4.58 so doesn't finish until 5.45. That never happens to Nina, who strategically turns her phone off seven minutes early so that she can leave at precisely 5pm and make the 5.08 train.

By the time Gabrielle has changed her shoes and begun to walk across the nearby oval to the train station, it's nearly 6. She enjoys the walk: the feeling of the soft grass giving way beneath her Converses and the muggy air that breaks beads of sweat across her skin. It's a pleasant reprieve from the artificial air of the office.

This exact moment—between finishing work and arriving home—is Gabrielle's favourite time of day. The frustrations of being berated, talked down to, made fun of and ignored are behind her, while the reheated single-serve meals eaten alongside a monotonous stream of reality television remain at least an hour away. Right now, her heart is pumping with the exertion of the walk, her calves ache slightly and sweat is trickling down her arms and back. Gabrielle is feeling real, physical sensations and they drown out everything else.

'Heads!'

A hard voice breaks the silence and Gabrielle looks up in time to see a red oval-shaped ball flying hard and fast in her direction, arcing and tipping end over end. Without thinking, she drops her bag and reaches her arms out to save herself from being pummelled in the face. The ball stings and makes a satisfying 'thwack' as she catches it with both hands.

'Here!'

A figure waves from almost 50 metres away.

Squinting into the sun, Gabrielle punts the ball in the general direction of the voice. She isn't sure if her kick is accurate, but it makes the distance. 'Still got it', she murmurs to herself, thinking of the time she won longest kick in Year 6.

As Gabrielle picks up her bag, a figure runs in her direction. The woman is tall and tanned, with clearly defined shoulders and well-muscled legs. She's wearing a yellow and black singlet with the words 'Westview Hawks' emblazoned across the chest. Tight black bike shorts wrap around her thick quads and her body is shiny with sweat.

'That's one helluva kick! You play?'

'Oh, nah. I did AusKick in primary school but stopped after 12s because there wasn't a comp. That's just left over from the old days.' Gabrielle laughs awkwardly and doesn't know what to say next.

'Well, you should! My team, the Hawks'—at this, she points to the writing on her singlet— 'are recruiting. We really need some height.' The woman looks her up and down, nods and smiles amiably. 'You'd be a good ruck. We—'

A whistle blows in the distance.

'—sorry, got to go!' The woman turns and runs in its direction.

Light on her feet, she spins quickly back around, now jogging backward. 'By the way, my name's Groucho!' Then she turns back to face the way she's running and takes off.

Groucho's figure casts a long black shadow against the green grass and Gabrielle stands for a frozen moment, watching the woman's back muscles move as her arms pump a steady, powerful rhythm. Gabrielle's heart pounds as well.

'I reckon it's a great idea, Gabs. It'll be good for you.'

'Mum. Do not encourage her. Footy's too rough for women. Look at all of them doing their ACLs in the *AWFL*.'

'It's called the AFLW Darren. And she's strong, she'll be fine.'

'She's not fit enough. Do you have any idea how much you have to run to play footy? Before I did my back, I –'

'Oh my god Darren, we've heard enough about your glory days. They're over, it's Gab's turn. She used to row. She's got the fitness in her.'

'I'm here, you know.' Gabrielle interrupts, taking a large glug from a can of Jim Beam. She's dressed comfortably in denim cut-off shorts and a flannel shirt with the sleeves rolled up. Finishing her drink, she stands, stretches and then makes her way to the fridge for another. She resists the urge to nick a sneaky forkful of Mum's famous potato salad.

It's a Saturday afternoon and they're having a barbecue at her Mum's place. Gabrielle loves being there. The scratched up old lino and shelves cluttered with familiar nick nacks remind her of days when she wasn't so numb.

Mum is bustling around the kitchen, washing and chopping vegetables, while Darren's stepped outside to warm up the barbie. Darren's boys—13 and 17—are wrestling in the pool, while his daughter, Maddie, who's 15, is scrolling on her phone at the kitchen bench.

'Why don't you swim with your brothers, Mads?' Gabrielle's Mum asks kindly. Maddie blushes a furious red and mumbles something un-intelligible.

'She's on her rag!' Connor, the youngest, bursts into the room, dripping wet and searching for food but satisfied with causing trouble for his sister instead.

Connor dodges a swipe from Gabrielle's Mum, while Maddie looks like she wants to disappear into the floor.

'Come on, Mads. Let's watch the game.' Gabrielle grabs another Jim Beam from the fridge for herself and a coke for Maddie. The two escape to the living room to watch the women's Dees play against Richmond.

Maddie sits cross-legged on the floor, barely a metre from the TV, while Gabrielle settles into her dad's cracked brown leather La-Z-Boy. Away from her dad and brothers, the kid pipes up, giving Gabrielle the background of each player, showing her their Instagram profiles and explaining what they do in their day jobs.

'Wait, you're telling me these women work all day in offices and then play footy like this on the weekend?' Gabrielle's gobsmacked.

'Yup! Some of them even work at banks, like you!'

The commentator's voice raises in pitch with excitement as one of the Dees players breaks away from the pack. She punches out a quick handball to a teammate—Pearce—who's flying down the wing at impossible speed and receives the pass with quick but steady hands.

Pearce's legs pump, pushing her ahead of her nearest opponents. She drops the ball for a bounce, fumbles for a second, picks it up again without losing speed. She's approaching the 50-metre mark. Just before the defender can lay down a tackle, Pearce launches a barrel from downtown. It lands just short of the goal line but dribbles through untouched. Pearce collapses to her knees, exhausted but elated, and her teammates rush to pick her up, slap her on the back, shower her in adulation.

Maddie jumps up and down with excitement and even Gabrielle finds herself cheering with delight.

The first training session is harder than Gabrielle could have possibly imagined. She feels too big, too uncoordinated, too ungainly compared to the other women, who barely break a sweat.

The team runs 40 metre sprints and the mids jet off like greyhounds, striding with practiced ease, reaching the line before Gabrielle makes it halfway. Her shoes pound the ground and she imagines that she's leaving heavy footprints on the grass.

Gabrielle enjoys the drills. Falling into the steady rhythm of the kicking and running patterns, she hits all her targets and doesn't drop a single mark. The coach tells her that her hands are safe as houses.

Toward the end of training, the coach instructs the team to run a fast lap of the oval—400 metres. Nearly half a kilometre. Gabrielle's never run that far in one go in her life. The women groan but do as they're told, lining up from fastest to slowest before the coach blows his whistle, signalling them to begin.

Gabrielle is way behind everyone else, plodding heavily. Twice, she has to slow to a walk, but Groucho and Sneaks jog back after they've finished to run alongside her. The women shout and clap and Gabrielle picks her pace back up to a fast run.

With 50 metres to go, Gabrielle's lungs are bursting and her legs burn. She wants to give up. Wants to collapse on the ground and never move again. But they're all watching so she has to keep going. One foot in front of the other. Pain in every step. The entire team is cheering at the finish.

Gabrielle's legs fold and she tries to lie down but Whizza and Bluey pull her up, slapping her on the back. She's surrounded by women high-fiving and grinning, applauding her for being the worst.

'Mate, ripper effort.'

'I came last.'

'But it was hardest for you. Those little mids can run a lap like that in their sleep. Fuck, they do it for fun. When's the last time you ran 400 metres?'

'Never.'

'Exactly. You put way more into that than they did.'

Later that night, Gabrielle eats a chicken schnitzel, an entire broccoli and two baked potatoes. Just before she tumbles into bed, she notices that she doesn't feel the dreary sadness that usually accompanies this part of her day. Her mind is clear and she can feel every muscle in her body aching pleasantly. Sleep claims her instantly and she has no time to worry about the day ahead.

By Round 4, Gabrielle can run a lap of the oval. She's still the slowest in the group, but she doesn't feel like dying at the end. Training becomes a place where little is expected of her except to show up and try her best.

One night, they practice contested marking. The coach kicks the ball into the pocket and the entire team rushes forward all at once to try and win it. As the tallest, Gabrielle takes the mark every time.

'Fuckin' hell, Gabbo. Give someone else a chance!' Whizza yells out good-naturedly. 'Yeah Gabbo, ya ball hog.'

'Bloody hell. Nobody can take a mark against Gabbo over here!'

It's the first time she stands out at training in a positive way; the first time she's the best at something. It's gives her teammates a real reason to say her name—a new version of her name. She likes it.

Impressed by Gabbo's form, the coach lets her have a go of rucking during match simulation. It's difficult against Big T—the main ruck—who's dominant and experienced. But in the final play, Gabbo wins a tap. She hits it to Groucho who slams a huge dump kick to score a lucky goal. Groucho, Sneaks and Whizza all jump onto Gabbo's back in an exaggerated celebration, then pull her to the ground, creating a laughing pile of arms and legs. Big T pours the contents of her drink bottle on the lot of them.

Game day is different; game day is terrifying.

So far, during games, Gabbo has sat in the back line, taking responsibility for the kick-ins and stopping the opposing team from scoring. If her team wins, Gabbo doesn't feel like she's contributed. If they lose, she carries the burden of responsibility for the loss, castigating herself for every goal kicked against the Hawks under her watch.

The coach tries to make her understand. 'Gabbo, they have to get the ball past every single other player on the team before it even reaches you. Most of the time, you're pretty fuckin hard to beat.'

'Pfft. Because I'm huge.'

'Well, ya can't teach tall.'

Gabbo looks forward to team dinner at the local after the game. The Hawks commandeer a long table outside where they order jugs of beer and eat as much as they can. For once, she doesn't eat the most. Nobody is eyeing her as she takes huge bites of sloppy parma and stuffs her mouth with greasy chips slathered in gravy. For the first five minutes after the food arrives, the team is silent with satiation.

Once the food is finished and the drinking becomes more serious, she doesn't talk much, simply allows the conversation to wash over her. Company is enough. After dinner, the young kids catch taxis to nightclubs in the city and the older women return home to their families.

Gabbo watches as Groucho and Sneaks steal a kiss at the bar while they wait for their drinks and she feels that familiar tug of loneliness. It's different to the weeknight boredom of eating meals for one. This time, it's more urgent.


Quarter three, Round 5. Big T goes down. Her cries of pain echo around the field and even the opposition grimace in sympathy. The dreaded ACL.

A stellar season—BOG three games in a row—done and dusted for the year, maybe forever. Volunteers carry Big T off the field and tears of disappointment streak her muddy face.

'Gabbo, you're rucking!' The runner delivers the message then dashes back to the sideline.

'Go get 'em Gabbo! Show 'em how it's done'. Bluey yells encouragement.

'I don't know if I can—'

Groucho clasps Gabbo by the shoulder, pulling her closer so that they're nose to nose. Gabbo can't avoid eye contact. 'You can do this.'

She speaks softly, spilling conviction into Gabbo.

'Just like at training.' Then she winks, buoyant with confidence. The teams line up to begin the final quarter.

The umpire strides into the centre square with the ball.

The mids circle, hungry for the tap.

Gabbo's heart beats. She's never felt more nervous in her life. Her arms tingle with anticipation and her legs thrum.

The whistle blows, the umpire releases the ball into the air and, just like at training, Gabbo pushes off the opposing ruck, jumps, raises her arm and whacks the ball as hard as she can. She hits it cleanly, sending it sailing through the air and into Groucho's outstretched hands.

The players scuffle messily for the ball and Gabbo runs to the contest, arriving as the umpire calls for another ball up. There's no time to catch her breath before the ball is thrown again.

Somehow, Gabbo is up there with it. Again, she beats her opponent. Again, Groucho catches the tap.

Groucho handballs to Rach.

Rach is tackled but holds onto the ball, writhing around on the ground to wrench it free. The umpire calls another ball up.

Gabbo wins again.

And again.

And again.

Gabbo isn't thinking anymore. There isn't time and she doesn't have the energy. She's been reduced to a single purpose: follow the ball, be there for the ball up, win the tap. Repeat.

At some point, they score.

Back to the centre. No time for water.

Again.

She's so tired. But she has a job to do and there's nobody else to do it.

Her body takes over. Her muscles, lungs and legs take the lead. For the first time in her life, Gabbo is winning. With her size; with her strength.

Gabbo's senses are alive and she can feel everything. All the pain but also all the joy.

The final siren cuts through the air and she hears screaming from the sidelines: Mum and Maddie have come down to watch. They're flushed with excitement and calling out her name. Maddie is looking at her the same way she watches those superhero women who work normal jobs during the day and play footy on weekends.

The Westview Hawks have made the finals, an achievement not seen by the men for over 10 years and the first time for the women. The unexpected success has filled the coach's sails and he's transformed from a relaxed retiree to a drill sergeant. Gabbo's mobile phone is blowing up on the desk beside her. He wants her at training early to practice stoppages. She'll have to leave right on 5 to make it. It's 4.45.

Her phone rings. It's an elderly member who often calls to check her account balance because she doesn't know how to use internet banking. Usually, Gabbo finds her frustrating. Today, she entertains the old bird to draw out the conversation until 5 so she can finish on time.

4.50. Gabbo asks Mrs Inglewood about her grandchildren and listens to her describe her granddaughter's bathroom renovation.

4.51. Nina's phone rings. Gabbo grins as she listens to Nina attempting to rush the slow-speaking member who's fallen victim to a diet-pill scam.

4.59. Gabbo ends the call with Mrs Inglewood and surreptitiously switches off her phone. 5pm. Success. Gabbo turns off her computer and picks up her packed bag.

As she stands, so does Erin, appearing behind the divider like an unwanted meerkat. 'One sec, Gabrielle!' Her voice is unnaturally high.

5.02. 'Is this important, Ez? I've got footy training.'

Gabbo makes a show of pulling her bag over her shoulder to demonstrate that she's leaving. 'Can Nina do it? I've already shut down my computer.'

Nina—still on the phone—twists her mouth in revolt at the suggestion.

Erin continues as if Gabbo hasn't spoken. 'We've just received a notice from Visa about this client's ATM dispute. It's been rejected. You'll have to tell them they won't be receiving a refund.'

Gabbo's stomach drops. This will be a long conversation and an angry member.

'But Ez, that isn't even my case. Can't you do it? You know they'll want to escalate anyway.'

'No, Gabrielle. I've noticed over the past few weeks that your customer service skills have really declined. This will be good for your professional development.'

'Can it wait 'til tomorrow? I really have to go. Our team have made finals and—'

'Gabrielle, this footy thing of yours isn't really all that important. You're going to have to make the call and work a bit past 5 for once.'

Erin places the client's file on Gabbo's desk and then sits back down at her own to shut down her computer. Gabbo continues to stand, seething.

'Hurry up. The sooner you start your computer up again the sooner you can get to training.' Erin smirks at Nina as she says this. 'Nina, you're done. Do you want a lift to the station? Sorry you missed the 5.08.'

Gabbo doesn't sit. Her heart is loud in her ears and her arms feel funny. Erin continues to pack up, not realising that Gabbo isn't following her instructions.

When Erin stands again, keys in hand and bag on her shoulder, she finally notices Gabrielle.

'What are you doing?' Erin tilts her head slightly, looking put out. Nina stops what she's doing and stares openly at the unfolding confrontation.

'What do you mean, what am I doing?' Gabbo keeps her voice low and steady, barely containing her rage.

'I mean, why aren't you calling that member?'

'Because it's not my fucking case. So, it's not my fucking job.'

'What did you say—'

Gabrielle steps out from behind her desk so that the plasterboard divider no longer separates the two women. Then she takes a step forward so that they're standing barely a handspan apart.

It's only a small step, but it brings her and Erin closer than they've ever stood before. It brings Gabbo's significant size into perspective and makes Gabbo feel, like on the field, momentarily powerful. Looking down at Erin, Gabbo's anger is replaced by pity and quietly blooming self-assurance.

'I fucking quit...' Gabbo speaks quietly. Erin takes a step back in mute shock. '...You fucking bitch.'

'Hurry up Gabbo, it's about to start!' Mum is in the living room calling out to Gabbo, who's in the kitchen refilling everyone's drinks.

'Hang on, I've gotta bring Queen Muck in there her pinot!'

Gabbo re-enters the lounge room carrying a Jim Beam for herself and a sweating glass of light gold wine for Ruby, who's cosily sandwiched on the couch between Mum and Maddie.

Darren is sitting on the La-Z-Boy with his feet resting on the coffee table, staring vacantly into the screen of his phone.

'Thanks babe,' Ruby says as she reaches for the glass. Gabbo gives her a quick kiss on the head as she passes it over. The kiss is chaste but Darren frowns from behind his screen anyway.

'Get a room, you two!'

'Oh, shush Daz.' Mum berates Darren and he glowers.

After Gabbo quit the bank, she had to work out what to do with her life. She looked at uni, TAFE, online courses and, after months of indecision, even begging for her job back. Her coach recommended that she join a gym.

Gabbo was thrilled when the Hawks won the semi-final. The following week, they went down to the eventual premiers in the prelim by a red-time goal. It was a bittersweet ending, but enough for the women. Not for the coach. After sipping a taste of victory, he had the premiership in his sights for the next season. With Big T out for good, he wanted Gabbo fighting fit to be the Hawks' main ruck.

So, Gabbo joined a gym. She went every single day, sometimes twice. It was one of the few places where, like footy, all that was expected of Gabbo was to show up and try. And, just like at footy, her size didn't matter. She didn't have to squeeze into cubicles and skirts or make herself smaller. At the gym, she could lunge wide and press tall, stretch her body, expand and grow.

As the months passed, muscles began to form and Gabbo's strength became formidable. After six months, Gabbo noticed that she drew stares when she exercised. Finally, Groucho suggested the blatantly obvious.

'You should be a personal trainer!' 'Who'd want me to train them?' 'Anyone with eyes in their head?' 'I'm—'

'—Ripped?' Groucho interrupted. 'Dedicated? Literally made to be a PT?'

The course took six months and, as soon as she was finished, the gym gave her a contract.

For the first three months, Gabbo's only clients were Groucho, Sneaks and Mum. But then pre-season training started and Gabbo was surprised to find her timetable peppered with women from the team. A new player, Ruby, signed up for three sessions a week.

By the end of the next season, Gabbo and Ruby had moved in together.

Gabbo's timetable really began to fill when she started training Maddie and her friends, prepping them for their pre-season with the Westview Hawks' junior women's side.

Maddie had always been a quietly good kick, her skills honed over weekends spent standing behind the goals for her brothers. One slow Christmas afternoon, while the boys were inside drinking, Gabbo asked Maddie to join her for a kick. The two spent an hour piffing the ball back and forth and it had felt good. Really good.

Drinks handed out, Gabbo, Ruby, Maddie, Mum and Darren settle into silence, watching the television in anticipation as the ad break ends.

'Welcome back to the 2024 AFLW Draft.'

Darren has put down his phone and is glaring at the television with a peculiar look of concentration on his face, as if he's losing some kind of internal struggle.

Maddie is gripping Gabbo's hand tightly, her calloused palm sweaty.

'And at pick number seven, Richmond Tigers take Maddison Walker, 18 years old from Westview in Melbourne.'

Ruby squeals.

'No fucking way!' Maddie is wearing the Richmond jersey that Dustin Martin signed for her in 2017.

Mum covers her face with her hands, helpless with joy. Darren shocks everyone by openly weeping.

'We did it!' Maddie turns to Gabbo.

'We fucking did it!'

# JOINT WINNER, POETRY

## MICHAEL LEACH

### STRATHDALE, DJA DJA WURRUNG COUNTRY, VICTORIA, AUSTRALIA

Michael Leach (@m_jleach) lives on Dja Dja Wurrung Country and works at Monash University School of Rural Health. Michael won the UniSA Mental Health and Wellbeing Poetry Competition (2015) and received a commendation in the Hippocrates Prize for Poetry and Medicine (2021). His poems can be found in *Cordite, Meniscus, Rabbit, Burrow, Verandah, Plumwood Mountain, Medical Humanities, the Medical Journal of Australia*. Michael's poetry books include the chapbook *Chronicity* (Melbourne Poets Union, 2020) and the full-length collection *Natural Philosophies* (Recent Work Press, 2022).

# EMERGENCE OF VOICE

In loving memory of my mother, Judy Leach (1953-2020), and my maternal
grandparents, Lily Wheeler (1923-2012) and Eric Wheeler (1927-2016)

i've
always
been shy

my
20th-
century
memories

    encompass
   bro    ken
      moments:

            the lights
              go out
            in my room—
            i pull bedding
            over my face
            & feel
            safe

            the door
            -bell rings—
            i run to Mum's side
            & then slide
            beneath
            the daybed

            schoolkids stare
            at bespectacled eyes—
            i hang my head
            low

& speak
to precious few

the school stage
show—
i stand
to one side
& shine lights
on stars

i've
always
been shy

my
21st-
century
memories

encompass
breakthrough
moments:

lights shine
on me—
I stand alone
on the stage
& recite
another's words

new kids look
at me—

I establish
eye contact
& speak
to them too

the final siren
sounds
—I high
-five teammates
& shake
hands with rivals

the lights
        go out
in my room—
I wrap myself
in ghosts
& feel
safe

i've
always
been shy

        yet   now
somehow

I stand up
        in front
of health care students
        to teach

                    them how
                    to care

i've
always
been shy

        yet   now
        somehow

                    I stand up
                        at weddings
                            & funerals
                        to recite
                    my free
                            verse

# ABOUT THE WRITERS

This collection of interpretations of the confidence theme was created by some talented writers. Here is some information about each of the commended writers from the Minds Shine Bright Writing Competition Confidence 2022.

CHARLOTTE FINN, poet, 'Treading on Water', is from Bulla, Victoria

C SULLIVAN, author of flash fiction 'Morning Chorus', is qualified in journalism but nowadays prefers the creativity and challenge of flash fiction writing. Since experiencing postnatal depression, she is passionate about shedding a light on this condition and dispelling the misconceptions so more women are inclined to seek support.

CLAIRE DALKIN, author of short story 'Microbial', is a high school tutor and support worker. Her work has been published by the Wyrd Harvest Press, along with flash fiction for local newspapers. The writing bug bit her when she was eight, when she had her first story read out in Assembly. She lives with her family in Sussex between the hills and the beautiful sea.

KATE FOULDS, author of flash fiction 'Acorn', is a Bendigo based mother, shop girl and short fiction/memoir writer who grew up on the family farm in Musk. She completed a post-graduate journalism cadetship at Kyneton's *Midland Express* and cultivated her craft at *The Bendigo Advertiser.* 'Grandma's Gift' was published in *Mother—Memories, moments & stories*, as part of the 2020 Bendigo Writers Festival programme. Several memoir pieces have been published on the *Stereo Stories* website: www.stereostories.com

JENNIFER HARRISON: poet of 'Grandmother'. Jennifer's ninth poetry collection *Sideshow History* is forthcoming from Black Pepper, Melbourne. In 2012 she received the Christopher Brennan Award for sustained achievement in Australian poetry. She is currently Chair of the World Psychiatry Association's Section for Art and Psychiatry.

MOCCO WOOLLERT, poet of 'Jessica at fifteen', came as a migrant from Germany. She is a recognised poet and author who lives in Brisbane. She writes in English, her second language,and in German. Her poems are published in newspapers and anthologies. Her memoir 'Bloody, Bastard, Beautiful' was published in July 2017. A series of 8 children's books was published in 2021.

KAREN LETHLEAN, author of short story 'Catch and Release', is a retired English teacher. With fiction 'Barbaric Yawp', 'Ken*Again', 'Pendulum Papers'. She has won a few awards through Australian and UK competitions. Including Best of Times, with 'Bum Joke'. In her other life Karen is a triathlete who has done Hawaii Ironman championships twice.

JULIET GUTHRIE, poet of 'the last heady days', is a first-year university student who enjoys writing about navigating late adolescence. She has been published twice in the *Shared Stories Anthology* and enjoys tutoring English.

CLARE LE, poet of 'Fossil', is a life-long lover of literature, storytelling and the Australian bush. Clare is strongly connected to the pocket of foreshore bushland she was given the freedom to explore and dream in as a child. Vivid moments of inner joy are captured in her work, only to elude her as they fossilise into memories.

ELLA MITCHELL, poet. 'Beautiful Things' is about realising that beauty is not found in physical attributes, rather in the belief that we are beautiful regardless of appearance. Learning to have confidence and love the bodies that carry us can be a difficult journey, but one that is worth embarking on. As a young woman who has struggled with physical appearance, I am still learning to be at peace with all of the imperfections that make me who I am, but it reassures me to know that others are on the same journey to self acceptance. All it takes is a little bit of confidence!

LENI MAAG, author of flash fiction, 'Sarah': Hi! I'm Leni, 20 years old and from Germany. I have been writing stories with a couple of intermissions for some time now. I especially enjoy it when I feel like I was maybe able to describe or express a feeling, an emotion or a situation of mine in a way that feels sufficiently adequate to me, which may have been hard to express or get across otherwise.. Thank you so much for reading!

DAVID EDWARDS, author of flash fiction 'Chilblains', is an emerging writer from Canberra. He works across a range of short form genres, with a focus on flash fiction and poetry. David's work explores themes of loneliness, social isolation, mental health and life with chronic illness. Influences on David's recent writing include Anne Sexton, Amos Oz, and Clarice Lispector.

JAYDAN SALZKE, author of short story 'Rite of Passage', is originally from Queensland, Australia and is a teacher turned writer who is intent on wielding the power of words to make our world better, not just noisier. In 2022, Jaydan is completing a Masters of Creative Writing, penning a short-form literature collection that explores the notion of intersectionality.

SADIE YETTON, poet of 'Party Song', is an 18-year-old from New Zealand. She resides in Auckland city. Her passions include songwriting, performing, and writing poetry and fiction. She hopes to pursue these things in the future.

RAFAEL S.W. poet of 'Stag Nation', is a creative writing graduate and a founding member of Dead Poets' Fight Club. He writes every single day and has been published in *The Big Issue* Fiction Edition, *The Sleepers Almanac*, and *Award Winning Australian Writing*. A regular contributor to Going Down Swinging online he also competes in poetry slams and giant-sized chess games.

AOIFE McFADDEN, author of short story 'Distorted Lens', is a writer from Adelaide, South Australia who loves to travel and has been all over the world, but can't find anywhere better than her hometown. She has an obsession with running and spends her days in scientific research, fantasising about how to turn it all into a story. Aoife has been scribbling into notebooks for fun since she learnt to write and is finally finding the confidence to share it all with the world.

DREW GRANT, poet of 'Night Owl'. 'I've been writing for most of my life, but always kept in secret. Motherhood has brought me out of my shell more than anything else ever could. I understand more of the world through the eyes of my daughter. Beauty lies in the most mundane of places if you are able to keep your eyes open.' Drew's inspirational image is of her daughter, 'her inspiration for all things.'

EVE NUCIFORA, author of flash fiction 'Trumpet', is a PhD candidate at the University of Canberra. Her creative-led research draws on feminist, psychoanalytical, and affect theories to explore ambivalence as a recurring motif in short prose fiction, expressed through sexuality, place, and sensation. Her stories have been published in *Axon* and *Meniscus* literary journals. Eve lives on Ngunnawal Country.

DIANA STOICESCU, poet of 'Debarked', from Bucharest, Romania. Researcher of togetherness. Planter of seeds. Gatherer of words. Exit point of consciousness.

PETER FITZGERALD, poet of 'Mudgee Railway Station', is a well travelled retired teacher, now dedicated writer. Peter has recently written creative stories for *Discover Central NSW* Magazine. He has been published with Queensland Independent Radio 'on air' and in a printed anthology. Since residing in Mudgee Peter has been published with a Mudgee Valley Writer's anthology. Peter is currently editing a Mudgee region anthology of his short stories.

OLGA PAVLINOVA OLENICH, poet of 'The Line of Trees', is a widely-published Australian writer whose work appears in local and international publications. Her prose and poems have been broadcast on national radio and have featured in national newspapers. Her poetry is published in various anthologies including *Writing the Country, Griffith Review*. Queensland (2019) and *Best Australian Poems* (Black inc. 2015).

HEATHER COMPTON, poet of 'Somewhere: 2021'. My writing aims to get people thinking about life in a new light—in a way that provides a little hope in a world that often seems less than perfect. I started writing from a young age, but have only recently started writing poetry. I read a lot, write a lot, and love staring out of the window for inspiration—or just at the birds. I like bending the rules of writing—especially if it helps get my message across in a way that I think resonates more with both myself and the reader.

LESLEY DAY, author of flash fiction 'Poached', is an innovative educator in English and Languages. She is passionate about writing and often uses her short stories and poems to reflect on the positive outcomes of challenging circumstances. Using poignant imagery and vivid descriptive language, Lesley crafts narratives that provide deep insight into the personal experiences and emotions of her characters.

AMELIA CARTER, author of flash fiction 'The Currawong', is a writer based in chilly, cosy, Canberra, where she spent several years studying linguistics at the ANU, which she found endlessly fascinating. She is inspired by the magic of language and how it connects people. She writes short stories and poetry in her spare time. This is her first published flash fiction.

JANEEN SAMUEL, poet of 'Parrot People', is a former veterinary pathologist who lives in South-West Victoria, surrounded by sheep and slumbering volcanoes. Many of her poems and short fiction have been published in various magazines and anthologies, while her half-finished novels sit unpublished in drawers and cupboards.

SUE HALL, author of flash fiction 'Barred Rock'. My early years revolved around my family and a preschool I set up on our property. In the latter part of my working life I became a free-lance editor, writing six non-fiction books and editing and proofreading fiction and non-fiction for others. In my spare time, I also wrote and illustrated two children's books. Now, in my retirement in Kerikeri, New Zealand, I am thoroughly enjoying the freedom and challenge of writing flash fiction and short stories at will, drawing on a life-time of experiences!

SCOTT HALLARN, writer of flash fiction 'Townscapes', is a Canadian writer living in Toronto. His short fiction has been published in the UK and Canada. He is also the author of two novels, *Sundays in the Solarium* and *An Afternoon in Phnom Penh*. Unresolved guilt and redemption are frequent themes in his writing.

ANNA RODWAY, author of short story 'Mabel', is a writer and theatre-maker currently based in southern NSW. She is one-third of independent company Three Birds Theatre, who are swiftly gaining recognition as exciting innovators of sharp, comedy driven theatre. She is in the midst of developing a web-series and completing a Master of English Studies at the University of Sydney.

MOROUJE SHERIF, poet of 'When the Sea Takes You, I Won't Come', is an aspiring artist who adores apricots and temperate climates. Growing up in the Mediterranean, she has a vicarious thrill for all feel-good artistic compositions and a budding introspection on the traverse of truth. Asides from writing, she enjoys judging dubious architecture, the colour sage, and the paradox of non-places to spark inspiration through the boundless facets of a flourishing mind.

REGINA DE BÚRCA, author of short story 'Sovereign', was raised in a bookshop in the West of Ireland, where her fascination with the Irish language and mythology began. In 2010, she graduated with an MA in Writing for Young People from Bath Spa University in England. Regina has had various short stories published and was longlisted for the Mercier Fiction Competition in

2017. In 2021, Regina produced the first Irish language version of the Rider Waite Tarot deck and is due to take part in an MA in Irish Mythology and Folklore in University College Cork this September.

JESSICA KILKENNY, the author of the short story 'Move', is an English teacher and writer working in Melbourne. When she's not writing, she likes working on textile projects and going on wintry walks with her dog.

SHOSHANNA ROCKMAN, 'Dragons don't smoke', is a poet, editor, copywriter, vet nurse intern and mother of five. Her poetry is a direct, acerbic and often humourful evocation of human nature and relationships; how we navigate, celebrate, collaborate, love and loss. 'My writing is a collision of chaos and courage.'

EVELYN MENARY, author of short story 'Victory Memorial', is a Canadian writer who loves writing until the magic happens—entering inside a story, listening, looking around and recording what unfolds. She has a Master of Arts degree in Psychology. Evelyn is an avid writer of journals and dream journals and has conducted numerous individual sessions and workshops on dream work, writing and life path transitions.

JERICHO ELLAO, poet of 'The Kingdom of the Overworld', attends Scotts College in Albury and is currently in year nine. He enjoys creating art, music—including classical guitar and piano; making short films and performing on stage. Jericho regularly attends the Albury Wondonga Eisteddfod and looks forward to developing a career in the arts as 'earth without art is just eh!'

LEE A BAGLIN, poet of 'Of Machines and Love'. A university graduate of 2016, Lee struggled with his mental and physical health. Lee returned to his passion in writing as a means to help battle his own demons.

STEVE FENDT, writer of short story 'Gone South'. As a writer, I'm fascinated by the power of place over the human psyche. Australia is my adopted country: I have lived here for twenty years, yet it seems ever strange and new to me. When I'm not writing, I like to spend my time sailing, birdwatching, playing music around the campfire—and simply being in nature.

Dr JENNIFER HURLEY, author of short story 'Tree of Knowledge', is an independent writer living on Wadawurrung country in Victoria. After a long career working in universities, she is now writing fiction that explores human connections as they intersect with gender and power, justice for Australia's first peoples, and the climate crisis.

KAREN LEE MILLS, poet of 'A Northern Flicker', is an emerging author, best known for her poetry, short article publications and her children's picture book, *Precious Artwork*. Karen is a public speaker and presents author talks in schools and local writers' groups. Karen resides in rural Victoria and enjoys hearing from her readers via email: karen@blessing.net.au. Karen is currently compiling a collection of her poems for future publication.

OLIVIA CAMPBELL, poet of 'The people of the art'.
As a poet and songwriter, Olivia arranges and layers
words and sounds to create pieces that offer embodied
experiences of poetry and music. She has several
years' experience as editor, and is nearing completion
of a Master of Publishing and Communications at the
University of Melbourne.

HANNAH SMALL, author of flash fiction 'Confidence in
Healing'. Born and raised in Melbourne, Hannah Small
moved to Canberra to study a Bachelor of Arts and
Bachelor of Medical Science (with First Class Honours).
She works in STEM and is passionate about gender
equity and nature conservation. In her writing, Hannah
explores the concepts of health and happiness and their
link to our external surroundings.